CHAINS

Laurie Halse Anderson

CHAINS

SEEDS OF AMERICA

ATHENEUM
BOOKS FOR YOUNG READERS
NEW YORK • LONDON • TORONTO • SYDNEY

ATHENEUM BOOKS FOR YOUNG READERS
An imprint of Simon & Schuster Children's Publishing Division
1230 Avenue of the Americas, New York, New York 10020

Also available in an Atheneum Books for Young Readers hardcover edition.
Book design by Lizzy Bromley
The text for this book is set in Regula.
Manufactured in the United States of America
First Atheneum Books for Young Readers paperback edition January 2010
22 24 26 28 30 29 27 25 23
The Library of Congress has cataloged the hardcover edition as follows:
Anderson, Laurie Halse.
Chains/Laurie Halse Anderson—1st ed.
Summary: After being sold to a cruel couple in New York City, a slave named Isabel spies for the rebels during the Revolutionary War.
ISBN 978-1-4169-0585-1 (hc)
1. New York (N.Y.)—History—Revolution, 1775-1783—Juvenile fiction. [1. New York (N.Y.)—History—Revolution, 1775-1783—Fiction. 2. United States—History—Revolution, 1775-1783—Fiction. 3. Slavery—Fiction. 4. African-Americans—Fiction. 5. Spies—Fiction.] I. Title.
PZ7.A54385Ch2008
[Fic]—dc22 2007052139
ISBN 978-1-4169-0586-8 (pbk)
0820 OFF

ABIGAIL ADAMS
once described her husband, JOHN, as
him whom my Heart esteems
above all earthly things.
I UNDERSTAND THAT FEELING.
That's why this book is dedicated
to my beloved husband,
SCOT.

Part 1

CHAPTER 1

Monday, May 27, 1776

YOUTH IS THE SEED TIME OF GOOD HABITS,
AS WELL IN NATIONS AS IN INDIVIDUALS.
–THOMAS PAINE, *COMMON SENSE*

THE BEST TIME TO TALK TO GHOSTS is just before the sun comes up. That's when they can hear us true, Momma said. That's when ghosts can answer us.

The eastern sky was peach colored, but a handful of lazy stars still blinked in the west. It was almost time.

"May I run ahead, sir?" I asked.

Pastor Weeks sat at the front of his squeaky wagon with Old Ben next to him, the mules' reins loose in his hands. The pine coffin that held Miss Mary Finch–wearing her best dress, with her hair washed clean and combed–bounced in the back when the wagon wheels hit a rut. My sister, Ruth, sat next to the coffin. Ruth was too big to carry, plus the pastor knew about her peculiar manner of being, so it was the wagon for her and the road for me.

Old Ben looked to the east and gave me a little nod. He knew a few things about ghosts, too.

Pastor Weeks turned around to talk to Mr. Robert Finch, who rode his horse a few lengths behind the wagon.

"The child wants to run ahead," Pastor explained to him. "She has kin buried there. Do you give leave for a quick visit?"

Mr. Robert's mouth tightened like a rope pulled taut. He had showed up a few weeks earlier to visit Miss Mary Finch, his aunt and only living relation. He looked around her tidy farm, listened to her ragged, wet cough, and moved in. Miss Mary wasn't even cold on her deathbed when he helped himself to the coins in her strongbox. He hurried along her burying, too, most improper. He didn't care that the neighbors would want to come around with cakes and platters of cold meat, and drink ale to the rememory of Miss Mary Finch of Tew, Rhode Island. He had to get on with things, he said.

I stole a look backward. Mr. Robert Finch was filled up with trouble from his dirty boots to the brim of his scraggly hat.

"Please, sir," I said.

"Go then," he said. "But don't tarry. I've much business today."

I ran as fast as I could.

I hurried past the stone fence that surrounded the white graveyard, to the split-rail fence that marked our ground, and stopped outside the gate to pick a handful of chilly violets, wet with dew. The morning mist twisted and hung low over the field. No ghosts yet, just ash trees and maples lined up in a mournful row.

I entered.

Momma was buried in the back, her feet to the east, her head to the west. Someday I would pay the stone carver for a proper marker with her name on it: *Dinah, wife of Cuffe, mother of Isabel and Ruth.* For now, there was a wooden cross and a gray rock the size of a dinner plate lying flat on the ground in front of it.

We had buried her the year before, when the first roses bloomed.

"Smallpox is tricky," Miss Mary Finch said to me when Momma died. "There's no telling who it'll take." The pox had left Ruth and me with scars like tiny stars scattered on our skin. It took Momma home to Our Maker.

I looked back at the road. Old Ben had slowed the mules to give me time. I knelt down and set the violets on the grave. "It's here, Momma," I whispered. "The day you promised. But I need your help. Can you please cross back over for just a little bit?"

I stared without blinking at the mist, looking for the curve of her back or the silhouette of her head wrapped in a pretty kerchief. A small flock of robins swooped out of the maple trees.

"I don't have much time," I told the grass-covered grave. "Where do you want us to go? What should we do?"

The mist swirled between the tall grass and the low-hanging branches. Two black butterflies danced through a cloud of bugs and disappeared. Chickadees and barn swallows called overhead.

"Whoa." Old Ben stopped the wagon next to the open hole near the iron fence, then climbed down and walked to where Nehemiah the gravedigger was waiting. The two men reached for the coffin.

"Please, Momma," I whispered urgently. "I need your help." I squinted into the ash grove, where the mist was heaviest.

No ghosts. Nothing.

I'd been making like this for near a year. No matter what I said, or where the sun and the moon and the stars hung, Momma never answered. Maybe she was angry because I'd buried her wrong. I'd heard stories of old country burials with singers and dancers, but I wasn't sure what to do, so we just dug a hole and said a passel of prayers. Maybe Momma's ghost was lost and wandering because I didn't send her home the right way.

The men set Miss Mary's coffin on the ground. Mr. Robert got off his horse and said something I couldn't hear. Ruth stayed in the wagon, her bare feet curled up under her skirt and her thumb in her mouth.

I reached in the pocket under my apron and took out the oatcake. It was in two pieces, with honey smeared between them. The smell made my stomach rumble, but I didn't dare nibble. I picked up the flat rock in front of the cross and set the offering in the hollow under it. Then I put the rock back and sat still, my eyes closed tight to keep the tears inside my head where they belonged.

I could smell the honey that had dripped on my hands, the damp ground under me, and the salt of the ocean. I could hear cows mooing in a far pasture and bees buzzing in a nearby clover patch.

If she would just say my name, just once . . .

"Girl!" Mr. Robert shouted. "You there, girl!"

I sniffed, opened my eyes, and wiped my face on my sleeve. The sun had popped up in the east like a cork and was burning through the morning mist. The ghosts had all gone to ground. I wouldn't see her today, either.

He grabbed my arm and pulled me roughly to my feet. "I told you to move," Mr. Robert snarled at me.

"Apologies, sir," I said, wincing with pain.

He released me with a shove and pointed to the cemetery where they buried white people. "Go pray for her that owned you, girl."

CHAPTER II

Monday, May 27, 1776

I, YOUNG IN LIFE, BY SEEMING CRUEL FATE
WAS SNATCH'D FROM AFRIC'S FANCYIED HAPPY SEAT: . . .
. . . THAT FROM A FATHER SEIZ'D HIS BABE BELOV'D:
SUCH, SUCH MY CASE. AND CAN I THEN BUT PRAY
OTHERS MAY NEVER FEEL TYRANNIC SWAY?
—PHILLIS WHEATLEY, "TO THE RIGHT
HONOURABLE WILLIAM, EARL OF DARTMOUTH"

"AMEN," WE SAID TOGETHER.

Pastor Weeks closed his Bible, and the funeral was over.

Nehemiah drove his shovel into the mound of dirt and pitched some into the open grave. The earth rattled and bounced on the coffin lid. Old Ben put on his hat and walked toward the mule team. Mr. Robert reached for coins to pay the pastor. Ruth drew a line in the dust with her toe.

My belly flipped with worry. I was breathing hard as if I'd run all the way to the village and back. This was the moment we'd been waiting for, the one that Momma promised would come. It was up to me to take care of things, to find a place for us. I had to be bold.

I stood up proper, the way I had been taught—chin up, eyes down—took Ruth by the hand, and walked over to the men.

"Pardon me, Pastor Weeks, sir," I said. "May I ask you something?"

He set his hat on his head. "Certainly, Isabel."

I held Ruth's hand tighter. "Where do you think we should go?"

"What do you mean, child?"

"I know I'll find work, but I can't figure where to sleep, me and Ruth. I thought you might know a place."

Pastor Weeks frowned. "I don't understand what you're saying, Isabel. You're to return with Mr. Robert here. You and your sister belong to him now."

I spoke slowly, saying the words I had practiced in my head since Miss Mary Finch took her last breath, the words that would change everything. "Ruth and me are free, Pastor. Miss Finch freed us in her will. Momma, too, if she had lived. It was done up legal, on paper with wax seals."

Mr. Robert snorted. "That's enough out of you, girl. Time for us to be on the road to Newport."

"Was there a will?" Pastor Weeks asked him.

"She didn't need one," Mr. Robert replied. "I was Aunt Mary's only relative."

I planted my feet firmly in the dirt and fought to keep my voice polite and proper. "I saw the will, sir. After the lawyer wrote it, Miss Mary had me read it out loud on account of her eyes being bad."

"Slaves don't read," Mr. Robert said. "I should beat you for lying, girl."

Pastor Weeks held up his hand. "It's true. Your aunt had some odd notions. She taught the child herself. I disapproved, of course. Only leads to trouble."

I spoke up again. "We're to be freed, sir. The lawyer,

Mr. Cornell, he'll tell you. Ruth and me, we're going to get work and a place of our own to sleep."

"That's enough." Mr. Robert narrowed his eyes at me.

"But Mr. Cornell–," I started.

"Shut your mouth!" he snapped.

The pastor cleared his throat. "Perhaps we should inquire . . ."

"Where is this Cornell?" Mr. Robert demanded. "Newport?"

"He left for Boston before the blockade," the pastor said. "Took his papers with him."

"The girl is lying, then," Mr. Robert said. "She knows the lawyer is absent and her cause cannot be proved. The sooner I'm rid of her, the better."

"It's the truth," I blurted out. Ruth looked up at me anxiously and gripped my hand tighter.

"I said, silence!" Mr. Robert yelled.

"Isabel, remember your place." Pastor Weeks fumbled with the latch on his Bible. "You and your sister belong to Mr. Robert now. He'll be a good master to you."

My insides went cold, like I'd swallowed water straight from a deep, dark well. This couldn't be happening. "Couldn't you send a message to Boston, seeking Mr. Cornell?"

"The matter is settled." Mr. Robert pulled on his gloves. "If I might borrow your wagon and man for the drive to Newport, Pastor, I'd be grateful. These girls should bring a decent price at auction."

"You're selling us?" The words flew out of my mouth before I could weigh them.

"Hush, Isabel," Pastor Weeks cautioned.

The cold inside me snaked down to my feet and up around my neck. I shivered in the warm spring sunshine. Ruth bent down and picked up a shiny pebble. What if we were split up? Who would take care of her?

I fought back the tears. "Pastor Weeks, please, sir."

Mr. Robert knocked the dust from his hat. "They should go quick. Your wagon will be back by nightfall."

The minister placed the Bible in his leather satchel and pulled it up over his shoulder. He studied the ground, his hands, Mr. Robert's horse, and the clouds. He did not look at me. "You'll be wanting to bring their shoes and blankets," he finally said. "They'll fetch a better price that way."

"True enough."

"I'll have a word with Ben. Explain matters."

Pastor Weeks walked toward his own slave, keeping a hand on the satchel so it didn't bump against his side.

My heart wanted to force my feet to run, but I couldn't feel them, couldn't feel my hands, nor my arms, nor any part of myself. I had froze solid, sticking to the dirt. We were sold once before, back when Ruth was a tiny baby, not even baptized yet. They sold all of us from the plantation when old Mister Malbone run up his debts too high. His bankers wanted their pounds of flesh. Our flesh.

One by one they dragged us forward, and a man shouted out prices to the crowd of likely buyers and baby Ruth cried, and Momma shook like the last leaf on a tree, and Poppa . . . and Poppa, he didn't want them to bust up our family like we were sheep or hogs. "I am a man," he shouted, and he was Momma's husband and our father, and baby Ruth, she cried and cried, and I thought Momma would shatter like a bowl when it falls off a table. Poppa fought like a lion when they came for him, the strongest lion, roaring; it took five of them with hickory clubs, and then Momma fainted, and I caught baby Ruth just in time and there was lion's blood on the ground mixed with the dust like the very earth was bleeding, and we left there, we three in Miss Mary Finch's wagon, and everything in the whole world was froze in ice for near two years after that.

I opened my mouth to roar, but not a sound escaped. I could not even mewl like a kitten.

CHAPTER III

Monday, May 27, 1776

RUN-AWAY FROM THE SUBSCRIBER, LIVING AT NO. 110, WATER-STREET, NEAR THE NEW SLIP. A NEGRO GIRL NAMED POLL, ABOUT 13 YEARS OF AGE, VERY BLACK, MARKED WITH THE SMALL-POX, AND HAD ON WHEN SHE WENT AWAY A RED CLOTH PETTICOAT, AND A LIGHT BLUE SHORT GOWN, HOME MADE. WHOEVER WILL TAKE UP AND SECURE THE SAID GIRL SO THAT THE OWNER MAY GET HER, SHALL BE HANDSOMELY REWARDED.

—NEWSPAPER ADVERTISEMENT IN THE *ROYAL GAZETTE* (NEW YORK)

THE SNAKE TOOK US TO MISS MARY'S house to collect our blankets and too-small shoes but nothing else. We couldn't take Momma's shells, nor Ruth's baby doll made of flannel bits and calico, nor the wooden bowl Poppa made for me. Nothing belonged to us.

As I folded the blankets, Mr. Robert went out to the privy. There was no point in grabbing Ruth and running. He had a horse and a gun, and we were known to all. I looked around our small room, searching for a tiny piece of home I could hide in my pocket.

What to take?

Seeds.

On the hearth stood the jar of flower seeds that Momma

had collected, seeds she never had a chance to put into the ground. I didn't know what they'd grow into. I didn't know if they'd grow at all. It was fanciful notion, but I uncorked the jar, snatched a handful, and buried it deep in my pocket just as the privy door creaked open.

As the wagon drove us away, Ruth turned to see the little house disappear. I pulled her into my lap and stared straight ahead, afraid that if I looked back, I might break.

By midday we were in Newport, following Mr. Robert up the steps of Sullivan's Tavern. I had never been inside a tavern before. It was a large room, twice as big as Miss Mary's house, with two wide fireplaces, one on each of the far walls. The room was crowded with tables and chairs and as many people as church on Easter Sunday, except church was never cloudy with tobacco smoke nor the smell of roast beef.

Most of the customers were men, and a few had their wives with them. Some seemed like regular country folk, but others wore rich clothes not useful for muck shoveling. They made haste tucking into their dinners, playing cards, paging newspapers, and arguing loud about the British soldiers and their navy and taxes and a war.

Ruth didn't like the noise and covered her ears with her hands. I pulled her toward me and patted her on the back. Ruth was simpleminded and prone to fits, which spooked ignorant folk. Noise could bring them on, as well as a state of nervous excitement. She was in the middle of both.

As I patted, her eyes grew wide at the sight of a thick slice of buttered bread perched near the edge of a table. We hadn't eaten all day, and there had been little food the day before, what with Miss Mary dying. I snatched her hand away as she reached for it.

"Soon," I whispered.

Mr. Robert pointed to a spot in the corner. "Stand there," he ordered.

A woman burst through the kitchen door carrying a tray heavy with food. She was a big woman, twice the size of my mother, with milky skin and freckles. She looked familiar and caused me to search my remembery.

"We'll have Jenny fatten up the British navy and make their ships sink to the bottom of the sea!" yelled a red-faced man.

The big woman, Jenny, laughed as she set a bowl in front of the man. The proprietor called her over to join us. She frowned as she approached, giving Ruth and me a quick once-over while tucking a stray curl under her cap.

"These are the girls," Mr. Robert explained.

"It don't matter," the proprietor said as he put his hand on Jenny's back. "We don't hold with slaves being auctioned on our front steps. Won't stand for it, in fact."

"I thought this was a business establishment," Mr. Robert said. "Are you opposed to earning your percentage?"

"You want to listen to my Bill, mister," Jenny said. "Advertise in the paper, that's what we do around here."

"I don't have time for that. These are fine girls, they'll go quickly. Give me half an hour's time on your front steps, and we both walk away with heavier pockets."

Jenny's husband pulled out a rag and wiped his hands on it. "Auctions of people ain't seemly. Why don't you just talk quiet-like to folks? Or leave a notice tacked up, that's proper."

"I recall an auction not twenty yards from here," Mr. Robert said. "One of Brown's ships brought up a load of rum and slaves from the islands. They must have sold thirty-five, forty people in two hours' time."

"Rhode Island don't import slaves, not for two years now," Jenny said.

"All the more reason why folks want to buy what I have to sell. I want this done quickly. I have other business to tend to."

"Is that our problem, Bill?" Jenny asked her husband. "He says that like it's our problem."

"Ease off, Jenny," Bill said. "The girls look hungry. Why don't you take them to the kitchen?"

Jenny looked like she had plenty more to say to Mr. Robert, but she gave Ruth and me a quick glance and said, "Follow me."

Mr. Robert grabbed my shoulder. "They've already eaten."

"No charge," Jenny said evenly. "I like feeding children."

"Oh." Mr. Robert released me. "Well then, that's different."

Jenny closed the kitchen door behind her and motioned for Ruth and me to sit at the table in the middle of the room. A cauldron of stew hung above the fire in the hearth, and two fresh pies were cooling by the window.

"Eat first," she said. "Then talk."

She cut us slices of brown bread and ham and poured us both big mugs of cider. Ruth gulped hers down quick and held out her mug for more. Jenny smiled and refilled it. I made short work of the food, keeping one eye on the door in case Mr. Robert walked in. The back door to the kitchen was wide open to let in the breeze. Should I grab Ruth's hand and try to escape?

Jenny read my mind. "No sense in running." She shook her head from side to side. "He'd find you right away."

I scowled at my bread and took another bite.

"I'd help you if I could," she said. "It'd be the least I could do for Dinah."

I wasn't sure I had heard her right. "Pardon me, ma'am?"

"You're Dinah's girl. Knew you when you walked in the door."

"You knew my mother?"

Jenny stirred the cauldron of stew. "Your mother and your father both. I held you when you were just a day old. I heard she passed away last year. My condolences."

She cut two pieces from the apple pie and gave them to Ruth and me. "I was indentured when I was your age. Old Mister Malbone had five of us from Ireland, along with near thirty slaves. Worked us all just as hard, but after seven years, I could walk away, thank the Lord. Dinah was real friendly to me when I first got there, helped me get used to a new place, and people ordering me around."

"I thought I knew you," I said.

She smiled warmly and snatched a piece of apple from the pie plate. "You always were the best rememberer I ever saw. We used to make a game of it. Tell you a line to memorize, or a song. Didn't matter how much time passed, you'd have the whole thing in your mouth. Made your parents proud."

A serving girl came through the door and the talk stopped. Once Jenny had loaded up her tray and sent her back out, she sat down next to me. "How did you come to be with that man?" she asked. "I thought you were at Miss Finch's place."

I quickly explained the dizzy events of the last two days.

"There's no telling what happened to the lawyer," Jenny said when I was finished. "Boston is a terrible confusion—first the King's army, and now Washington's."

"What should I do?" I asked. The words came out louder than they should have.

Jenny gently covered my mouth with her hand. "Shhh," she warned. "You got to use your head."

I grabbed her hand. "Could you take us? Please? You knew Momma . . ."

She slowly pulled her hand from mine, shaking her head. "I'm sorry, Isabel. I dare not."

"But—"

Bill opened the door and poked his head in. "He wants the girls. Best to hurry."

A thin woman stood next to Mr. Robert. Her plum-colored gown was crisp and well sewn, and expensive lace trailed from the small cap on her head. She was perhaps five and forty years, with pale eyebrows and small eyes like apple seeds. A fading yellow bruise circled her right wrist like a bracelet.

She looked us over quickly. "Sisters?"

"Two for the price of one," Mr. Robert said. "Hardest-working girls you'll ever own."

"What's wrong with them?" the woman asked bluntly. "Why such a cheap price?"

Mr. Robert's snake smile widened. "My haste is your good fortune, madam. These girls were the servants of my late aunt, whose passing I mourn deeply. I must quickly conclude the matters of her estate. The recent unrest, you know."

A man joined the woman, his eyes suspicious and flinty. He wore a red silk waistcoat under a snuff-colored coat with silver buttons, a starched linen shirt, and black breeches. The buckles on his boots were as big as my fists. "And what side do you take in the current situation, sir?" he asked. "Are you for the King or do you support rebellion?"

Conversation at nearby tables stopped as people listened in.

"I pledge myself to our rightful sovereign, the King, sir," Mr. Robert said. "Washington and his rabble may have taken Boston, but that's the last thing they'll take."

The stranger gave a little bow and introduced himself. "Elihu Lockton, at your service, sir. This is my wife, Anne."

Mr. Robert bowed politely in return, ignoring the muttering at the table behind him. "May I offer you both some sup and drink that we might be better acquainted?"

They all sat, and Jenny swooped over to take their orders. Ruth and I stood with our backs against the wall as Mr. Robert and the Locktons ate and drank. I watched them close. The husband was a head taller and twice the girth of most men. His shoulders rounded forward and his neck seemed to pain him, for he often reached up to rub it. He said he was a merchant with business in Boston, New York, and Charleston, and complained about how much the Boston uprising cost him.

His missus sipped Jenny's chowder, shuddered at the taste, and reached for her mug of small beer. She stole glances at us from time to time. I could not figure what kind of mistress she would be. In truth, I was struggling to think straight. The air in the tavern had grown heavy, and the weight of the day pressed against my head.

When the men took out their pipes and lit their tobacco,

Ruth sneezed, and the company all turned and considered us.

"Well, then," Lockton said, pushing back from the table to give his belly some room. "The wife is looking for a serving wench."

Missus Lockton crooked a finger at us. "Come here, girls."

I took Ruth by the hand and stepped within reach. Missus Lockton studied our hands and arms, looked at our feet, and made us take off our kerchiefs to look in our hair for nits.

"Can you cook?" she finally asked me.

"Not much, ma'am," I admitted.

"Just as well," she said. "I don't need another cook. What do you do?"

I put my arm around Ruth. "We can scrub your house clean, care for cows and pigs, work your garden, and carry just about anything."

"My aunt trained them up herself," Mr. Robert added. "And they come with blankets and shoes."

Lockton sighed. "Why not wait, Anne, and procure another indentured girl in New York?"

His wife sat back as Jenny arrived with coffee. "Indentured servants complain all the time and steal us blind at the first opportunity. I'll never hire another."

Jenny set the tray on the table so hard the cups rattled in their saucers.

Lockton reached for a plate of apple pie. "Are you sure we need two? These are uncertain times, dear."

Missus regarded Ruth. "This one looks simple. Is she addlepated?"

Ruth gave a shy smile.

I spoke before Mr. Robert could open his mouth. "She's

a good simple, ma'am. Does what she's told. In truth, she's a harder worker than me. Give her a broom and tell her to sweep, and you'll be able to eat off your floor."

Jenny poured a cup of coffee and set it in front of the missus, spilling a little on the table.

"She's prettier than you," Missus said. "And she knows how to hold her tongue." She turned to her husband. "The little one might be an amusement in the parlor. The big one could help Becky with the firewood and housekeeping."

Jenny pressed her lips tight together and poured coffee for Lockton and for Mr. Robert.

Missus bent close to Ruth's face. "I do not brook foolishness," she said.

Ruth shook her head from side to side. "No foolin'," she said.

The missus cocked her head to one side and stared at me. "And you. You are to address me as Madam. I expect obedience at all times. Insolence will not be tolerated, not one bit. And you will curb your tendency to talk."

"Yes, ma'am, M-Madam," I stuttered.

"What say you, Anne?" Lockton said. "We sail with the tide."

"I want these girls, husband," Madam said. "It is Providence that put them in our path."

"How much do you want for them?" Lockton asked.

Mr. Robert named his price. Our price. Two for one, us being sold like bolts of faded cloth or chipped porridge bowls.

"Wait," Jenny announced loudly. "I'll . . . I'll take them."

The table froze. A person like Jenny did not speak to folks like the Locktons or Mr. Robert, not in that manner.

Lockton stared at her as if she had grown a second head. "I beg your pardon."

Jenny set the kettle on the table, stood straight, and wiped her palms on her skirt. "I want them two girls. I need the help. We'll pay cash."

"Keep to your kitchen, woman." Madam Lockton's words came out sharp and loud.

Did she change her mind? Will she really take us?

Work in the tavern wouldn't be bad, maybe, and Jenny would be kind to Ruth. I could ask around about Lawyer Cornell's papers. When we found Miss Mary's will, I'd work extra to pay Jenny back for the money we cost her, fair and square. Ruth and me would stay together, and we'd stay here, close to Momma.

Please, God, please, God.

"Leave us," Lockton said to Jenny. "And send your husband over."

Jenny ignored him. "It'll take us a couple of days to get your money together," she said to Mr. Robert. "We'll give you free lodging in the meantime."

Mr. Robert's eyes darted between the two bidders. Ruth yawned. I crossed my fingers behind my back. *Please, God, please, God, please, God, please.*

Madam Lockton flicked crumbs to the floor with her handkerchief. "Dear husband," she said. "These girls are a bargain at double the price. With your permission, might we increase our offer twofold?"

Lockton picked at his teeth. "As long as we can conclude this business quickly."

Madam stared at Jenny. "Can you top the offer?"

Jenny wiped her hands on her apron, silent.

"Well?" Madam Lockton demanded.

Jenny shook her head. "I cannot pay more." She bobbed a little curtsy. "My husband will tally your account." She hurried for the kitchen door.

Mr. Robert chuckled and reached for his pie. "Well, then. We had a little auction here, after all."

"Such impudence is disturbing," Lockton said. "This is why we need the King's soldiers to return." He pulled out a small sack and counted out the coins to pay for us. "I thank you, sir, for the meal and the transaction. You may deliver the girls to the *Hartshorn,* if you please. Come now, Anne."

Madam Lockton stood and the men stood with her. "Good day to you, sir."

"Safe voyage, ma'am," Mr. Robert replied.

As the Locktons made their way through the crowded room, Mr. Robert dropped the heavy coins into a worn velvet bag. The thudding sound they made as they fell to the bottom reminded me of clods of dirt raining down on a fresh coffin.

Ruth put her arm around my waist and leaned against me.

CHAPTER IV

Monday, May 27–
Wednesday, May 29, 1776

WHAT A FINE AFFAIR IT WOULD BE
IF WE COULD FLIT ACROSS THE ATLANTIC AS THEY SAY
THE ANGELS DO FROM PLANET TO PLANET.
–LETTER FROM JOHN ADAMS TO HIS WIFE, ABIGAIL

IT TOOK TWO NIGHTS AND TWO DAYS for the *Hartshorn* to sail from Newport to the city of New York. Ruth and me were housed below the packet-boat's deck with six sheep, a pen of hogs, three families from Scotland, and fifty casks of dried cod. At the far end of the hold were crates of goods stamped LOCKTON & FOOTE and casks of rum with the same marking.

I spent most of the voyage bent double over a puke bucket, bringing up every scrap of food and swallow of brackish water I choked down. Ruth stood on a box looking out of a porthole, counting seagulls and waves in a whisper that could barely be heard over the creaking of the hull.

The seas calmed late on the second night, and I was able to walk a bit. Ruth was sound asleep in our hammock, thumb in her mouth. The hatchway to the deck was open and tempting. I climbed up the ladder slowly. The few sailors on watch saw me but didn't say a word.

The fat moon lit the water like a lantern over a looking glass. A clean, cold breeze blew from the north, pushing the ship so fast across the sea we seemed to fly. I sat on a crate facing the back end of the ship and hugged my knees to my chest. A mist of salty spray hung in the air.

The coastline of Rhode Island had long disappeared into darkness. I could not see where we came from or where we were going. Maybe the ship would spring a leak and sink. Maybe we would be blown off course and land in a country without New York or people who bought and sold children.

Maybe the wind would blow us in circles until the end of our days.

I wiped the mist from my face.

Momma said that ghosts couldn't move over water. That's why kidnapped Africans got trapped in the Americas. When Poppa was stolen from Guinea, he said the ancestors howled and raged and sent a thunderstorm to turn the ship back around, but it was too late. The ghosts couldn't cross the water to help him so he had to make his own way in a strange place, sometimes with an iron collar around his neck. All of Momma's people had been stolen too, and taken to Jamaica where she was born. Then she got sold to Rhode Island, and the ghosts of her parents couldn't follow and protect her neither.

They kept moving us over the water, stealing us away from our ghosts and our ancestors, who cried salty rivers into the sand. That's where Momma was now, wailing at the water's edge, while her girls were pulled out of sight under white sails that cracked in the wind.

CHAPTER V

Wednesday, May 29, 1776

THE INHABITANTS [OF NEW YORK] ARE IN GENERAL BRISK AND LIVELY. . . . IT RATHER HURTS THE EUROPEAN EYE TO SEE SO MANY SLAVES UPON THE STREETS . . . THERE ARE COMPUTED BETWEEN TWENTY-SIX AND THIRTY THOUSAND INHABITANTS . . . THE SLAVES MAKES AT LEAST A FIFTH PART OF THE NUMBER.
—LETTER WRITTEN BY PATRICK M'ROBERT, A SCOTSMAN VISITING NEW YORK

THE *HARTSHORN* DOCKED IN NEW YORK the next morning, just after a sailor brought down some old biscuits for our breakfast. I picked out the worms and tossed them through the porthole, then gave the biscuits to Ruth.

Madam Lockton's voice rose above the shouting sailors. "Bring those girls up," she said.

A fellow missing most of his teeth stuck his head down the hatchway and waved us over to the ladder. We climbed up, shading our eyes against the bright light of day. Men of all types and colors swarmed the deck, carrying casks and chests down the gangplank, scurrying up the rigging to tend to the sails, unloading gear, loading gear, and making me feel very small and in the way.

Ruth stood at my side and stared so hard, her thumb fell out of her mouth.

The ship was tied up at a long dock, one of many that jutted into the river. The sun sparkled off the water so strong I had to shade my eyes. Tall houses of brick and stone faced us, with rows upon rows of windows looking down at the street. They reached higher than the oldest trees back home. There were smaller buildings, too, all crowded shoulder to shoulder, with no room for a feather to pass betwixt them.

We had arrived soon after a heavy rain. Soldiers splashed through the glittering puddles, toting wood, emptying wagons, carrying buckets hither and fro, and standing about on corners conversating with each other. Some wore uniforms and carried long muskets. Others, in homespun clothes, dragged fence posts to a barricade.

There were ordinary people, too; maids with baskets over their arms moving into and out of the shops and cart men pushing their barrows over the cobblestones, calling out to each other and yelling at the dogs in their way. The working people were dressed muchly as we did out in the country, but there were a few gentry who stuck out of the crowd like peacocks wandering in the chicken pen. Some of the working folk were black. In truth, I had never seen so many of us in one place, not even at burials.

A wagon drawn by two thick-necked horses stopped just beyond the end of the dock. Not far behind it came a beautiful carriage drawn by two pale gold stallions and driven by a stout man in livery with a three-cornered hat on his head. He clucked to the horses to walk on until he stopped behind the first wagon.

The toothless sailor approached us again and pointed down to the dock where the crates and casks stamped LOCKTON & FOOTE were being stacked. "That's where you belong. Don't wander off or one of them soldiers will shoot you dead."

He laughed as he walked down the swaying plank. We followed with tiny steps, Ruth's hand in mine. As I stepped onto the solid dock, I stumbled.

"There you are!" exclaimed Madam Lockton, coming around the stack of crates. "Be careful with that," she said to two deckhands carrying a fine walnut chest. "That goes on the back of the carriage, not to the warehouse."

The men nodded and carried the chest toward the beautiful carriage with the golden horses at the end of the dock.

"Pretty horses," Ruth said.

A soldier at the end of the dock picked up his musket and stopped the two men carrying the walnut chest. There was a brief argument, then the sailors returned, still carrying their burden.

"What is this?" Madam asked as they set the chest at her feet. "I told you to put that on the carriage."

"Beggin' your pardon, ma'am," the sailor said, "but them fellas say all cargo has to be inspected at the wharf before it enters the city. Order of some committee what's in charge here."

"Inspected?" She lifted her chin. "Those are my personal belongings. They will not be inspected by anyone. I do not permit it."

Master Lockton had been half following the turn of events while supervising the unloading. As his wife's voice rose, he hurried to join her.

"Now dear," he said. "I told you there would be some inconveniences. We must be accommodating. Look, there's Charles. He'll straighten this out."

A second wagon had pulled up next to the first. A round, short man rolled off it and bustled up to the Locktons.

"What are you doing here?" demanded the round man. "You shouldn't have come back."

"Lower your voice, Charles," Lockton said. "Where are the men I instructed you to bring?"

The round man pulled a handkerchief out of his waistcoat pocket and wiped his face. "Washington's men took them all to work on the blasted fortifications. Oh, double-blast. Look there: Bellingham."

An official-looking man in a somber black coat had stepped out of a building across the street and was striding toward our little group, walking stick in hand. He was followed by a thin fellow carrying a book near as big as Ruth. Behind him walked a slave boy about my height, whose arms were weighted down with a wooden contraption and a small case with a rope handle. The boy wore a floppy red hat, his shirt sleeves rolled up to the elbow, the blue breeches of a sailor, and a pair of dusty boots.

"Bellingham is eager to arrest you," Charles quietly told Master Lockton. "I told you it was still unsafe. You should have waited."

"Anne." Lockton fixed his eyes intently on his wife. "Do not fail me."

She gave a little nod.

"You have a plan?" Charles asked.

"Everything is in order," Lockton said.

"Elihu Lockton!" Bellingham called, waving his walking stick. "Come join us, friend." Three more soldiers appeared and lined up a few paces behind him.

"Smile, everyone," Lockton commanded through clenched teeth. "Pretend to be happy rebels."

The Locktons and Charles walked to the land end of the dock. Ruth and me followed a few steps behind, little mice trailing behind dogs that were fixing to fight.

The boy in the red hat set down the case and fiddled

with the strange wooden thing. It was actually two strange wooden things: a folding desk and a small stool. After he set up both of them, the thin fellow laid the book on the desk, opened it to a blank page, and perched on the rickety stool. The boy opened the case and took out a bottle of ink and a quill, which he set next to the book. He closed and latched the case, then stepped back and put his hands behind his back, eyes ahead like he was a soldier too.

"Good day, Charles." Bellingham inclined his head toward Madam. "Missus Lockton."

Ruth started to raise her hand to wave at the man, but I grabbed it and held it down.

"Mister Bellingham," Madam replied. "How fares your good wife?"

"Happy that summer is nearly here. You know how she hates the cold."

"Please tell Lorna I shall call on her as soon as we are settled," Madam said.

"Very good," Bellingham said. "We thought you were in London, Elihu."

"London? Never!" exclaimed Lockton. "England offers us nothing but taxes, stamps, and bloodshed."

"How odd. Word from Boston is that you still lick the King's boots."

Madam drew in her breath sharply but said nothing.

"Why do you insult me, sir?" Lockton replied.

"We are at war, sir," Bellingham said in a voice that all could hear. Several of the dockworkers put down their burdens and stood up straight. "Insults are the least of my concern. I'm more worried about the British invasion."

Lockton shrugged. "I am a merchant with cargo to sell. Search my crates. If you wish, search the entire ship. You won't find the British fleet, I promise you. Those yellow-bellied cowards have sailed for Canada."

Bellingham took two steps and stood a fingertip away from Lockton. He lowered his voice. "I don't have time for your games. The Committee of Safety suspects you a Tory, in cahoots with Governor Tryon. You've come home to fight us who strive for freedom and liberty."

All work on the ship stopped. The air had suddenly grown warm. I glanced sideways. The soldiers guarding the crates had picked up their guns. The clerk at the desk was the only one who seemed unrattled. He opened the ink bottle, dipped his pen, and scratched something across a blank page. I caught the boy behind the clerk sparing a quick look at Ruth and me. His eyes were dark gray, the color of the sea during a storm.

"'Freedom and liberty' has many meanings," Lockton finally said. "Am I free to return to my home? Shall I be at liberty from the improper meddling of your Committee?"

Bellingham held his position a moment longer, then he took one long step back. "Search the cargo," he commanded the soldiers, who laid down their weapons and picked up crowbars.

"Very well," Lockton said. "Am I under arrest?"

"Not until I find something," said Bellingham.

"Then I'm leaving. My wife is exhausted and needs me to accompany her home. Charles will stay and supervise."

The round man sputtered twice but didn't say a word.

"Enjoy your homecoming," Bellingham said. "It may be short."

The soldiers had started to go through the crates and call out the contents, the clerk writing down the details in his big book.

Lockton motioned with his elbow again. "Come, dear," he said firmly.

Madam refused to move. "We cannot leave without my chest."

"Now, wife," he said. "It will be sent along."

"It travels with me," Madam said crisply. "Mister Bellingham!"

Bellingham, bent over the clerk's inventory book, looked up. "Ma'am?"

"Does your battle for liberty entitle you to search through the private linens of a lady?"

The dock fell silent again. It was one thing for a gentleman to threaten another with arrest. The topic of a lady's linens was delicate.

Bellingham cleared his throat and stood up straight. "Well, ah, the rules . . ."

"Do I gather, sir, from your hesitation, that you are unsure of the etiquette involved? Perhaps you lack the proper authority." She carefully set herself on the walnut chest in question.

"Oh, no, Anne, please," Lockton groaned. "Do not do this, my dear."

Madam ignored him. "I demand that Mr. Bellingham write to his Congress in Philadelphia. If they give permission for common soldiers to rifle through my personal goods, then I will surrender. Until that letter arrives, I shan't move. I shall guard my dignity day and night."

Charles shifted nervously from foot to foot. Lockton pinched the space where his nose met his forehead. The soldiers studied the tips of their boots. Bellingham muttered something impolite, and the boy standing behind the clerk fought hard not to smile.

My own lips twitched. A woman defending her

underclothes from a battalion of soldiers was comical. I didn't dare laugh, of course.

But Ruth did. She giggled, a sound like a small silver bell. A bell tolling disaster.

Madam Lockton flew off the chest and pointed her finger at us. "Which one of you made that noise?" Her face flushed with rage, her eyes darting back and forth between us.

"I did, ma'am," I quickly lied. The smile on Ruth's face faded as she figured that something bad was unfolding.

Craaack! Lightning struck from a blue sky; Madam slapped my face so hard it near threw me to the ground. The sound echoed off the stone-faced buildings. Ruth grabbed at my skirts and helped me stand straight again. She was confused but kept her mouth closed, thank heavens.

My cheek burned, but I fought back the hot tears and tried to swallow the lump in my throat. No one had ever slapped my face like that, not once in my whole life. *Better me than Ruth, better me than Ruth.*

Madam sat back on the wooden chest and looked calmly at her husband, as if nothing had happened. The soldiers all went about their business, one of them whistling. The only person who looked my way was the boy in the red hat. He kept his features froze in a mask, but he swallowed hard.

Lockton shrugged. "You see, Bellingham? I don't have time for your war. I have enough battles in my own household."

Bellingham sighed and waved at the soldier closest to where Madam sat. "You there. Carry the lady's belongings to her carriage."

He did not mention me. I was already forgotten, dismissed, though the outline of her palm and fingers still burned on my skin. For an instant, I saw myself pushing her off the dock into the water below, but I blinked twice and the vision vanished. I took Ruth by the hand.

Madam rose gracefully. "Thank you, Mr. Bellingham."

Lockton offered his arm again to his wife, and this time, she took it. Bellingham lifted his hat as they passed. Ruth and me trailed close behind.

As we approached the carriage, the driver jumped down and opened the door. Lockton helped his wife as she stepped up and settled on the padded seat. "Well done, my dear," he murmured. "Well done, indeed."

Madam blushed. "'Twas all your doing." She smoothed her skirts. "Put the little girl up with the driver."

"What about the older one?"

She leaned forward to stare at me, standing just behind the master. "Send that one to fetch us some clean water. I doubt Becky has had word of our arrival yet."

Lockton looked puzzled. "How will she know where to find the pump? Or how to get home, for that matter?"

"Charles will find someone to assist her."

"I'll take her, sir."

Lockton turned around. The boy had removed his red hat and bowed politely. "I'm Curzon, sir. Mister Bellingham's boy. My master needs me to fetch new quills up Vandewater Street. I could show your girl the way."

The driver and the soldier had finished strapping the walnut chest to the back of the carriage. The driver spoke gently to Ruth and took her by the hand to meet the horses. She giggled and went eagerly.

Lockton studied the boy, then looked over to Bellingham, who was inspecting one of the opened crates with a nervous Charles by his side.

"Excellent idea," said Madam.

"You know where our house is?" Lockton asked Curzon.

"One of the proudest in our city, sir," the boy answered as he put his hat back on his head. With him standing this close, I could see the gold ring in his right ear, like a pirate's, and a long, thin scar that ran along the left side of his chin. "South side of Wall Street, just past Smith."

Lockton grunted and glared at me. "Be quick about your business, no dawdling, understand?"

I curtsied, bewildered at the speed of it all. Yesterday I had been aboard a ship. The day before that, sold in a tavern. The day before that, I woke up in my own bed and watched an old woman die. My belly ached again, as if I were still at sea and the waves were throwing me off balance.

"Well?" Lockton demanded.

"Yes, sir," I whispered.

He looked at his wife. "This one might be simple too." He climbed into the carriage, closed the door, and rapped at the ceiling with his knuckles. "Go, driver."

The carriage rolled away, Ruth sitting up straight, with a big grin, the golden horses tossing their manes, hooves flashing in the sunshine. She waved to me as they drove away.

I bent down, dipped my fingers in a puddle, and scrubbed the spot where that woman hit me.

CHAPTER VI

Wednesday, May 29, 1776

WE ARE TOLD, THAT THE SUBJECTION OF AMERICANS MAY TEND TO THE DIMINUTION OF OUR OWN LIBERTIES; . . . HOW IS IT THAT WE HEAR THE LOUDEST YELPS FOR LIBERTY AMONG THE DRIVERS OF NEGROES?
—ENGLISH AUTHOR SAMUEL JOHNSON IN HIS POLITICAL PAMPHLET, *TAXATION NO TYRANNY*

"THIS WAY," THE BOY SAID AS THE carriage turned the corner. He headed away from the waterfront quick, without looking back. I picked up my skirts and ran after him.

"Please, slow down," I called.

He pushed ahead. I tried to follow. We hurried past the biggest houses I had ever seen, past shops and taverns and manufactories, past city folk walking like their shoes were on fire. But I could not move fast enough, and I was losing sight of him in the crowd.

"You best slow down!" I called. Folks about me muttered and frowned. The boy stopped in front of a tavern and waited, his mouth twisted in irritation.

I trotted up to him so angry that steam came off the top of my head. "You offer to help, then you abandon me." The words spilled out of my mouth. "Where are we going? And why did she send me to buy water? Don't people here know about digging wells?"

He waited for a moment, then said, "You ask a lot of questions."

"You give dull-witted answers," I shot back.

"Country girls are slow-moving, vexing creatures," he said.

"You're the vexatious one," I said. "Running off and leaving me like that."

We stood glaring at each other, him with his arms crossed over his chest, me trying to catch my breath. Inside the tavern, a woman argued with a man about a leaking cask of beer. On the street corner, an army officer yelled orders at four soldiers building a barricade out of logs, large stones, and barrows full of dirt.

My heart finally slowed, my brow cooled off, and I wanted to give myself a nasty pinch. *Fool.* I should have kept my temper. Now he would truly leave and I would be lost in this horrible place, and there was no telling what Madam Lockton might do to Ruth in my absence.

Apologies did not come natural to me, but I had no choice. "I am sorry I spoke so rudely."

"Hmm," he said. "I am sorry I caused you a fright, Country."

"Thank you. And my name is Isabel, not Country."

"Apologies again, Miss Country Isabel," he said with a smile. "I should have explained before. We're headed up to what folks call the Tea Water Pump. Rich people get their water from there 'cause it tastes the best. But first I must deliver a message for my master. Stay here."

He ducked inside a stationer's shop briefly and came out carrying a small parcel wrapped in brown paper and two fresh rolls, steaming hot, with butter oozing from their middles.

"Follow this a' way."

We walked the length of an alley to a small courtyard. Someone had planted a garden there, and the first plants had come up: peas, cabbage, and pennyroyal. Curzon handed me a roll and pointed to a tree stump. "Figured you'd want to set and eat a bite."

"I have no money," I said. "I can't take this."

"It cost me nothing," he said. "The baker's daughter likes the lad who works the press. She brings him extra breads and pies. Go ahead, eat."

Half of my roll disappeared in one bite. It was the first decent food I'd had since Jenny's kitchen. Curzon watched me without saying a word. When I licked the butter off my fingers, he gave me his roll.

"I et a large breakfast," he said.

My pride wanted to turn it down, but my belly was stronger. The second roll vanished as quick as the first.

"Thank you," I said when I finished. "I'm beholden to you for that. Can we go now? I need to get back to my sister."

He set his package on the tree stump. "The littler one is your sister? That's why you took the blow meant for her, isn't it?"

A breeze ran through the courtyard, fluttering the leaves of the young pea plants and blowing cool across my cheek where Madam struck me. "She needs watching over."

He nodded. "How long have you been with the Locktons?"

"Three days."

Curzon listened carefully as I told how Madam and her husband bought us. "Lockton is a dirty Loyalist," he said when I finished.

"Loyalist or rebel, I don't care." I stood up from the stump and brushed the back of my skirt clean. "Can we go?"

He nodded, picked up his package, and led me out of the alley. "You feel beholden to Lockton?"

"Pardon?"

"He's going to feed you and your sister, give you a place to sleep. He can order you sold, beat, or hung, if the mood takes him. That could make a person feel a kind of loyalty."

I stopped, considering this. "Someday I'll find that lawyer and Miss Mary's will and that'll free us. Until then, we need to eat, work, and stay together. So yes, I guess I'm loyal to Lockton."

The words tasted bitter. Being loyal to the one who owned me gave me prickly thoughts, like burrs trapped in my shift, pressing into my skin with every step.

We paused at a corner while a soldier drove a cart filled with barrels down the street. After we crossed, Curzon spoke so quiet I had to lean in to catch his words. "You might be better served if you placed your loyalty with us."

"Who is 'us'?"

"My master and those he serves, the rebels, the Congress. We're fighting for freedom from people like Lockton."

"I'm just fighting for me and Ruth. You can keep your rebellion. How much longer till this pump?"

He stopped beside a barricade. The brim of his hat cast his face in shadow. "You might hear things. At the Lockton house."

"What kinds of things?"

"Useful things. Things that might help you get to that lawyer and your freedom."

I frowned. "I don't like riddles. Talk plain."

"New York is a ball tossed between the Loyalists and

Patriots," he said, scratching at the scar on his face. "Right now the Patriots hold it."

"So?"

"Lockton has returned to hurt our cause."

"Why don't they arrest him?"

"It's not that simple. Plenty of folks hereabouts haven't decided which side they favor. One day they cheer General Washington, the next day they toast the King. Putting Lockton in jail could turn them against us."

He started walking again, nattering on and on about plots and conspiracies and battle plans and secrets, but truth be told, my mind drifted. I cared not a fig for politics nor soldiers. I was worried about my sister, and my cheek still hurt.

"Will you help us or not?"

He stared at me intent as I tried to figure his meaning. It slowly dawned.

"You want me to be a spy?" I asked. "Are you funny in the head? Do you know what they would do to me?"

"Shhh," he warned. "Keep your voice down. You just have to listen and alert me if you hear anything important. You won't be in any danger."

"You are a crazy fool. How do you know I won't tell Master Lockton you sought me out?"

"Wouldn't matter if you did. He knows he's under suspicion. Might do you some good, bring you favor in his eyes if you told him. But it would be a mistake. Lockton won't reward you. The Patriots can."

"Reward?"

"Colonel Regan is the officer in charge. He could send you back to Rhode Island, maybe, help you find that lawyer and his papers."

I pondered this. Was he lying? Could I trust this strange boy, filled with war and secrets? What would Momma do?

I shook my head. "It's too dangerous. I'll have enough to do with chores and watching Ruth and keeping out of Madam's way."

"All you have to do is to listen for talk of the King's troops."

"See, there you go again, proving you're a fool. They won't say anything in front of me."

"You are a small black girl, Country," he said bitterly. "You are a slave, not a person. They'll say things in front of you they won't say in front of the white servants. 'Cause you don't count to them. It happens all the time to me."

There was truth in his words, hard truth, a hammer striking stone.

"If you hear something, come to Bellingham's house in the night, across from where your ship docked this morning. I sleep in the shed room. Tap on the window and I'll awake."

I touched my cheek. I couldn't. I shouldn't.

"I can't," I said. "I promised Momma I would take care of Ruth. Now can we please go?"

CHAPTER VII

Wednesday, May 29, 1776

I HIRED A GIRL TO CLEAN [THE HOUSE], IT HAD A CART LOAD OF DIRT IN IT . . . ONE OF THE CHAMBERS WAS USED TO KEEP POULTRY IN, AN OTHER SEA COAL, AND AN OTHER SALT. YOU MAY CONCEIVE HOW IT LOOK'D. THE HOUSE IS SO EXCEEDING DAMP BEING SHUT UP, THAT THE FLOORS ARE MILDEWD, THE SEALING FALLING DOWN, AND THE PAPER MOULDY AND FALLING FROM THE WALLS.
—LETTER FROM ABIGAIL ADAMS TO HER HUSBAND, JOHN

IT WAS NEAR A MILE FROM THE TEA WATER Pump back down the island to the Lockton house, a long journey carrying heavy buckets that stretched my arms into sore ribbons.

I forgot the pain when Curzon stopped, pointed, and said, "There 'tis."

The house was made of blocks of cream-colored stone and was wider from side to side than Jenny's tavern. I tilted my head up and counted: four floors, each with big windows facing the street. There were balcony railings on the roof. There were even windows peeking out at foot-level, cellar windows, which meant five stories in one house.

A curtain moved.

"Make haste," Curzon said. "If you value your life, don't use the front door."

The sun caught the ring in his ear and blazed as he tipped his hat to me.

I hurried through the side gate. The mansion was twice as long as it was wide. A large plot stretched behind it with a cistern, a privy, a poor excuse for a garden, and at the far end, a carriage house and small stable.

"You there!"

I turned around. A tiny woman wearing a green calico skirt, a nut-brown bodice, and a dingy shift stood in the open door to the kitchen. She tossed a pan of dirty water onto the flagstones and pushed a strand of graying hair out of her eyes with the back of her hand.

"What's your business here?" she demanded.

"I'm Isabel. I'm the . . . Master Lockton brought us from Newport."

The anger drained out of her face. "You're the new girl gone for the water. Lord help us. Did you get lost?"

"I don't think so. Curzon–"

"Funny little boy, ring in his ear?" She shook her head. "That's Bellingham's boy. You stay away from him. Bring in that water. We've a world of work to do."

Her name was Becky Berry, ". . . though it'll be mud if I don't pull this house together in a flash," she said as she poured the fresh water into a pot and swung it over the kitchen fire. She barely stopped talking long enough to draw a breath. "Eight months! They vanish to Boston for eight months and then show up with no warning and wanting tea. Tea! I could get tarred and feathered for brewing tea," she muttered.

She turned around. Her face marked her as being of middle years, dotted with freckles and pox scars. Her chin was narrow and pointed like a shovel, and her smile was missing several teeth. "The rules here is simple: do what Madam says. You know where the Tea Water Pump is; you'll go up there every day. You'll go with me to market when I need you to. Don't go north of Chambers Street, or wandering off past Mulberry, less Madam writes you a pass. You don't want folks thinking you're trying to run. That don't work here. You been a housemaid before?"

I shook my head. "We lived on a farm. Pardon me, ma'am, Miss Becky, but can you tell me where my sister is?"

"Your what?" Her eyebrows went up. "Ooohhh . . . that little girl."

I nodded. "Ruth."

"She's slow, ain't she?"

I didn't dare explain until I figured what kind of person Becky was. "She's good-natured."

Becky walked into a pantry crowded with shelves of crockery. "Not going to cause me trouble?"

"Never," I lied. "Where is she, please, ma'am?"

Becky came out carrying a tarnished silver teapot and a stack of china cups and plates.

"Madam Lockton told me to give the little one a bath and feed her." She went back to the pantry and shouted a little so I could hear her. "She's in the privy. Your sister, I mean, not the madam."

I let out a long breath and stepped toward the door.

Becky came back carrying a small chest. "Where do you think you're going?"

"To fetch Ruth."

"Oh, no, you are not," Becky said. "Madam wants her outside peeling potatoes. You're to work in here."

"But . . ."

Through the window, I watched Ruth leave the privy and walk straight to a bench. She hopped up on it, pulled a potato from the sack next to her, and started peeling with a small knife, her feet kicking in the air under the bench. She looked like a little bird on a twig. I relaxed some; she was safe and happy enough.

Becky brushed at the cobwebs clinging to her skirt. "But nothing. If Madam sees you idling and jawing out there, there'll be the devil to pay." She paused. "She can be a harsh mistress to slaves."

I waited for her to say more, but she shook her head once and handed me a broom.

"Me, I see things different." She picked up a pile of rags and a jar. "You do what you're told and we'll get along fine. Now follow me and pay attention."

Becky led me down a narrow corridor to the front entry hall, where a grand staircase curled upward. A tall grandfather clock sat at the foot of the stairs, pecking away at the hour as if a crow trapped inside were trying to break loose. The walnut linen chest that Madam had fussed over at the dock was set in front of the clock.

Opposite the chest was the door that led to the street. Two other doors with tarnished brass pulls faced the hall. Becky pointed to the door on the right. "That there's the master's library. You don't step foot in it without permission. He don't like his things touched."

"A library with books?"

"And maps and papers all in a jumble. It's a wonder he can find anything." She opened the door on the left and entered, me at her heels. "This is the good parlor, where I'll serve the tea. The drawing room is upstairs. We'll clean up there later. Open them windows."

The room was crowded with furniture draped with cloth. The air was thick and stale. I pulled aside the heavy drapes and stretched on my toes to push up the window. The sills were dusty and the corners were spun thick with spiderwebs studded with dead flies. I went to open the next window as Becky laid out a rag on each sill.

"Wipe down the windows and sweep the floor before you uncover the furniture," she said.

The second window was stubborn. I pushed as hard as I could until it suddenly flew up and I near lost my balance. Becky grabbed me before I tumbled outside.

"Easy on," she said as I regained my balance. "You're no good to me with a cracked head."

Three soldiers wearing homespun shirts and carrying muskets walked past the window, laughing loudly.

"I wish they'd all go home," Becky muttered. "Soldiers is a nuisance."

"You don't like the rebels?" I asked.

Becky put a finger to her lips and pulled me away from the window. "Listen to me good. Them that feeds us"–she pointed upstairs–"they're Loyalists, Tories. That means we're Tories, too, understand?"

"Yes, ma'am." I nodded. "But . . ." I hesitated, not sure if I was allowed to ask questions. "Master Lockton claimed he was a Patriot on the docks."

Becky fought to open the final window. A cool breeze flowed through the room and stirred the dust. "He was faking to protect his skin. Some folks switch back and forth. One day they're for the King, the next, it's all 'liberty and freedom, huzzah'! A tribe of Mr. Facing-Both-Ways, that's what you'll find in New York. But you know what never changes?"

I shook my head. "No, what?"

"Madam wants lemon cakes with her tea. She is terrible

fond of cakes, is Madam. Lady Clarissa Seymour is coming to hear all the news from Boston."

"A lady? A royal lady?"

Becky laughed. "Close enough. She's the master's aunt; she's rich and old, and owns land in three countries. The master hopes to inherit the lot when she dies, so they treat her like the Queen herself. To her face, at least."

The grandfather clock in the hall bonged loudly, four times, startling us both.

"Wretched clock," Becky muttered. "I'm off to the baker. Finish sweeping in here, and dusting. After that, polish the teapot and bring in the firewood. Don't stop moving, whatever you do."

CHAPTER VIII

Wednesday, May 29–Thursday, June 6, 1776

. . . WE HAVE IN COMMON WITH ALL OTHER MEN
A NATUREL RIGHT TO OUR FREEDOMS WITHOUT
BEING DEPRIV'D OF THEM BY OUR FELLOW MEN. . . .
WE WERE UNJUSTLY DRAGGED BY THE CRUEL HAND
OF POWER FROM OUR DEAREST FRIENDS AND SUM OF US
STOLEN . . . AND BROUGHT HITHER TO BE MADE SLAVES FOR
LIFE IN A CHRISTIAN LAND THUS ARE WE DEPRIVED
OF EVERY THING THAT HATH A TENDENCY TO MAKE
LIFE EVEN TOLERABLE . . .
–PETITION FOR FREEDOM FROM A GROUP OF SLAVES
TO MASSACHUSETTS GOVERNOR THOMAS GAGE,
HIS MAJESTY'S COUNCIL, AND THE HOUSE OF
REPRESENTATIVES, 25 MAY 1774

THE DAYS STARTED EARLY IN THE Lockton kitchen. Since Becky lived in a boardinghouse on Oliver Street, it fell to me to wake first and build up the fire. She did the proper cooking, and I did near everything else, like washing pots and plates and beating eggs till my arms fell off for Madam's almond jumbles and plum cakes with icing. If not in the kitchen, I was removing colonies of spiders, polishing tables and chairs, or sweeping up a mountain of dust. I saved the cobwebs, twisting them around a rag and storing them by our pallet in the cellar.

Cobwebs were handy when a person had a bloody cut.

Madam complained every time she saw me: I left a streak of wax on the tabletop. I tracked in mud. I faced a china dog toward the door after I dusted it, which would cause the family's luck to run out. At the end of every scolding, I cast down my eyes and said, "Yes, Madam."

I kept careful track of her the same way as I used to mind the neighbor's bull when I took the milk cows out to pasture. She had not hit me again, but always seemed on the edge of it.

Mostly Madam slept late, wrote letters, and picked out melodies on a badly tuned spinet. A few times, she and her husband conversated fast and quiet about Mr. Washington and when the King's ships would arrive for the invasion. They argued fierce on Thursday night. Lockton shouted and called Madam rude names before storming out of the house, the front door crashing behind him.

I vowed not to cross neither of them.

Madam went to bed early that night, so we did too. Ruth snuggled next to me and fell asleep quick. I lay awake, praying hard but gaining little comfort.

I was lost. I knew that we were in the cellar of a house on Wall Street, owned by the Locktons, in the city of New York, but it was like looking at a knot, knowing it was a knot, but not knowing how to untie it. I had no map for this life.

I lay awake and stared into the darkness.

Madam called for tea in her bedchamber the next morning and sent for Ruth, who was pumping the butter churn with vigor.

"Why would she need Ruth?" I asked as I wiped my sister's hands and face with a damp rag.

"Why does she do anything?" Becky asked. "I'm to climb to the attic to fetch the cast-off clothing in an old trunk. Maybe she'll set the little one to rip out the stitches so the dressmaker can use the fabric. This best be the last of the day's fanciful notions. My knees don't like all this upping and downing of the stairs."

Ruth stayed in Madam's chamber for hours. I spilled the fireplace ashes on the kitchen floor, then kicked over the bucket of wash water I brought in to clean up the mess. I stubbed my toe and near cut off my finger whilst peeling an old, tough turnip.

When I could stand it no more, I snuck out of the kitchen and tiptoed down the hall. I could hear the sound of Madam's voice from the bottom of the stairs, but not the words she was saying. I wanted to march up there and tell Ruth to come back and finish the butter.

I did not. I forced myself to work.

Becky took a tray of cookies and a pot of tea upstairs late in the afternoon. I pounced when she returned to the kitchen.

"Is Ruth well? Why does Madam keep her?"

Becky chose her words with care. "Madam has taken a liking to your Ruth, on account of her being so tiny and quiet." She sat at the kitchen table. "She means to use her for a personal maid."

"Pardon me?"

"Most of Madam's friends have a slave to split wood and carry chamber pots, like you. If Madam has a slave dressed in finery, well that makes her more of a lady. Ruth can fan her when she's hot, or stir the fire when she's cold."

I forgot myself and sat down across from Becky. "She's making Ruth into a curiosity?"

Becky nodded. "Aye, that's a good word for it."

I went cold with anger, then hot, then cold again. It wasn't right. It wasn't right for one body to own another or pull strings to make them jump. Why was Madam allowed to hit me or to treat Ruth like a toy?

"Take care," Becky warned, pointing to my lap.

I looked down. My hands were clenched into fists so tight the cords that held my bones together could be seen. I released them.

Becky leaned across the table and spoke quiet. "I don't imagine you like this much. Can't say I blame you. But don't lose your head. Madam is not afraid to beat her slaves."

I rubbed my palms together. "Do they own more than us?"

"Half a dozen down to the Charleston place, none up in Boston. Never been to the Carolinas, so I don't know how they get along. But you need to calm yourself and heed what I am about to tell you."

"Yes, ma'am," I said stiffly.

"Two, three years ago, there was another girl here, slave like you. She talked back. Madam called her surly and took to beating her regular-like. One day she beat her with a fireplace poker."

"Did she die?"

"No, but her arm broke and didn't heal right. It withered and hung useless, so Madam sold her."

I could not hold the hot words in my mouth any longer. "She best not come after me with a poker. Or hurt Ruth."

Becky leaned back and studied on me a bit. "You ain't never going to say something like that again, not in my kitchen. I get paid decent here, and I won't let some girl like you get in the way of that. Wearing pretty dresses ain't going to hurt the little one, so wipe that look off your face and fetch me some more wood."

After that, Ruth's every waking moment was spent with Madam. Though we worked in the same house and slept under the same blanket, we had little time to talk. Ruth was permitted to sleep until the sun rose, went to bed when Madam retired, and rarely had to work in the kitchen or garden.

I lay awake every night, heart filled with dread, recalling the dangerous offer made by the boy in the floppy red hat.

CHAPTER IX

Thursday, June 6, 1776

. . . HUNDREDS IN THIS [NEW YORK] COLONY ARE ACTIVE AGAINST US AND SUCH IS THE WEAKNESS OF THE GOVERNMENT, (IF IT CAN DESERVE THE NAME) THAT THE TORIES OPENLY PROFESS THEIR SENTIMENTS IN FAVOUR OF THE ENEMY, AND LIVE UNPUNISHED.
—LETTER OF WILLIAM TUDOR,
WASHINGTON'S CHIEF LEGAL OFFICER, TO JOHN ADAMS

I WAS STUCK ON THE BACK STEPS with a pile of dull knives and a whetstone. It was a dreary job. First, spit on the stone. Next, hold the knife at the proper angle and circle it against the stone; ten to the left, ten to the right, until the blade was sharp enough to slice through a joint of beef like it was warm butter.

As I sharpened, I imagined using the knife to cut through the ropes that tied us to New York. I'd slice through the ocean, and Ruth and me would walk on the sand all the way home. *Ten circles to the left* . . .

Ruth was abovestairs, standing by whilst Madam prepared herself for company. The master was locked in his library. Becky was somewhere in the crowd watching General Washington parade down Broadway with five regiments of soldiers. The sounds of beating drums and whistling fifes, and the cries of "Huzzah! Huzzah!" blew toward me over the rooftops.

I pushed everything out of my mind, save my task. *Ten circles to the right . . .*

Becky came back from the parade an hour later, overflowing with stories. She nattered on about the spectacle whilst assembling the tea things for Madam and Lady Seymour, who had come again to call. I pretended to listen. Truth be told, I didn't notice when she left carrying the tray.

Ten circles to the left, ten circles to the righty, all make the blade sharp and mighty. Ten circles to the left, ten to the right . . .

Becky called for me twice before I heard her proper. Her voice was high and tight. ". . . I said to hurry! You want to get me put on the street? Madam wants you in the parlor."

The knife near slipped from my hands. "Is it Ruth?"

"No, the Lady Seymour wants to see you. And the master just arrived with gentlemen friends all calling for food and drink. Hurry!"

I washed up in the cold water bucket, quickly pinned on a clean apron, checked my kerchief was on proper and followed Becky to the parlor. She rapped lightly on the door and pushed it open. "The new girl, ma'am," she said, setting a plate of fresh-baked strawberry tarts on the table.

"Show her in," Madam said.

Becky waved at me to enter.

Madam and an older woman sat at the table, but my eyes were drawn behind them, to my sister, dressed up as Madam's pretty pet in a bleached linen shift, a navy-blue brocade short gown, and a full skirt patterned with lilacs. When she saw me, she clenched her hands together and bit her lower lip. Her eyes were red and swollen with crying.

My belly went funny and my mind raced. Why had she been crying? Was she sick? Scared? Did Madam hurt her?

Becky poked me gently in the back. This was not the time for questions.

I quickly dropped into a curtsy, bowing my head. When I stood up, the older woman, the lady aunt with all the money, gave me a shadow of a smile. She was smaller than Madam and wore a silk gown the color of a mourning dove and gray lace gloves. Her hair was curled high and powdered snow white. A necklace set with black stones shone from her neck. There were deep lines at the corners of her eyes and around her mouth, but I couldn't tell if they were from laughing or from crying.

She turned in her chair and looked at Ruth, then back at me. "And these two girls are the sisters?" she asked.

Madam reached for a tart. "That's what the man said."

The older woman sipped her tea. "What is your name, girl?" she asked me.

"Isabel, ma'am," I said. "Isabel Finch."

"Ridiculous name," Madam said. She opened her fan and waved it in front of her face. "You are called Sal Lockton now. It's more suitable."

I forced myself to breathe in slow and regular instead of telling her that my name was not her affair. "Yes, ma'am."

She glanced at my feet. "And you must wear your shoes. This is a house, not a barn."

Ruth stepped out of her corner. "Isabel."

Madam snapped the fan shut and rapped it against the edge of the table, startling us all. "What did I tell you about silence?" she said roughly.

Ruth raised one shaking finger to her mouth and said, "Shh."

"Precisely." Madam set the fan in her lap and reached for a piece of sugar with silver tongs. When she plopped it in the cup, the tea overflowed into the saucer.

Ruth stood there like a carved statue, her finger still held to her lips. I took another breath, slower than the first, and tried not to think on the newly sharpened knives on the kitchen steps. Lady Seymour curled her fingers around the teacup, her gaze marking first Madam, then Ruth, then me. She said nothing.

"Would you like Sal to serve you and Lady Seymour while I wait on the gentlemen?" Becky asked.

"Absolutely not. Show her the library and make sure the men are fed. And bring fresh tea. This has already gone cold."

We curtsied and left the parlor. Ruth's sad eyes followed me to the door.

Ten circles to the left, ten circles to the righty,
all make the blade sharp and mighty.

Back in the kitchen, Becky took a large silver tray off a high shelf in the pantry. "Hold this." She loaded the tray with plates of cold sliced tongue, cheddar cheese, brown bread, and a bowl of pickles. I could not stop thinking about the way Ruth had jumped when Madam shouted, nor the tears in her eyes.

Becky took down a second tray and set upon it four goblets, two bottles of claret wine, and a crock of mustard. She swung the kettle back over the fire to heat up more water, picked up the tray with the wine, and said, "Hop to."

I followed her to the front of the house. "But, what about my shoes?"

"The master won't notice long as he gets his grub." Becky

balanced the edge of the tray on her hip and knocked on the door on the right side of the front hall. When a deep voice answered, she opened it.

Lockton looked up as we entered. "Oh, good. Sustenance," he said, pushing aside a stack of newspapers to clear off the desk.

The room was the same size and shape as the parlor, but two of the walls had bookcases built into them. A large painting of horses jumping over a high hedge hung on the third wall. A thin layer of dust lay over everything. The front windows were open, bringing in fresh air and noise from the street; carts rolling over the cobblestones and church bells in the distance mingled with the voices of the four men who sat around the enormous desk.

One man looked poorer than the others; the cuffs of his coat were frayed and his hands were stained with ink. Next to him sat a man with suspicious gray eyes and a liver-colored coat with a double row of gold buttons fastened over a large pudding-belly. The third man wore something on his head that looked more like a dead possum than a wig, but his coat was crisp and new and the buckles on his shoes gleamed. The fourth was Master Lockton, looking like a cat who had just swallowed the last bite of a juicy mouse.

Becky set her tray on a sideboard. I held mine as she poured the wine and served the gentlemen. Then she had me hold the food tray so that she could serve the tongue and cheese. Talk halted as the men started in on their meal.

"Becky!" Madam called from across the hall.

"Go see to her," Lockton told Becky. "The girl can stay here. Does she know where the wine is?"

"Yes, sir," I said.

Becky and Lockton both stared at me. I had spoken out of

turn. My job was to be silent and follow orders. Ruth had already learned that. *Shhhhhh* . . .

"Keep the wine flowing and the plates full," Lockton said. "My friends eat more at my table than their own."

As Becky left, Goldbuttons drained his wine, then raised his goblet. I hurried to pour him another, and topped off the drinks of the other men. Lockton gave me a curt nod when I was finished. "Stand over there," he said, pointing to the corner where the two bookshelves met each other.

I gave a wordless curtsy and took my place.

The men dove back into their conversation. "Who has been arrested because of the oath?" demanded Lockton.

"Fools unschooled in the art of fence-sitting," said Goldbuttons.

"Plank-walking, you mean," said Inkstained.

Shabbywig leaned forward and pointed his finger at Inkstained. "Don't you turn the coward on us. Not when we're this close."

"Close?" argued Inkstained. "Do you see His Majesty's ships in the harbor? I don't. I might argue that England has fled and the rebel traitors have won."

"Lower your voices," Lockton said with a scowl. He closed the windows with a loud *bang,* then returned to his seat.

"His Majesty's ships are very close, closer than you know. This rebellion will be smashed like glass under a heavy boot, and the King will be very grateful for our assistance."

The mention of the King caught my ear. I studied the wide boards on the floor and listened with care.

Goldbuttons popped a piece of cheese into his mouth and talked as he chewed. "I sincerely hope you speak the truth, Elihu. These rebel committees are multiplying faster than rabbits in the spring. They've just about ground business to a halt."

"Have they interfered with you directly?" Lockton asked.

"Every waking moment," Goldbuttons said. "The latest bit of nonsense is a Committee to Detect Conspiracies. They've sent the hounds after us, old friend."

"Have you written to Parliament? They need the specifics of our difficulties."

"Parliament is as far away as the moon," complained Inkstained.

As the other men argued about Parliament and letters of protest and counterletters and counter-counterletters, Shabbywig stabbed at the last pieces of tongue on his plate and shoved them into his mouth. He turned in his seat to look at me, held up his plate, and grunted. If I had ever done such a thing, Momma would have switched my behind for having the manners of a pig. Even Miss Mary Finch had asked with a "please" and a "thank you" when Momma served her dinner.

This is New York, I reminded myself as I crossed the room and took the plate from his hand. *The rules are different.* I loaded his plate down with the last slices of tongue and set it in front of him before retreating to my corner. *Everything is different.*

My belly growled and grumbled in its cage. The smell of the tongue and mustard and the cheese filled the room and made my mouth water. I had eaten a bowl of corn mush at sunrise and only dumplings at midday. To distract the beast in my gullet, I tried to read the names of the books on the shelves without turning my head. My eyes were as starved for words as the rest of me was for dinner.

It was hard to read from the side like that. I wanted to pull down a book, open it proper, and gobble up page after page. I wanted to stare into the faces of these men and demand they take me home. I wanted to jump on the horse in the painting and fly over the hills. Most of all, I wanted to grab my sister by the hand and run as fast as we could until the cobblestones disappeared and there was dirt under our feet again.

"Girl," Lockton said. "Bring us more bread, sliced thin. And some of Becky's apricot jam. I've missed the taste of that."

I curtsied and hurried out of the room, leaving the door open a crack so I could easily open it when I came back with my hands full. Across the hall came the quiet conversation of Madam and Lady Seymour. I paused but heard no mention of Ruth.

Shhhhh . . .

There was fresh bread on the kitchen table, but it took a piece of time to find the crock of jam. I used one of my sharp knives to slice the loaf, set out the slices on a clean plate, and put the plate and jam on a tray. It was taking me too long to finish a simple chore. I feared the master would be angry with me, and I was angry at myself for being afraid.

I was just about to push open the library door with my foot when the master said, "Compliments of His Majesty, gentleman. There's enough money here to bribe half of the rebel army."

I stopped and peered through the crack.

Madam's linen chest, the one that she had fussed about when we arrived, was in the middle of the library floor, the top thrown open. Underskirts and shifts were heaped on the floor beside it. Lockton reached into the chest and pulled out two handfuls of paper currency.

"Huzzah!" said Inkstained as Goldbuttons let out a low whistle.

"Do you have a man ready?" Lockton asked.

"Two," Shabbywig answered. "One will operate out of Corby's Tavern, the other from the Highlander."

"Good." Lockton crossed back to his desk. I could no longer see him, but his words were clear. "Every man willing to switch sides is to be paid five guineas and two hundred acres of land. If he have a wife, an additional hundred acres. Each child of his blood garners another fifty."

"Makes me want to marry the next lady I clap eyes on," Goldbuttons said.

Lockton chuckled.

I gave the door a little push and it swung open. "Sir?" I asked in a hushed tone.

"Enter," Lockton said.

I walked in. The other men did not look my way. I was invisible to them until they needed something.

"Jam," he said with a smile. "Put it right here."

I placed the tray in front of him and took my place again in the corner. The men spread the jam on the bread and drank their wine, discussing politics and war and armies over the stacks of money on my master's desk. The smell of apricots filled the warm room. It put me in mind of the orchards down the road from Miss Mary's place.

I kept my face still as a plaster mask, but inside my brainpan, thoughts chased round and round. By the time the men rose to leave, I knew what I had to do.

CHAPTER X

Thursday, June 6, 1776

THE PEOPLE [OF NEW YORK]—WHY THE PEOPLE ARE MAGNIFICENT; IN THEIR CARRIAGES, WHICH ARE NUMEROUS, IN THEIR HOUSE FURNITURE, WHICH IS FINE, IN THEIR PRIDE AND CONCEIT, WHICH ARE INIMITABLE, IN THEIR PROFANENESS, WHICH IS INTOLERABLE, IN THE WANT OF PRINCIPLE, WHICH IS PREVALENT, AND IN THEIR TORYISM, WHICH IS INSUFFERABLE.
—LETTER FROM PATRIOT COLONEL HENRY KNOX TO HIS WIFE, LUCY

LADY SEYMOUR WAS THE FIRST TO leave, followed soon after by the gentlemen in the library. Lockton and Madam retired upstairs, releasing Ruth for the evening and leaving me with the cleaning up. For supper we ate the remainders from the plates of Inkstained and Goldbuttons—cold tongue and brown bread. Ruth ate three bites, then laid her head down on the table.

When Becky left for the night, I held my sister's hand and walked her down the steep stairs. Our bed was a thin mattress stuffed with old corn husks in front of the potato bin. I helped her out of her skirt and removed my own.

Just before I blew out the candle I asked, "Why were you crying in the parlor today, before Becky and me came in? Did Madam hurt you?"

Her eyes puddled with tears, and she shook her head from side to side. "No foolin'."

"Did you play or fuss? Was Madam angry with you? Did she hit you?"

She sniffed and wiped her nose on the sleeves of her shift. "Shhh," she said again.

That wretched woman beat Ruth, I just knew it. She would beat Ruth into total silence if I let her.

I kissed her tears and we knelt to pray. When we finally laid down, my fingers felt along the edge of my blanket, looking for the rip that Momma had sewed up with tiny feather stitches. She wouldn't let anyone hurt her children.

"Where's my baby?" Ruth muttered, half-asleep. She asked this every night.

"That bad man stole your doll baby," I reminded her. "The skinny one who stole us. He took everything."

"Everything?"

I hugged her close. "Almost everything. But I'll get it back. Don't worry. Just go to sleep."

"I can't sleep without my baby." There was a stubborn note in her voice.

"I'll make you another doll, I promise, but not tonight. Want me to sing to you?"

I didn't wait for an answer, but started in on an island lullaby that Momma had loved. Ruth lay quiet, her breath steady and slow. By the time the song was over, she was fast asleep.

I waited a full hour, until the clock struck eleven, then slipped out from under the blanket and put my skirt back on. I did not stuff my feet into my shoes. I'd be faster and quieter without them.

I climbed up the cellar stairs, freezing with every groan of the old wood. *If Madam or Lockton come across me, I'll say I'm on my way to the privy.* They couldn't be angry about that. A body must follow the call of nature, even in the dead of the night.

The kitchen was so dark I walked slowly, my hands feeling in front of me so I wouldn't bump into the table or knock over a pitcher on the sideboard. I paused at the back door. The sound of Lockton's snoring came from above, like faraway thunder. *I'm on my way to the privy,* I reminded myself. *No harm in that.* I carefully opened the door and stepped outside.

The night air was crisp and smelled faintly of salt. I tiptoed down the back steps and flew past the privy and around the side of the house to the gate, which hid in shadows. My heart pounded so loud I felt sure it would wake the entire street.

I had only to open the gate latch and step out.

My hand would not move.

If I opened the gate, I would be a criminal. Slaves were not allowed out after sunset without a pass from a master. Anyone who caught me could take me to the jail. If I opened the gate, a judge could order me flogged. If I opened the gate, there was no telling what punishment Madam would demand.

If I opened the gate, I might die of fright.

I leaned my head against the gate. I could not open the gate, but I had to open the gate. This house was not a safe place. I had to get us out. But there was no way to get out, no way to run away off an island, no way to run with a little girl. The secret of Madam's linen chest was the only key I held.

Watch over me, Momma.

I opened the latch, slipped out the gate, and ran.

I thought it would be easy. I would run straight to the shed behind Bellingham's house, tap on Curzon's window, tell him the news, and hurry home. It was nighttime, after all, and folks would be asleep.

Not in New York. Not in a city occupied by the Continental army.

At the end of the block there were soldiers on watch in front of City Hall; a dozen or so men standing around a campfire, with more dozing on the ground. One man was trying to read a letter by the firelight, another was roasting a small piece of meat at the end of a stick. Their guns were close to hand. I crept as close as I dared, but there was no way to sneak past them. I swallowed hard and turned around to head east, away from the firelight.

The next corner was dark and lonesome. I turned south, then west again, then was forced north for three blocks by loud soldiers spilling out of taverns. The crowded buildings confuddled me. I tried to be brave like Momma or Queen Esther in the Bible, but I just knew there were hobgoblins awalking in the dark, looking to steal the breath from a girl's body.

I hid when I heard voices and when a horseman galloped down the middle of the street. The horse's hooves sparked off the cobblestones and sounded like a hammer striking a forge. I chased up and down streets and alleys, sticking to the shadows and shying away from the flickering streetlamps. I ran.

Finally the street emptied out onto a wharf. I had reached one of the two rivers that sheltered New York Island, but I couldn't tell if I was looking at the East River or the North. I ventured out farther into the street. Relaxed men told loud jokes to each other on the waterfront, a tin whistle played, and a small dog yipped. The masts of ships grew thicker to my right. That was my heading.

The shapes of the buildings and the outline of the wharves soon became familiar. There was the dock the *Hartshorn* had tied to, and there was Bellingham's building. I snuck down the alley to the shed window that Curzon described.

This was the end of my quest. I took a deep breath, said a prayer, and rapped on the glass.

Nothing happened.

I started to rap again, then stopped. *What if this is the wrong window, the wrong house? What if the person within thinks me a thief in the night or a murderess? What if–?*

"Country?"

A puzzled voice called to me from the shadows of the back end of a tavern, a few buildings down. Every window in the tavern was lit up, and the air loud with the angry shouts of men deep in argument.

"Are you speaking to me?" I said, trying to keep my voice from shaking.

"What are you doing here?" Curzon stepped out of the shadows and motioned for me to join him.

I dashed toward him, keeping to the edge of the tavern candlelight. "I have news."

"Of Lockton?"

"And more." I quickly told him everything I had seen and heard.

"Is the money still there?" he finally asked.

"A portion," I said. "The gentlemen took some with them, but Lockton placed the rest back in the chest. Then I was sent to fetch more wine. The chest was gone by my return."

He nodded gravely.

"Will this be enough to send us home?" I asked. "Can they get us on a ship tomorrow? I can have Ruth at the docks by sunup."

He raised both of his hands. "Go home and sleep, I'll take your news to Master Bellingham. I expect the Committee will visit Lockton tomorrow. Whatever you do, don't let on that you were the informant."

"Why not?" I asked. "How else can I claim what's mine?"

"The colonel will know who you are and how to find you. Until you hear from him, you're just the new Lockton girl."

"But not for long," I said, trying to sound braver than I felt.

"Not for long," he agreed. "Go home now."

I hesitated. "I don't know how. I got lost coming here."

He chuckled softly. "It's easy enough once you know the way." He gave me the directions.

"Thank you," I said, picking up my skirts. "Thank you for everything."

"Go quick." When I was halfway up the alley, he called after me. "Ho there, Country."

"What?"

"Well done."

CHAPTER XI

Friday, June 7, 1776

THERE IS NOTHING MORE NECESSARY THAN GOOD INTELLIGENCE TO FRUSTRATE A DESIGNING ENEMY, & NOTHING REQUIRES GREATER PAINS TO OBTAIN.
–LETTER OF GEORGE WASHINGTON TO ROBERT MORRIS

IT FELT LIKE BECKY SHOOK ME AWAKE the moment I fell asleep.

"Make haste, girl," she hissed. "You didn't start the fire. Why are you still abed?"

"Haste" was the word of the day. No matter how hard I tried, I couldn't catch up. It did not help that Madam was in a mood.

"Girl," she said to me as I prepared to sweep the kitchen floor, "the bedding needs to be aired."

"Yes, ma'am." I set the broom back in its place and went upstairs, where I stripped off the bedding, carried it outside, and pegged it to the line. Just as I finished, Madam opened the back door.

"Why are you dawdling so?" she yelled. "The floor in here is filthy, and the banister needs to be polished. And I told you to wear your shoes in my house."

After I squeezed my feet into those small, dreadful shoes,

it was back to the sweeping, and then the polishing of the banister with soft rags and beeswax scented with lemon. When I made it halfway up the stairs, Madam yelled at me for airing the bed linen on a day that threatened rain. At least she did not call for Ruth's company. Becky had set my sister to scrubbing the back steps. Ruth hummed so loudly it put me in mind of a swarm of bees in clover.

As I gathered in the sheets, I watched the gate, waiting for the rebels to arrive to arrest the Locktons and reward me with our liberty. We would be given proper cabins on the ship, I was sure of it. No more riding in the hold with barrels of salt cod. Ruth and me would have a cabin fit for ladies, with bunks and blankets and pillows and three meals every day.

Yes, indeed, that was my future.

"Aren't you done yet?" Becky yelled from the back door. "We have to prepare the drawing room."

I shook away my daydreams.

The drawing room on the second floor wasn't a room where folks sat with paints and colored chalk to draw pictures, like I'd figured. It was another parlor, three times the size of the one downstairs. We removed the sheets covering the furniture. A dozen chairs with needleworked seats were scattered around the room, organized around tables with delicate legs. A low settee stood in front of the fireplace, and a mirror framed in mahogany hung above the mantel, flanked by oil lamps fastened to the walls.

"Why this room has to be prepared is beyond me," Becky muttered as we folded the sheets together. "No staff to speak of, the larder half-empty, the city getting ready to explode, and she wants this turned out and polished. Of all the foolish—"

A loud beating on the front door interrupted her.

"Dash it all!" Becky exclaimed as she clattered down the stairs. "Keep folding!" she called to me.

Not for love nor money. I peered out a front window.

The group of men clustered on the front steps did not look like angels, but they could have been in disguise. Four wore the coats, breeches, powdered wigs, and hats of merchants; one had papers tucked under his arm. Six soldiers stood behind them, all wearing uniforms but carrying long metal bars instead of guns.

Becky opened the door and the men filed inside.

I stepped out into the hall and peered down the stairs. The man with the papers under his arm had removed his hat. It was Master Bellingham.

My heart sang.

A door slammed overhead as Madam flew out of her chamber. "What is the meaning of this?"

I pressed myself against the wall so she could rush by me, then followed her down the stairs. The soldiers had split into two groups. Half went into the front parlor, and the other half into Lockton's library. Both groups set to removing the windows, prying them out of their casings with the long bars.

"What are you doing to my windows?" Madam demanded.

Bellingham approached her. "No need to fret, ma'am. We are all called to make sacrifices."

"Sacrifices?" Master Lockton asked as he hurried in. "This is thievery. What right have you to destroy my home?"

There was a horrific crash in the parlor as the hooks that held up the heavy draperies flew off the wall and landed on the floor. Plaster dust swirled.

Bellingham removed the papers under his arm. "You surprise me, Elihu," he said. "I thought a Patriot such as yourself would welcome the chance to contribute to the army."

Beads of sweat stood at the edge of Lockton's wig. "How does that pertain to the ripping down of my house, James?"

Bellingham patted Lockton's shoulder. "We need your lead, friend. For ammunition. Good people throughout the city are donating all the lead they own. The Provincial Congress will compensate you, of course. In due time. I've invoices prepared."

Madam frowned. "How is it possible to turn windows into bullets?"

"The counterweights are made of lead, ma'am," Bellingham explained. "And your drapery pulls."

"This is an outrage," Lockton fumed.

"No, Elihu," Bellingham said. "This is war. Even our churches are making the sacrifice, delivering their bells to be recast as cannon. Surely you do not rate your home above the houses of God?"

The soldiers left the library, deposited the lead weights by the front door, and headed up to the second floor, knocking their shoulders against the paintings of the Lockton ancestors that lined the staircase.

I wanted to shout that they should search for the money in the linen chest. Instead, I shrank against the wall to let them pass.

"They haven't restored the windows to the frames," protested Lockton.

"Where are they going?" Madam asked.

"There are plenty of carpenters who will assist with the windows, if you don't feel up to the task yourself, Elihu," Bellingham said.

"Sir!" shouted a soldier upstairs. "We've found it!"

Bellingham dropped his manners and bounded up the stairs, two at a time. Madam and Lockton followed close on his heels. I trailed behind.

The bedchamber was a large room made small by the four-poster canopy bed that sat as high as a carriage, two massive armoires, and a half-dozen men with red faces. Madam had once again set herself on her walnut linen chest, which sat in front of the hearth.

Why was it up here?

". . . of all the insults, of all the assaults on the dignity of a woman," she said to Bellingham, "this, sir, is the lowest, the most base. I shall see to it that every leader in every land knows–"

"Madam," Bellingham said sternly. "If you do not take your person from that chest, I shall order these soldiers to remove you."

"You would not dare," she said.

"Yes, he would, dear," Lockton said. "Please, wife, let these men do their work with no further delay. There is nothing to worry about."

He seemed to hide a message beneath those words, for Madam relaxed some and stood with grace. "If you insist, husband," she said.

"Perhaps you would prefer to go belowstairs," Lockton suggested. "The girl can heat some wine to calm your nerves."

Madam shook her head. "No, dear. I shall remain by your side."

Bellingham gave the sergeant a quick nod. The man knelt in front of the chest and opened the latch.

Deliverance! They'll arrest them both and reward me mightily. We'll leave this horrid place by sunset.

One corner of Lockton's mouth turned up in a sly smile as a blushing soldier removed the shifts and underskirts. My heart skipped a beat. Why were dirty linens still in there? Becky gathered all the washing yesterday.

The soldier looked up at Bellingham. "That's all, sir. Clear down to the bottom."

I wanted to shout, *The money is underneath the false bottom!* but pressed my lips together. Bellingham knelt and checked for himself, knocking the wooden sides.

Lockton's grin had spread to both sides of his mouth. "Would you care to inspect all of our clothing, James? Perhaps you'd send a man to root through the potatoes and parsnips in the cellar."

He had hidden the money elsewhere, that's why he was at ease. Bellingham rose to his feet and stood with his hands behind him. Would he turn on me, accuse me of making a false report and expose me to the Locktons?

No. He searched through his papers until he pulled out one that he handed to Lockton.

"You are summoned to the New York Provincial Congress for suspicion of aiding the enemy, Elihu. I am placing you under arrest. These soldiers will escort you."

He nodded his head. Two soldiers grabbed Lockton by his elbows. His smile vanished.

"Wait," Madam said. "You can't arrest him. He's done nothing."

"To the contrary, ma'am," Bellingham snapped. "He has put the lives of thousands in jeopardy."

The men filed by me without another word. Bellingham kept his face straight ahead, but as he passed by, he cut his eyes at me. They drilled a hole right into my fear of discovery.

There was the clatter of boots on the stair treads, then boots on the marble steps outside, and then the crash of the front door slamming. They were gone.

Madam stared blankly at the empty doorway.

"Ma'am?" I asked quietly.

Her eyes turned to me, then she blinked, as if she suddenly realized who I was and where she stood.

"Don't just stand there, girl. These linens need to be washed. I can't think how Becky missed them. I shall speak to her about her laziness."

And then she fainted.

CHAPTER XII

Friday, June 7, 1776

BY VIRTUE OF THE AUTHORITY VESTED IN US
BY CERTAIN RESOLUTIONS OF THE CONGRESS OF THE COLONY
OF NEW-YORK OF THE 7TH DAY OF JUNE, . . . DO THEREFORE
SUMMON YOU TO APPEAR BEFORE US . . . TO SHOW CAUSE (IF
YOU HAVE ANY) WHY YOU SHOULD BE CONSIDERED
AS A FRIEND TO THE AMERICAN CAUSE . . .
—SUMMONS FROM THE NEW YORK
PROVINCIAL CONGRESS TO A SUSPECTED TORY

BECKY SENT ME TO FETCH THE LADY Seymour to help Madam get through having her husband arrested like that. The old lady lived two blocks north of Trinity Church, the one with spires that scraped the sky.

"It's one of them old Dutch-style houses. Got a red door and a knocker looks like a heart," Becky said. "Can't miss it."

The house was not far from City Hall, along a street where soldiers with heavy axes were chopping down the row of tall poplar trees. "Fortifications," a soldier explained to a cart man. "To protect against the invasion. Any day now, they say."

The red door made the house easy to find. I walked through a beautiful garden around to the back. Neatly trimmed boxwood hedges created a path lined with young betony plants, lavender, day lilies, and honeysuckle. Momma would have admired the roses. My fingers itched to pluck up the scraggly weeds that were crowding them, but I dared not.

I knocked at the back. The door was opened by the whitest girl I'd ever seen. Her skin was pale as water except for two flame-colored spots on her cheeks. Her eyebrows and eyelashes were near invisible, and her eyes a mix of pewter and blue. She wiped her hands on her apron and said something I didn't understand.

"I've come for the Lady Seymour," I explained. "Madam Lockton requires her presence."

She frowned. *"Wat wilt u?"*

"What did you say?" I asked.

"Een ogenblik alstublieft," she said before she closed the door in my face.

What was an ogenblik? New York was stranger every passing day. I knocked again, but there was no answer. I was about to walk home, when I heard Lady Seymour's voice through an open window. A moment later, the door opened, and she stood there in the kitchen.

I curtsied, proper-like. "Pardon, ma'am, but they've arrested the master. Madam is poorly."

She nodded. "They've been hunting Loyalists all day. I told Anne it would come to this. Come inside, child. Isabel, is it not?"

The kitchen was larger than the Locktons', with a tiled hearth and copper pots hanging on the wall. A smoke-colored cat curled itself around my ankles, its tail in the shape of a question mark.

"Please, sit down. You must be hungry."

I perched on the edge of a chair.

Lady Seymour poured me a mug of fresh milk. My surprise at having a proper lady do so must have shown on my face.

"You could use some building up," she said as she pushed a plate of molasses cookies to me. "Eat and tell me everything." She turned to her servant, who stood by the hearth. *"Wil je alsjeblieft even de meubels afstoffen?"*

The strange girl bobbed once and left the room, the pale pink ribbons from the back of her cap trailing behind her.

"She speaks only Dutch," Lady Seymour explained. "And shows no inclination to learn English, I'm afraid. Now, a bite, and the events."

I chewed the cookie quickly, took a sip of milk, and recounted near everything, tho' I neglected to mention my role as the household spy. She listened carefully as I spoke and asked plenty of questions.

"Did Elihu say anything to the men who arrested him? Did he give them any names?"

"Not in my hearing, ma'am."

She sat back in her chair. "He's in no danger so long as he stays silent." She broke off a piece of cookie, popped it into her mouth, and chewed. "I imagine Anne is in a lather."

"Yes, ma'am," I said carefully. "She told Becky to pack the trunks for Charleston."

Lady Seymour shook her head. "I don't blame her, but fleeing would ensure that the rebels would take everything."

"Yes, ma'am," I mumbled. I took an overly large bite of the cookie, certain she would send me back straightaway.

She tapped her forefinger on the table as she pondered, her rings flashing in the light. "Right," she said firmly, having come to a decision. "I will write a note for you to take to the lawyer's office before you go home, and another for Anne, telling her that Elihu will be soon set free."

The Dutch girl came back in the kitchen and said something I could not make out at all. Lady Seymour rose from her chair and motioned for me to stay seated. "Finish those cookies, please, and drink a second glass of milk. You can't run errands for me unless properly nourished."

CHAPTER XIII

Saturday, June 8–
Friday, June 21, 1776

I DESIRE YOU WOULD REMEMBER THE LADIES,
AND BE MORE GENEROUS AND FAVOURABLE TO THEM
THAN YOUR ANCESTORS. DO NOT PUT SUCH UNLIMITED
POWER INTO THE HANDS OF THE HUSBANDS. REMEMBER
ALL MEN WOULD BE TYRANTS IF THEY COULD. . . .
THAT YOUR SEX ARE NATURALLY TYRANNICAL IS A
TRUTH SO THOROUGHLY ESTABLISHED AS TO ADMIT OF
NO DISPUTE, BUT SUCH OF YOU AS WISH TO BE HAPPY
WILLINGLY GIVE UP THE HARSH TITLE OF MASTER FOR
THE MORE TENDER AND ENDEARING ONE OF FRIEND.
–LETTER OF ABIGAIL ADAMS TO HER HUSBAND, JOHN

THE FRONT DOOR OPENED THE NEXT morning as I walked down the stairs carrying Madam's chamber pot. It was Master Lockton, back from being arrested. His clothing was rumpled, and he looked as if he'd not slept. He paused when he saw me.

"Tell Becky I require strong coffee and food. Where is your mistress, and what is she doing?"

"Above, sir." I gripped the handle of the chamber pot tightly. "Packing."

He stormed past me, bellowing for his wife.

As I dumped and washed out the chamber pot, I gave thanks. 'Twas clear he did not think me a spy.

When I went back inside, there came a ruckus and much shouting from the second floor. I joined Ruth and Becky at the foot of the staircase, the three of us listening with big ears as Lockton and Madam shouted at each other.

"Shhhh!" Ruth said, putting her finger to her lips.

"That's right, little 'un," said Becky. "They don't pipe down soon, the whole neighborhood will turn out to watch."

Crash!

"Bet you that was the wash pitcher," she said.

Craaash!

"And the basin," she added.

"Do they often fight like this?" I asked.

"Often enough," Becky said. She stopped as Madam cried out in pain. "The master likes to be obeyed. He's not happy she wants to head for Charleston. And she don't want to stay here."

Lockton lowered his voice some, but he was still angry and scolding.

"Should we do something?" I asked. "Perhaps Lady Seymour could calm him."

Becky shook her head. "'Twould fire him up even more. Best not to discuss these things."

Ruth stuck her thumb in her mouth.

Once the fighting had ended and the master had been served his meal, I took a cool compress and mug of cold ale up to Madam. As she applied the compress to her swollen, split lip, she scolded me for not scraping candle wax that had dripped on the floor.

"It caused me to fall," she said. "Do you see what your clumsiness has cost me?"

We both knew it was a lie. There was no wax on the floor. A few drops of blood stained the edge of the carpet.

"What do you have to say for yourself?" she asked.

I didn't like picking up the blame and carrying it, but I had no choice. I bowed my head. "I beg forgiveness, ma'am, and promise it will not happen again."

She removed the compress and winced. "It had better not."

In the weeks that followed, the master had me serve him whenever his companions visited. I listened closely to their conversating, but they blew only hot air, complaining about the Congress and the weather and the effect of war on business. I was relieved to hear that the printer, Inkstained, had fled the city with his wife and children. Lockton was certain that he had told the rebels about the money and the plan to bribe the American troops. My secret was safe.

Becky brought back peas, greens, and gossip from the marketplace: the British fleet was in the harbor, no, the fleet had sailed for Jamaica, no, the Congress had negotiated a peace, no, the British planned to kill us all while we slept.

"Gossip is the foul smell from the Devil's backside," that's what Momma always said. I tried to ignore the wild stories and stay alert for something, anything, I might use to secure our freedom.

Becky had been quite happy to give me the chore of hiking up to the Tea Water Pump every day. After my first few visits, it became the favorite part of my day. The pump was set in a little shed at the edge of the Common, a big gathering place ringed by army barracks, the poorhouse, and the jail. There were trees and fields to the north of the Common and the burying place for Africans. The air was cleaner up there, easier to breathe.

A week after Lockton returned home, Curzon stood with me in the line of servants waiting for water. I was desperate to ask him questions but knew they had to wait until we were alone.

When my turn came, I handed my buckets to the ancient slave who worked the pump handle, a man old as dirt, with stone-gray hair and skin the color of the night sky. He carried a country mark on his face, three straight lines that had been cut into his right cheek when he became a man in Africa. Poppa had a mark that looked close to it. It made me feel kin to the old man, and I smiled and curtsied polite whenever I saw him.

"Thank you, Grandfather," Curzon said to the man as he handed us the full buckets.

I was surprised. "He's your grandfather? I didn't know that."

The old man chuckled softly and reached for the buckets of the girl standing behind me. "I'm the grandfather of everybody and everything." He pushed down on the handle of the pump and water flowed. "Mind how you go, missy."

Curzon waited until we were two blocks down Queen Street before he asked me about Lockton's affairs.

"He traveled to Fairfield in Connecticut two days ago and came home late last night," I said. "I thought he was on a parole, that he had to stay in New York. Why don't they arrest him?"

Curzon looked behind us and from side to side before answering. "They don't have enough men to follow him," he explained. "And his aunt has powerful connections, both here and in England. There must be solid proof before they dare arrest him again. Should you ever come in possession of letters sent to him or maps, or—"

"—or if I find the King hiding in our pantry," I interrupted.

"The Congress would give you a medal for that," he said with a grin.

"I would rather have passage home on a fast ship."

"You don't want to sail anywhere, not now," he said, doffing his hat and bowing to three officers passing on horseback.

I likewise bobbed in the direction of the gentlemen and waited for them to draw out of earshot before speaking again. "Why not?"

"The Royal Fleet is fast approaching and is eager for battle and spoils. If you sailed now, you'd likely be captured and sold to the islands."

"Idle gossip and pipe smoke," I said. "You hear it on every street corner. It's a wonder we don't all choke to death on it."

"Where you see smoke, you find fire, Country. Don't worry. The day of our liberty will soon dawn. This country is going to be free, and you and me with it."

"For a boy with a little head, you sure do have big dreams. I just want what's owed me."

"You need to be patient," he said with a frown. "The army has bigger fish to fry than you and your sister."

"And I have bigger fish to fry than your army," I said with a whole lot more confidence than I truly felt.

The sun set later and later in those weeks. The extra light was welcome and put to good use. I aired out our pallet and blanket and tidied our cellar corner. The potato bin was near empty, and Ruth asked to play in it as if it was a little house. I would not let her. Instead, I made her a cornhusk doll, painting a face on it with pokeberry juice and fashioning a gown for it with a piece of cambric from Becky's scrap bag.

One night, feeling out of sorts and reckless, I crept up the stairs. It was after midnight, and Lockton and his wife slept heavily. I snuck into the library and took a book from the shelves—a story called *Robinson Crusoe* by Mr. Defoe. I sat by the glowing coals in the kitchen hearth and read until I could hold my eyes open no longer.

When the fat moon rose the next night, I planted the mystery seeds I had taken from Momma's jar. I did not know what they would grow into, but planting them deep in the cool dirt was a comfort. Thunder boomed in the distance as a summer storm approached. *I ought check the cows,* I thought. Storms made them nervous. More thunder rolled, and then a third wave.

Fool, I scolded myself. The cows were in our old life, not this one.

The moon climbed higher and the air returned to stillness and waiting. I took myself to bed and did not dream.

CHAPTER XIV

Saturday, June 22, 1776

LIFE VERY UNCERTAIN, SEEMING DANGERS SCATTERED THICK AROUND US, PLOTS AGAINST THE MILITARY, AND IT IS WHISPERED, AGAINST THE SENATE. LET US PREPARE FOR THE WORST, WE CAN DIE HERE BUT ONCE. MAY ALL OUR BUSINESS, ALL OUR PURPOSES & PURSUITS TEND TO FIT US FOR THAT IMPORTANT EVENT.
—LETTER OF CONGRESSIONAL DELEGATE ABRAHAM CLARK TO ELIAS DAYTON

THE NEXT DAY I CARRIED A BASKET of eels from the fish market to Wall Street, thinking only of hot eel pie for supper. I had not eaten eel pie since Momma died, Miss Mary Finch not being fond of it. But Master Lockton enjoyed the dish, so fat eels weighed down my basket. I fervently hoped Becky would chop off their heads and strip off their skins. It made me go all jumbly in the belly to chop off heads.

I entered the kitchen and set the basket on the table. Ruth hummed quietly to herself, shelling peas into a large wooden bowl, and Becky chopped kale.

Madam walked in from the front hall, her hair half-fallen out of her cap, and stains of sweat under the arms of her dress. She crossed the room, peered out the back door, crossed her arms over her chest, and tapped her foot with impatience, then disappeared into the next room.

"I require you, girl," she said.

Becky looked at me, eyes wide and warning.

"Ma'am?" I asked.

Madam came back into the kitchen carrying a silver tray. She shoved it into my arms. "You will serve your master and his companions."

Becky slowly shook her head back and forth. "Are you sure, Madam, that's what the master requested?" she asked slowly. "'Tis hard to interpret the ways of menfolk, them being so complex and all, but surely when he said 'Let nothing disturb us,' that was indeed his true meaning?"

"Be quiet, Becky," Madam snapped. "You have the manners of a donkey and the voice of a goose."

Becky said nothing more but chopped faster.

Madam paced back and forth. "The mayor of New York is a supremely important man, could well be the next Royal governor. It is hardly appropriate to welcome him into our home without offering refreshment."

She turned to me. "You will not put one foot wrong."

When the tray was loaded so heavily I could scarce lift it, Madam preceded me down the hall and waited by the closed door to the library.

"Go on!" she told me, without offering to help.

I kicked at the door with my shoe and called out, "Wine, sir, and a bite to eat!"

"Leave us!" responded Lockton.

Madam knocked on the door with a not terribly refined fist. "Come now, Elihu, show some graciousness."

Deep voices in the room conferred, then the door was

unlocked and opened. Madam stepped toward the opening, but Lockton filled the frame.

"Thank you, dear," he said. "The girl can serve us. I'll send her to you if I am in need of anything more."

Madam tried to look beyond him to the distinguished guest but could not see through the thick form of her husband. "Very well," she said, loudly. "I shall be composing a letter to our cousins in London, our cousins who are so well regarded by His Majesty."

"Excellent suggestion, dear."

He stepped out of the way so that I might enter.

There were only two men besides Master Lockton—Goldbuttons, wearing a shabby waistcoat of black wool, and the third man, who I took to be the mayor. The mayor had on a fine wig, properly powdered and pulled back, with a curl at the end of his queue, a sable coat and matching breeches, a maroon waistcoat, and a white silk cravat tied loosely around his neck, atop his shirt. The windows were all closed, but sun streamed in, heating up the room to a slow simmer and bringing forth the ripe stink of underwashed gentlemen.

A broad, brightly colored map of the coastline was spread on the master's desk, weighted at each end by a heavy book. Lockton removed one of the books and the map curled up on itself, clearing the desk for the plate of Gloucester cheese and rye bread and the bowl of strawberries I set there.

"My most sincere apologies for the interruption," Lockton said. He took a glass of wine from me. "Pray, sir, continue."

Goldbuttons took a hasty bite of cheese before speaking. "It has proved more difficult to bribe the Patriots to change sides than we anticipated. Those who are fed up with the situation prefer to melt out of the city and walk home to Massachusetts or North Carolina."

I removed the serving tray and retreated to my corner. The horses in the painting still leapt the fence. I fought the temptation to reach for the adventures of Mr. Crusoe on the shelf. Instead, I centered my eyes on my feet and my thoughts upon a slice of eel pie.

"They turn down the offer of hundreds of acres?" Lockton said.

"The land offered by the King is distant from their farms." Goldbuttons buttered a piece of bread. "My fellow reports they simply want peace and the chance to get in a good crop of wheat."

"Idiots," said Lockton.

"The news from Philadelphia is that Congress is close to declaring independence," Goldbuttons continued.

I fought the urge to yawn. The master and his friends could complain about the Continental Congress at such length I feared my ears might drop off.

Lockton plucked a strawberry from the bowl and pulled the leaves from it. "And Admiral Howe continues to delay the invasion. It's maddening. The Crown must smash this rebellion into dust so we can return to our former lives with a sense of order."

"And higher profits," Goldbuttons added.

If Madam only knew how dull these gatherings were, she would not have been so anxious to barge her way in. I would have happily chopped off the heads of a barrel full of eels to escape another afternoon trapped with men whose voices droned on and on and on like rumbling, dusty grindstones.

The mayor set his goblet on the desk. "The time for

bribery and persuasion is past. This is the hour when we must unsheathe our swords."

Swords?

Lockton shook his head. "We've been over this, David. Our task is to hold this city loyal, nothing more."

The mayor leaned back in his chair. "Holding is not enough. They're coming after us, raiding our homes for lead and our stores for anything they desire."

Goldbuttons wiped the cheese from his fingers with a handkerchief. "I agree with Elihu. A Loyal New York cuts off New England from the other colonies. The rebellion will wither like a vine cut off at the roots."

"Cut off a vine and it will grow back," the mayor said. "You must pull it out of the ground and burn it to ensure it is dead."

Lockton put the strawberry leaves in the bowl. "Is there a plan afoot to destroy them?"

"Most definitely." The mayor's voice was quiet, but steely.

This was not idle prattle about Congress. I stood still as possible.

The mayor scratched at the mustard stain on his cuff. "General Howe delayed the invasion, hoping the revolutionary fervor would die down. On the contrary, independent sentiment now burns as far away as Georgia, as well as the western frontier."

I am a bookcase, I thought. *I am a piece of furniture, not a girl who will remember every word spoken in this room.*

"The cry for liberty has proved powerful," Lockton said.

"The beast has grown too large," the mayor said. "If it breaks free of its chains, we are all in danger. We need to cut off its head."

Goldbuttons frowned. "How so?"

"We must kill their commander."

Lockton drew in his breath sharply.

"With Washington gone, the revolution will collapse," predicted the mayor. "War will be averted and countless lives saved. Our world will return to the former state of tranquility we enjoyed before all this nonsense."

The study fell so silent, I feared the men would hear my heart beating. *Kill General Washington?*

"No," Lockton said, shaking his head. "Not possible. He is a gentleman. Capture him, arrest him, yes, but we dare not harm him."

The mayor ticked off the reasons on his fingers. "All of the American leaders have committed treason against the King. You cannot deny that. Treason is the highest offense under English law, worse than murder. And what is the punishment for treason, my friends?"

Neither Lockton nor Goldbuttons answered.

"To be hung by the neck until dead, then have your body chopped into four pieces, which are sent to the four corners of the kingdom," the mayor continued. "Others propose we send sections of Washington's corpse to Charleston, Philadelphia, and Boston. They want to keep the fourth bit here, to be displayed in front of City Hall."

The room fell silent again. I could hear the ticking of the hall clock through the wall.

Lockton shook his head again. "You cannot guarantee Parliament would rule treason. It's too dangerous."

"If we dispose of Washington, Parliament will do whatever we ask."

"But how can you accomplish this?" asked Goldbuttons. "The man is surrounded by an entire army."

"We have a man in the Life Guards committed to our plan.

He spends his days within two arms' length of the general. On our signal, he will act."

"And this is why you need the money," Lockton said.

There was the sound of a lid being removed and the jangling of keys. Lockton took a key ring out of the blue china snuff jar on the corner of the desk. He unlocked the top drawer and removed a tall stack of currency, enough to buy a village or two.

I let my eyelids droop as if I were a'dozing.

"The risks are too high," Goldbuttons said in a shaky voice. "If we are discovered, we are dead men."

"Think not upon the risks, but the rewards," suggested the mayor.

I peeked.

Lockton tugged at his collar to loosen it. "Suspicion will fall on my neck first, David. I require assurance that my role will not be betrayed."

"You have my word on it," the mayor said.

"Your promise is not enough, sir." Lockton pushed a sheet of paper, a quill, and the inkstand across the desk to the mayor. "Write down the names of those who know of this plot."

"Why?" Goldbuttons asked.

"The paper will serve as my insurance should I fall into rebel hands again. It will motivate you and our friends to do everything possible to secure my release."

"How?" Goldbuttons was still frowning, but the mayor reached for the quill.

"If we do not come to Elihu's aid, he will betray our names to the enemy," the mayor said softly. "He is showing us his weakness."

"Planning ahead is my strength," Lockton said. "Do not forget your own name, sir."

I closed my eyes again. The quill scratched across the paper. Goldbuttons shifted nervously in his chair.

"There," the mayor said.

I opened my eyes the tiniest bit. Goldbuttons quickly read the paper. "A vast conspiracy, indeed." He handed it to Lockton, who read the names and smiled.

"We are keeping good company." He handed the money to the mayor and lifted his empty glass. "I believe this calls for a toast, gentlemen."

I did not step forward with the wine bottle. Lockton needed to believe I was a sleepy servant, unaware of his plans.

"Sal!" he snapped.

I drew back my head and acted befuddled.

"Wine," Lockton said.

I crossed the room and emptied the last of the wine into his glass.

Lockton frowned. "Fetch another bottle," he said.

"Yessir." I curtsied and left the room, pondering how I could pass this news along to Curzon.

That was when the blood-curdling screams started in the kitchen.

I dropped the bottle and ran.

CHAPTER XV

Saturday, June 22, 1776

As for young Children liable to be attacked with this Distemper, you must begin with giving them wholesom Food . . . Apply to their Heads a small Plaister of Treacle, which must be renewed every eight Days. Let them always have some pleasant and agreeable Smells, let their common Drink be aromatized and sweetned with a little Cinnamon, Anise, Coriander, and Sugar.
—Noel Chomel and Richard Bradley,
Family Dictionary. Containing the most experienced Methods of improving Estates and of preserving Health . . .

"It's the Devil!" Madam screamed as I opened the door to the kitchen.

Ruth had fallen at her feet and lay there, her body shaking violently. Peas were scattered across the floor.

What I feared the most had happened.

Madam snatched the broom from Becky's hands and raised it over her head. "She has the Devil in her!"

"No, Madam, it's an illness!" I cried. "An ailment, nothing more."

Madam brought the broom down on the small, twisted body. Ruth couldn't raise her hands to protect herself. The seizure held her fast, her arms and legs stiff and trembling, her eyes wide, but not seeing.

"Out, Devil!" Madam shouted as she again raised the broom over her head.

"No!" I threw myself on top of my sister. The broom came down on my back, once, twice, but it didn't matter. I had to keep her safe until the storm passed.

The broom handle cracked, and Madam tossed it aside. I heard Becky yell something, then Lockton's loud voice boomed, "Enough!"

The room quieted, except for the soft bumping of Ruth's limbs on the floor. I looked up. Madam held a chair, prepared to throw it at us. Her husband pulled it out of her hands. Ruth's body suddenly went limp.

"What is the meaning of this?" Lockton asked.

"She's possessed," Madam sputtered. "I will not have a demon-child in my house, Elihu."

I ran my hand over Ruth's face and spoke to her softly. Her eyelids fluttered and her mouth moved. "Come back to me, baby girl, come back, Ruth," I whispered. "Wake up now. It's gone, blown away. Come back, Ruth."

She looked confused; she always did after a fit. I helped her to sit up. A little blood had soaked through the kerchief at the back of her head where it hit the floor. The wound would need some cobwebs.

Lockton sent Becky to the study with the wine. He bade Madam to sit on the chair she had nearly broke over my head, took a seat himself, and addressed me gravely.

"Your sister has the falling sickness," he said. "Does this happen often?"

"No, sir." Ruth wiped her tears on my sleeve.

"This is not a matter for inquiry," Madam said. "I will not have evil in my house."

Becky walked back in, poured cider into a chipped mug,

and handed it to Ruth, who took a large mouthful.

Madam took a step backward. "The child's curse will poison us all. I want her sold, Elihu, sold today."

Sold?

"Wife–," started Lockton.

"You can't sell her!" I burst out.

"Hold your tongue, girl," Madam commanded.

Ruth drank the last of the cider and stood up.

Lockton reached out and set his hand on her shoulder. "They are sisters, Anne. One must remember that."

"Please, Madam," I said. "She's too little. She'll be hurt."

The room fell silent except for the plopping sound of peas falling to the bottom of a wooden bowl. Ruth was picking up the peas that she'd spilled. The sound reminded me of pebbles plunking into a deep pond.

Becky carried a mug of cider to Madam. "Look there. The little one is already back at her chores. And she did a fine job sweeping earlier."

"How often do these fits take hold of her?" Lockton asked me. "Speak truthfully."

"Sometimes once a day, sir, sometimes weeks will go by."

"Once a day?" Madam's voice rose again.

"Ho, Lockton!" the mayor called from the study.

The master studied my sister, then tugged his waistcoat over his belly. "The girl is harmless and useful," he said. "She will work in the kitchen with Becky. That is my decision. Do not disturb me again with womanly prattle."

The kitchen fell silent as the master walked away. When we heard the door to the study close, Madam pointed at Ruth. "Don't let her near the milk. She'll curdle it. And don't get used to her presence here. Elihu will soon see reason."

She stalked off, leaving a sour smell in the air.

Ruth crawled under the table to pick up the peas that had rolled there. I watched her and tried to stop my hands from shaking. "What will happen to us?"

"No way of telling." Becky pulled an eel from the basket. "It's near impossible to hire help, what with folks running off in fear of the war."

She cut off the eel's head. "Long's you two can stay out of trouble"—she grabbed the eel's skin at the neck and pulled it all the way off—"I imagine you're safe enough."

I bent down to help Ruth with the peas.

CHAPTER XVI

Sunday, June 23, 1776

A REPORT PREVAILS HERE THAT A MOST VILE DEEP LAID **PLOT** WAS YESTERDAY DISCOVER'D AT **NEW YORK**, I HAVE NOT BEEN ABLE TO ASSERTAIN THE PERTICULAR FACTS . . . , HOWEVER 40 PERSONS ARE APPREHENDED & SECUR'D, AMONG THEM IS THE MAYOR OF THE CITY. WHAT BASENESS ARE OUR ENEMIES NOT CAPABLE OF, WHO WOD WISH TO BE CONNECTED WITH A PEOPLE SO DESTITUTE OF EVERY VERTUE, GOD FORBID IT SHOD EVER BE THE FATE OF AMERICA.

—LETTER OF CONGRESSIONAL DELEGATE WILLIAM WHIPPLE TO JOSHUA BRACKETT

RUTH FELL ASLEEP QUICK THAT NIGHT, my arms around her. I had washed out the blood from her kerchief and hung it to dry. There was a lump on her head, but it would go away.

Madam's threats would not.

I slowly pulled my arm out from under my sister. She sighed and curled into a tiny ball.

I had pondered the problem all day and half the night. No matter how many times I turned it round, I found the same answer.

We had to flee the city.

I sat up and pulled the blanket over Ruth, tucking it under her feet to keep them warm.

The wings that could spirit us away were hidden in the master's desk. I had to take the list; it would buy us our freedom. But Bellingham would not listen, not after the incident with the linen chest. I had to deliver it straight to the army.

The sound I had been waiting for broke through; the low roar of Master Lockton's snores, starting up just as the grandfather clock chimed midnight.

I put on my skirt and made my way to the bottom of the stairs. The hour was upon me.

'Twas time to act.

The moon was my friend.

It lit up the library enough for me to make my way without stumbling into anything. The snuff jar stood on the corner of the desk. I held my breath as I lifted the lid, put my hand inside, and slowly pulled out the keys. I crouched behind the desk and examined them in the moonlight. Only one was small enough to fit into the top drawer's lock.

I inserted the key and turned it gently to the right. There was a dull *clunk*. The drawer slid open a hair. I forced myself to remain still and count to twenty.

Lockton's snores continued above, regular as waves crashing against the side of a ship.

I pulled open the drawer and peered inside. It was crowded with abandoned quills, a rusty tinder box, and a few coins and pound notes, which I was sore tempted to take. I felt through the drawer with careful fingers. What had he done with the list? Was it in his coat pocket? I reached into the back of the drawer and pulled out a black hair ribbon. Had he given it to Goldbuttons for safekeeping?

There!

From the farthest reach of the drawer I pulled out a single sheet, folded once. I held it up to the light and quickly read; it was a list of names, with the mayor's at the bottom. He had titled it "Committee to Preserve the King's Peace."

I tucked the paper in my pocket, tied it tight, and slipped it under the waistband of my skirt where it could not be seen. I closed and relocked the drawer, then carefully returned the keys to their hiding place.

I tiptoed back through the house and slipped outside, quiet as a ghost.

The air was hot and dripping, as if the city were wrapped in a wool blanket just pulled from a boiling pot. I made my way along the streets seen only by cats, rats, and a slave hurrying by with a bundle on her head. Since she carried a lantern, and no doubt had a pass from her master, she was allowed to be out walking after dark.

I was not.

The woman said nothing as she passed by me but started singing the second verse of "Yankee Doodle" in a strong voice, which I thought curious indeed.

I listened close to the words. "*Father and I went down to camp, Along with Captain Gooding; And there we saw the men and boys, As thick as hasty pudding. . . .*"

She was sending me a message.

I dove behind a log barricade just as two soldiers turned the corner, talking intently to each other and sweeping the street with their eyes. I said a quick prayer of thanks to the singing woman for her help.

When the echoes of the soldiers' boots had vanished, I moved on, staying away from the lights of the sentry fires, passing under the dark shadow of King George's statue in the Bowling Green, and hurrying to my destination.

The Battery was the fort at the southern tip of the island, with high walls and cannons that pointed over the water to discourage enemies. It was headquarters of the Patriot army in New York. Even if General Washington was elsewhere, here I could find an officer who would understand the value of the list.

I marched past the rows of tents set up on the grounds outside of the fort, trying very hard to ignore the men and boys who stared as I walked by. As I neared the gate, a sentry stepped out and blocked my way. "Do you have a pass, girl?"

I swallowed hard and tried to remember the name of the colonel who worked with Master Bellingham. *Fagen, Jaden, McReadan* . . .

"Well?" A few other soldiers drinking coffee outside of their tents had stopped talking to observe.

"Please, sir," I said, polite and firm. "I've come with an urgent message for . . ." *Regan!* "For Colonel Regan, sir."

"Tell me, and I'll see that he gets it."

"I cannot," I said. "I must deliver it to him personally, sir."

"Who's your master?"

Telling a lie would not benefit me. "A Loyalist, sir, who would beat me bloody if he knew I was here."

He looked me over and yawned. "Come on, then. I could do with a walk to keep me awake."

I followed him inside, past a room of men sleeping on the floor, along a hall to a small room where a low fire smoldered in the hearth, a chair drawn up before it. The moonlight had broke free of the clouds again and lay in gray pools beneath the windows. A table stood by the door, where a heavy-set man scratched away on a piece of paper, his work lit by a half-dozen candle stubs that would soon burn out.

The soldier drew himself up to his full height. "This girl has a message, sir. Claims it must be delivered in person."

The man lifted a hand in the air and continued with what he was writing. I tried to make out what it was, but his scribble was dreadful bad. Finally, he laid down his quill, moved his spectacles high on his nose, and peered through them at me.

"What is it?" he rasped. His voice sounded raw, like it had been run against a grater. An onion poultice was tied around his neck.

I dropped in a polite curtsy. "I have information for Colonel Regan."

"Who sent you? Who is your master?"

"I cannot say."

"Then who will vouch for you?"

"Ah, I vouch for myself, sir. I am new in the city and know only a boy named Curzon."

One caterpillar eyebrow lifted above the glasses as he recognized the name. "Bellingham's Curzon?" He coughed loudly and sprayed drops of spittle on the page. "He's all bluster." He dipped his quill in the ink pot and continued to write. "Take her away, sergeant. I am too busy for this."

My escort grabbed hold of my arm. "Come now."

I tried to break free. "Please hear me out." I shook my arm and twisted. "They want to kill him."

I pulled with all my might and lost my footing. Both the sergeant and me stumbled against the table. The ink bottle overturned and poured across the table and papers. The sick man jumped up with a mighty curse and several ugly statements about my character.

"They want to kill the general!" I finally pulled free of the sergeant's grasp. "I have proof."

The man was concerned only with rescuing his papers from the spreading pool of ink. "Sergeant, remove this bird-wit!"

"Do not touch her." The commanding voice came from the center of the room.

The sergeant stood at attention. The man with inky hands did too, swallowing hard and wincing at the pain in his throat. A figure rose from the high-backed chair that stood in front of the hearth. He wore the dark blue coat of an officer, with buttons and buckles that reflected the firelight. His features stayed in the shadows, but I could see a book in his left hand, his finger marking the page.

"Leave us," he ordered.

"Yes, sir," the sergeant said.

"As you wish, Colonel Regan, sir," said the man whose clothes were stained blue by the papers he clutched to his chest.

When the door was pulled behind them, Colonel Regan returned to his seat. "Come here," he told me. "Show me what you've brought and tell your story, but keep your voice low. The walls have ears."

"Yes, sir." My voice strangulated a bit.

The colonel tugged at his coat as he sat down. He was not wearing a wig as did most gentlemen. His own hair was dark, pulled back into a neat queue, and tied with string. His eyes were sunk deep into his face, with dark hollows underneath them.

"Well?" He set the book on his lap, finger still marking the place he left off reading.

I weighed my words before I spoke. "I am in a position to trade with you, sir."

"What kind of trade?"

"My sister and I were wrongfully taken from Rhode Island. I mean to get us back there."

"You want passage home in exchange for what you know."

"Yes," I said, lifting my chin a little. "Sir."

He nodded gravely. "If your information is as useful as you think it is, I shall personally look into your case, miss."

That was far from a berth on a swift ship, but I had little choice.

"They plan to kill General Washington."

He closed the book, set it on the floor, and leaned forward, his elbows on his knees. "Tell me all."

I handed him the list and quickly told him everything I knew. He interrupted a few times with questions and had me repeat the mayor's words. Then he bade me to wait by the dying fire as he left the room, and soon reappeared with four other men, all clearly dragged from their beds. I was fighting to stay awake myself, but I repeated the story to the larger assembly.

A quarrel began instantly, the arguments flying across the room.

"How do we know Lockton didn't send her with a false story?"

"That's just a list of names. Anyone could have written it."

"I know the mayor's handwriting. And those are dyed-in-the-wool Loyalists, every one."

"I don't believe they've turned a Life Guard. Those men are the finest we have. This is nonsense and I'm going back to bed."

"Her story confirms what we've heard from other sources." This from Colonel Regan. He explained that several spies had brought him the same rumor earlier in the day. He walked to the hearth and looked at the glowing embers. "All that remains is to decide what to do with the information. Who has the list?"

A man wearing his uniform coat over his nightshirt waved the paper in the air.

"Return it to the girl."

"Why on earth would we do that?" he asked.

"I want her to plant it back where she found it. 'Tis best they believe their plan is still secret. That improves our chances of rounding them up."

The man handed the list back to me. I thought for a moment about tossing it on the fire, for it suddenly seemed frightful dangerous, but I folded it back in my pocket.

"Do you think you'll be able to return it to his desk?" Colonel Regan asked me.

"Yes, sir," I said.

"If you hear anything else, anything at all, you come and find me, do you understand?"

"Yes, sir." I hesitated. "And you'll soon help my sister and me get home."

His eyes darted to his companions, then back to me. "I shall do what is in my power," he promised.

"Thank you, sir."

"She'll need the code to get back into camp," said the man in the nightshirt. "The new regulations go out at dawn."

"Agreed." Colonel Regan bent down so that his face was level with mine. "Do not tell this to another soul, on pain of death. Do you swear?"

"I swear," I whispered.

"The code is 'ad astra.' Repeat it, please."

"Adastra?" I had never heard such a word, but then again, I'd never before spoken a code.

"Two words: 'ad astra.' It's Latin; it means 'to the stars.' Will you be able to remember it?"

"I never forget a thing. Sir."

CHAPTER XVII

Sunday, June 23–
Friday, June 28, 1776

AMONG ALL THE SPECIES AND DEGREES OF SLAVERY THAT HAVE EXCITED THE ATTENTION OF MANKIND . . . THERE IS PERHAPS NONE MORE PITIABLE THAN THAT OF THE ILL-SOOTED WIFE. SHE IS BOUND BY TIES FROM WHICH NOTHING BUT DEATH CAN RELEASE HER, AND WHATEVER HER SUFFERING AND HER WRONGS IS COMPELLED BY DELICACY AND A REGARD FOR PERSONAL REPUTATION . . . TO SUBMIT TO THEM IN SILENCE, AND CONCEAL THEM FROM OBSERVATION.
—UNSIGNED COLONIAL-ERA LETTER

WHAT WITH MY BUSY NIGHT AS A true spy, code word and all, and the heat in the upper gallery of Trinity Church, I fell sound asleep during the sermon the next morning. I woke when the people around me stood, so startled that I popped up from the pew and near toppled over the railing.

The next two days were long and hot as I awaited word from Colonel Regan. Master Lockton did not notice that his list of coconspirators was a little handworn; he was too busy visiting the mayor at his home in Flatbush and spending hours at his warehouse reviewing his accounts.

Madam took her meals upstairs. Only Becky was allowed

to serve her because of Madam's fear of the demons she claimed inhabited Ruth. Becky said Madam sat sighing by the window and shuffling a deck of playing cards over and over. We did not bother keeping Ruth away from the milk, of course. Instead, we kept one ear open for the thud of Madam's feet on the stairs. When she approached the kitchen, one of us would whisk Ruth down to the cellar.

Ruth understood none of this. She did not complain about the egg-sized lump on her head or anything else. After we finished our business in the privy each morning, I took her to check our mystery garden. The green shoots were two hands tall but gave no clue about their identity. It was perfect growing weather, especially for flowers and corn and strawberries. It was perfect weather for going home.

I practiced the code over and over until it felt like a prayer in my mouth. *Ad astra, ad astra, ad astra.* I was desperate to talk to Colonel Regan about our release from the city but dared not leave Ruth alone in the house with Madam Lockton. The thought of Madam putting Ruth up to auction was a constant torment, like bees darting in and out of my sight, daring me to swat at them.

The gossip from the market was fantastical. Becky brought back tales of sea monsters chasing the British fleet and a two-headed calf born outside Philadelphia that portended all manner of disaster. Folks were prickly and fearful. Loyalist shopkeepers had been tarred and feathered by angry mobs and their shops destroyed. Each day dawned hotter than the one before.

Ad astra, ad astra, ad astra.

Two mornings after my meeting with the colonel, a visitor pounded at the kitchen door. I was kneeling on the other side of it, polishing the lock with an oily rag and rottenstone. The noise near gave me apoplexy.

When I opened the door, I was shocked to see not a messenger, but the rotund figure of Mr. Goldbuttons. Instead of wearing a hat or coat, he had a long cloak draped over his head, and his wig sat askew.

He stormed past me toward the stairs. "Is your master still abed?" he shouted back at me.

"Yessir."

Goldbuttons dropped his cloak on the floor and ran up the stairs as if his breeches were on fire. A moment later, Master Lockton bellowed like a stuck bull, then thudded heavily across the floor and yelled for Becky.

The plot to kill Washington had been uncovered.

I was sent to fetch Madam home, for she had gone to call on a friend. Goldbuttons had vanished by the time we returned. Madam hurried to the library and told me to fetch her ivory fan from her bedchamber for she was feeling faint from heat and excitement. As she opened the door, I caught glimpse of the master pacing frantically, his nightcap still on his head.

He looked up and saw us. "Thank heavens. There is much to do and no time. The worst has happened, Anne."

I started up the stairs to fetch the fan, moving slow as possible to overhear their words.

"What is the meaning of this, Elihu?" Madam demanded.

"Listen carefully," Lockton interrupted. "The rebels know. I've sent for a cart. We must burn my papers."

"Dear God protect us," Madam prayed. "How much do they know? Wait one moment."

I took the steps two at a time and was near the top when Madam stepped into the hall and pointed at me.

"Forget the fan, girl. We need firewood for the library," she said sternly. "Now."

Lockton and Madam were exchanging heated words across his desk by the time I bought in an armload of wood and a few coals from the kitchen in the copper coal carrier. They seemed not to notice as I walked in.

"You are abandoning me?" Madam asked.

"You'll be safer here." Lockton dumped a folio of papers on his desk and rooted through the mess. "Aunt Seymour isn't leaving, and we have credit with all the merchants."

"Your aunt despises me," Madam said. "You must stay to defend our name and honor."

I arranged the wood so that it would not catch quickly, set the hot coals underneath it, leaned forward, and blew gently.

"I am guilty, Anne. They won't give me a parole this time. But as soon as the rebels are driven out, I shall return."

"What if they arrest me?" Madam asked. "Let me go with you."

"You must stay to keep them from stealing all that we own."

Madam picked the blue china snuff jar off the desk and flung it against the wall. It shattered and left a mark on the plaster. "I will not!" she shouted. "I will not be left at the mercy of our enemies while you slink away!"

Despite my best intentions, the kindling wood caught hold of a spark and burst into flame.

Master Lockton crossed the room to pick up the keys that had been hidden in the jar. He placed them in his pocket, then, without warning, hit Madam with all the force in his arm. She flew into the bookcase, causing several books to tumble to the ground. I almost reached for her but was afraid to anger Lockton any further.

"I command you to stay here, Anne. This is your duty and you will obey me." He turned to me. "The fire is satisfactory. Leave us."

"Yessir."

As I closed the door, Madam started in again, begging him to take her with him, or at least to let her know where he was going.

A carpenter soon arrived and nailed the master into a large crate marked CHEESE. As the final boards were being put into place, Lockton told Madam that he would first head north, then to Dr. van Buskirk's house in Bergen County.

Three men loaded the heavy crate onto a cart driven by a man I had never seen before.

Becky tended to Madam's battle wounds with ointment and medicinal wine. I offered to fetch Lady Seymour, but in truth, I planned to run the news of Lockton's escape to the rebels as fast as I could. Madam insisted we all stay in the house with the doors and windows locked. She passed the night burning packets of papers in the fire and demanding gallons of tea and fresh biscuits.

When the soldiers arrived at dawn to arrest the master, his business papers were all ash and the crate of "cheese" was long gone. The angry soldiers tore through the library but found nothing, save for the shards of the snuff jar. These they stomped under their boots before they departed.

Becky went to market and left me to clean the mess. She returned with a freshly killed hen and a basket full of beet greens. Before Becky could remove her bonnet, Madam shuffled into the kitchen.

"What news?" Madam demanded. Her red eyes perched above dark rings from a sleepless night. A livid purple welt had raised on the left side of her face where Lockton had struck her. Most of the bruises on her arms and shoulders were hid under her gown, but she walked stiff and sore as an old crone.

Becky gave her the gossip from the market stalls. Conspirators who plotted against the American cause had been arrested all over the city and in several close-by villages. The mayor, two doctors, a shoemaker, a tailor, a chandler, a gunsmith, a drummer, and a fifer were all charged with treason and a host of other offenses.

"How did they uncover the plot?" Madam asked.

I picked up the beheaded chicken and carried it to a basin. I held it by the feet so the last of the blood could drain out before I plucked it.

Becky hung her hat on its hook and pinned on her apron. "One of the conspirators flapped his mouth and the story poured out. Hickey, his name is, a tall Irishman who served in General Washington's Life Guards."

"Did anyone mention Master Lockton?"

"Only that he was one of them that got away, ma'am. They caught one feller trying to cross the East River. Couldn't row hard enough against the tide. The master is well out of harm's way."

"Which is more than I can say about myself," Madam muttered, gingerly rubbing the violet bruises on her wrist.

CHAPTER XVIII

Friday, June 28, 1776

. . . RECEIVED INFORMATION THAT A MOST
HORRID PLOT WAS ON FOOT BY THE VILE TORY'S
OF THIS PLACE . . . TO ASSASSINATE . . .
HIS EXCELLENCY, AND THE OTHER GENERAL
OFFICERS—BLOW UP THE [GUNPOWDER] MAGAZINE,
SPIKE THE CANNON, ETC. . . . HOPE THEY WILL RECEIVE
THE PUNISHMENT DUE SUCH INFAMOUS WRETCHES.
—JOURNAL OF SAMUEL B. WEBB,
WASHINGTON'S AIDE-DE-CAMP

SHORTLY AFTER THE CLOCK STRUCK ten on Friday morning, thousands of boots echoed against the cobblestones of Broadway. Every soldier in New York was marching up island to attend the hanging of Thomas Hickey, the man who almost assassinated General George Washington.

Becky urged me to go. "There's nothing like a good hanging, is there?" She gave the face of the grandfather clock another swipe with the dust rag. "Keep an eye on your sister, though. Little ones disappear in big crowds."

"What about Madam?" I asked.

"Nothing to worry about there, eh?" Becky pointed upstairs, where Madam lay atop the coverlet on her bed, asleep. She had stayed muddy in strong wine since Lockton fled the city.

The thought of a hanging turned my belly, but Colonel Regan would likely be there. Perhaps he would provide an escort for Ruth and me direct from the gallows to the wharf.

"Go on," Becky said again. "It'll be good for you to get some air. Fetch a bucket of water home with you, mind. I wager Madam will wake with a thumping headache."

Ruth and I found ourselves in a tide of people moving north. The wave spread out once it reached the Commons, where the prison, the barracks, and a large sugarhouse stood. Beyond the hills to the north lay the African Burial Ground and beyond that, the big pond called the Collect. This was the one spot in the city where twenty thousand folk could gather. I could scarce credit the number, but it was on everyone's lips.

Ruth watched the crowd with big eyes and shy smiles for strangers, but she did not release my hand and kept her doll baby clutched tight to her. I half expected to see vendors selling cinnamon water, boiled sweets, and currant cakes, and a conjure man who could juggle two balls and a stool. There were none in sight, but the air of high spirits made it feel like a fair day.

I took Ruth by the hand and led her around the back side of Bridewell Prison, toward the Tea Water Pump, where there were other slaves and servants gathered. I nodded polite and murmured my "Good day" to the old man we called Grandfather and the others who were familiar.

Ruth sat in the dust. I turned our bucket upside down, sat on it, pulled a length of string from my pocket, and wove it into a fanciful pattern around my fingers.

"Cratch-cradle!" Ruth said, clapping her hands. We lost ourselves in play, our fingers making Candles, Triangles, Diamonds, and the Manger.

Suddenly there came a rough shout from the center of the Commons. The crowd muttered, some folks craning their necks to see. Ruth giggled and held out her hands to me. She had made a complete mishmash of the string and could not untangle her fingers from the knot.

There came another shout, then the drummers started beating their snares. The noise crackled like lightning.

"Game's over," I said to Ruth, freeing her hands and pulling her to her feet.

The crowd surrounding the Commons had swelled to include the entire army and every soul in the city except for Madam and Becky. I scanned the rows of officers lined up behind the gallows, looking for Colonel Regan. I could pick out General Washington astride his big gray horse at the center of the line. Next to him was the rather large figure of Colonel Knox and countless other officers I could not name. Colonel Regan was not to be seen, but he could have been rows to the back. *Blast.* I should have realized they would be in formation, not scattered amongst the common folk.

Another shouted order echoed off the stone front of the prison. Near one hundred soldiers stepped out of the ranks and snapped to attention. The bayonets fixed to the ends of their long muskets flashed in the sun.

The drummers continued beating, sweat trickling down their faces.

"Bet you never saw this out in the country," a familiar voice said in my ear.

I whirled with a gasp.

Curzon laughed at my astonishment. "Miss me?" he asked.

"What are you doing here? Where have you been?" I asked, fighting to keep my voice low. "Much is afoot."

He nodded his head toward the gallows. "So I see."

I opened my mouth to ask the first of a thousand questions, but he quickly put a finger to his lips. "Shhhh," he warned.

Ruth put her arms in the air and grunted. She was tired of staring at the backsides of the people crowding around us.

I shook my head. "You're too big to pick up."

"No, she's not." Before I could protest, Curzon tossed his ridiculous hat at me and lifted Ruth up to a perch on his left shoulder. She squealed with delight and a little fear and hung on to his neck so tightly he looked to choke.

I glanced at the red hat in my hands. A name was written on a scrap of fabric affixed to the crown–*James*.

"James?" I wondered aloud. If he heard me, Curzon took no notice. His eyes raked the crowd, looking intently but giving no clue about what he sought.

I cupped a hand to my mouth and whispered in his ear. "When will they send for Ruth and me? Colonel Regan promised to help."

"The world turns upside down every day." He kept his eyes straight ahead and one hand on Ruth's back to hold her steady. "The time will come, you'll see."

The drums beat faster. My heart sped up to match the rhythm.

The drums stopped.

"Here he comes!" someone called.

A guard marched Hickey out of the prison and across the yard to the gallows, his uniform dirty but buttoned. He kept his eyes on the steps that led up to the platform. He did not look at the rope that awaited him.

The crowd had recovered its voice and was screaming vile curses. Cabbages, rotten apples, and a dead cat were thrown in the direction of the traitor. He flinched as an egg sailed past his nose, but the men holding his elbows kept their backs straight and their boots marching forward.

Hickey was halted in front of the captain of the guard. The captain said something that we couldn't hear, then he pulled the sword from his scabbard, and sliced the epaulets off Hickey's shoulders. He folded them and placed them in his pocket, then brought the sword down in a sweep across the front of Hickey's chest, neatly slicing off the buttons from the traitor's coat. The buttons fell one by one into the dust.

Ruth stopped giggling.

A preacher stepped out of the crowd and approached Hickey, a Bible in his hand. The captain nodded curtly at the preacher and said something else to Hickey, again too low for us to hear. Hickey said nothing, but he had started to tremble. The captain spat on Hickey's boots, took one step back, and slid his sword home into the scabbard. The preacher murmured to Hickey and got no response, so took him by the hand and led him to the wooden stairs that led up to his fate.

"He's crying," I said.

"Good," Curzon said.

When he got to the top of the steps, Hickey turned around so the hangman could bind his wrists behind him. The drummers started beating their snares again, louder than before. The aide on horseback next to General Washington spoke, and the general leaned forward to hear better. He was by far the tallest man in sight. He agreed with whatever the aide said and patted his horse's neck. The animal tossed his mane and pawed at the ground.

The crowd had grown so loud that Ruth released Curzon's neck and covered her ears with her hands. She whimpered once. I held out my arms and she slid into them. I lowered her to the ground. She stood near on top of my shoes, grasped my apron, and stuck her thumb in her mouth.

The hangman led Hickey to the center of the platform. He placed the knotted noose around Hickey's neck, tightened it, then helped him climb onto an upright barrel. The captain of the guard raised his hand. The drumming stopped.

The crowd fell still.

The captain of the guard unrolled a sheet of paper and read the charges in a loud voice. "Thomas Hickey, you have been court-martialed and found guilty of the capital crimes of mutiny and sedition, of holding a treacherous correspondence with, and receiving pay from, the enemy for the most horrid and detestable purposes, and you have been sentenced to hang from the neck until dead. You are a disgrace to your country."

He rolled the paper back up. "May God have mercy on your soul."

With that pronouncement, the hangman kicked the barrel away.

The crowd gasped.

I covered Ruth's eyes with my hands and closed my own.

CHAPTER XIX

Sunday, June 30–
Monday, July 1, 1776

SIR, WE HAVE BEEN TOO LONG DEAF. WE HAVE TOO LONG SHOWN OUR FORBEARANCE AND LONG-SUFFERING. . . . OUR THUNDERS MUST GO FORTH. AMERICA MUST BE CONQUERED.
—ALEXANDER WEDDERBURN, SOLICITOR GENERAL OF ENGLAND, TO GEORGE III, KING OF ENGLAND

"MOST HEARTILY WE BESEECH THEE with thy favor to behold our most gracious Sovereign Lord King George, and to replenish him with the grace of thy Holy Spirit"—the minister paused to draw breath—"and bless our gracious Queen Charlotte, their Royal Highnesses George Prince of Wales, the Princess Dowager of Wales, and all the Royal Family . . ."

The reverend had so much beseeching to do for the royal family, I thought we'd be stuck in church for a week. Trinity was an Anglican church, filled with prayers for England, burning incense, and ministers in fancy dress. It discommodated me some to attend, but Madam gave me no choice. At home we went to the Congregational church, with ten pews, windows that looked out on the ocean, and a preacher who always wore black. I liked it better. Incense made me sneeze.

"We humbly beseech . . ."

They did a pack of beseeching at Trinity. The church was more than half-empty compared to the first Sunday Madam brought us, what with so many folks melting into the countryside, like Master Lockton. Martha Washington and her ladies were north on the island and those left in the pews were Loyalist. This made matters easier for the reverend, who could pray the way he wanted without worry of insulting men who owned the rebel cannons.

Ruth bounced her cornhusk doll on her lap and flew it through the air. Some folk grumbled about servants and slaves being forced to sit in the upstairs gallery. To my mind, being in the upstairs meant we were closer to God, and our prayers got there first. Besides, nobody upstairs fussed when Ruth played on the floor.

"Lighten our darkness, we beseech thee, O Lord; and by thy great mercy defend us from all perils and dangers—"

I beseech thee, O Lord, by Thy great mercy take us home, by the hand of Colonel Regan, take us home, in all Thy glory, take us home, ad astra, ad astra, ad astra . . .

Ruth tugged on my skirt. It was time to stand up again and pray. Below us, Madam leaned against the sturdy figure of Lady Seymour, who had come to the house early and forced Madam out of bed and into a Sunday dress. She covered the bruises still visible on Madam's face with a thick white layer of Molyneux's Italian Paste and told her she must not show weakness.

We sat down again. Up. Down. Up. Down. Yon minister could never make up his mind. My belly grumbled. Good thing the service was drawing to a close. Just a little more beseeching, a few amens, and we'd head home for cold pigeon pie and sour pickles.

Ruth's fingers drifted to her nose for some unsightly digging. As I reached for her hand, the front door of the church slammed open with a thud. The reverend near fainted with surprise.

A young boy ran halfway down the center aisle. "Beggin' pardon, Reverend," he shouted, "but the British have sailed into the harbor!"

The British army was hardly marching down Wall Street, but ten ships had docked downriver on Staten Island. Ruth and me followed behind Madam and Lady Seymour as we strode with the crowd to the Battery as fast as our skirts would allow.

Madam quivered with excitement but was wise enough not to say a word, for we found ourselves in a crowd of rebels furious about the arrival of King George's boys. Someone fired a cannon a stone's throw from where we stood. Gunpowder smoke drifted across the crowd as soldiers started running every which a'way, carrying on about "orders this" and "orders that." Someone fired a musket, and a woman shrieked. Two more muskets blasted. Rough voices commanded the firing to cease. Mothers chased after their children. Five men in frontier leggings and leather shirts sprinted past us, rifles at the ready.

Should I grab Ruth and run for the barracks? Could we slip away to sanctuary in the commotion? I looked for Colonel Regan but saw him not. None of the men were familiar to me. Had I waited too long?

The cannons fired once more, then fell silent. The ships were too far away to be hit, and the cannonballs fell into the river. Another musket cracked fire, but this was more distant. The crowd had settled some, and soldiers were lining up in orderly fashion, thanks to their barking officers.

"Everyone please disperse," shouted a broad-shouldered man in a crisp blue coat and a sleek, freshly powdered wig. "There is no danger here. Go about your business."

"Come now," Madam said. "We will leave this rabble."

She walked away with Lady Seymour. I went to follow them, but Ruth would not move. She stood rooted to the ground, trembling against my leg as if a gale were blowing.

"Ruthie?" I patted her back. "It's over now. The noise is gone, no more bangs." I reached to pry her fingers from me. They were stiff and shaking. She was in the grip of a fit, a small one. *Oh Lord, I beseech thee . . .*

Madam had stopped and was watching us. "Come along, girl," she snapped. "Turn your sister loose and run ahead to prepare the meal."

Ruth quivered, her teeth chattering in her head.

"She's a wee bit frightened, ma'am," I explained. "Never heard a cannon go off before."

"Neither have I," added Lady Seymour. "She'll feel better once she starts to walk."

Please, Lord. "Hear what Missus said, Ruth? Walking is the best thing." *Please keep her on her feet. Please make it stop.* "We've work to do, baby girl." My voice was as false as my smile. "Please."

I stepped forward, pushing Ruth ahead as I went. The trembling stopped, but her body went limp. I picked her up and settled her on my hip, her head on my shoulder as if she had fallen asleep.

Lady Seymour frowned in concern. "Is she poorly?"

Madam cast a suspicious eye at us.

"No, ma'am," I lied. "Just tired."

"She is not suffering her particular ailment, is she?" Madam asked, her voice cutting like a blade.

"No, ma'am," I lied again. "She helped carry out the ashes this morning, and it tired her."

Madam glared a moment longer.

Lady Seymour stepped in front of Madam. "The heat affects small children more than most. Make sure your sister drinks some water before any more chores."

"Yes, ma'am. Thank you, ma'am." I bobbed a clumsy curtsy and walked as fast as I could with the limp burden in my arms, beseeching with every step.

British ships continued to sail up the river all the day and all the night. Madam set us to polishing the silver in the hope that we'd soon be serving dinner to the British high command. On Monday morning Becky sent me to the washerwoman with a giant basket of dirty tablecloths and serviettes. So many ships had arrived by then—hundreds, folks said, with thousands of soldiers—that we could see the patches of white sail far down the harbor.

The washerwoman's home stood empty. A neighbor said she had fled at first light, terrified at the thought of invasion.

She wasn't the only one.

I carried the basket of linen back to the house on Wall Street, put a pot of water over the fire, and gathered the soap and the scrubbing board. Becky was off in search of a seamstress, so Ruth helped me haul the water to the washtub in the backyard. I gave her a small bucket and sliver of soap and she got to work washing a pair of stockings and singing to herself. She showed no ill effects of the small fit at the Battery. It had been a brief shower, not a thunderstorm.

As I scrubbed, my mind ran in circles, like a dog chasing its tail. I should take Ruth and march down to the Battery. I should demand payment for helping with the arrests. No. No demands. I should politely ask the colonel to fulfill his promise, as a gentleman would. I should write a letter to the general. I should beg Curzon to beg Mr. Bellingham to beg whoever to get us out.

I flopped the tablecloth into the rinse tub and started in on a shift that had gotten mixed in with the table linens. Ruth dropped her stockings in the rinse bucket and loaded her bucket with rocks.

"We don't wash rocks, Ruth," I explained.

"But they dirty," she said.

"That is a truth," I said. The rocks were dirty and washing them kept her calm and away from Madam. "Scrub away, lass."

There was no use in begging anyone. The chances of them listening to me were as good as a snowball's chance in the Devil's bake oven.

I reached for the soap as Ruth flung her half-washed rocks, now muddy, not dirty, into the rinsing tub with the clean tablecloth. Before I could scold her, the back door slammed. I saw the flash of a yellow gown by the kitchen window. Madam had been watching us, no doubt displeased that Ruth was washing rocks with the tablecloths.

We must escape. Soon.

CHAPTER XX

Tuesday, July 2–
Tuesday, July 9, 1776

. . . THE CONGRESS HAVE JUDGED IT NECESSARY TO DISSOLVE THE CONNECTION BETWEEN GREAT BRITAIN AND THE AMERICAN COLONIES, AND TO DECLARE THEM FREE AND INDEPENDENT STATES; AS YOU WILL PERCEIVE BY THE ENCLOSED DECLARATION. . . . I AM DIRECTED . . . TO REQUEST YOU HAVE IT PROCLAIMED AT THE HEAD OF THE ARMY, IN THE WAY YOU SHALL THINK MOST PROPER.
—LETTER FROM JOHN HANCOCK,
PRESIDENT OF THE CONTINENTAL CONGRESS,
TO GENERAL GEORGE WASHINGTON

THAT WEEK UNSPOOLED SLOWLY WITH hot days and muggy, breathless nights. Militia units from the surrounding colonies piled into the city. Ordinary folk skedaddled out of it as fast as their horse or feet would carry them. The extra soldiers were not the cleanest sort, or maybe they were too busy drilling and making gunpowder cartridges to wash. Whatever the cause, New York soon smelled like a garbage pit mixed with a fresh mountain of manure. The stench cooked under the midsummer sun.

Madam's moods changed with the tide. One moment she floated on clouds of fancy, imagining her grand life once the British beat the rebels. Next she fell into melancholy, grumbling about the lazy British commanders floating at anchor off Staten Island, observing New York through long spyglasses but making no move to invade. She now carried with her a brocade pouch suspended from a red satin cord. Within the pouch lay a green flask filled with a calming elixir prescribed by the doctor. He advised her to drink from it whenever the need arose. She also took to walking around the house in her stocking feet, trying to catch me unawares as I scrubbed or dusted or polished, often with Ruth at my side. She said nothing during these encounters but watched us with hungry hawk eyes. It unnerved me.

The week after Hickey's hanging, Becky suffered a mild attack of the ague that had befallen so many soldiers. She grew pale and sweaty but did not require purging or leeches. In her stead, I went to the market. Our needs were fewer now that we no longer fed the master and his companions. 'Twas a good thing, for farmers were afeard to come into the city, and there was less to choose from. More people fled every day, including the wives of General Washington and Colonel Knox and Brigadier Greene, her that folks said was such a big flirt.

I searched for Curzon every day, but Bellingham's affairs kept him out of sight. I was afraid to seek out Colonel Regan, afraid that word would get back to Madam and our lives be put in jeopardy.

Ten days after the British flooded the river with their ships, news that the Congress had declared independence arrived in New York. The Declaration was read to the troops from the steps of City Hall. The men cheered so loud it seemed to shake the whole island. I hurried from the egg seller to see the cause of the commotion.

The cheering men danced and marched down Broadway,

tossing their hats into the air and shouting across the river at the silent ships of England. They gathered into a mob on the Bowling Green around the massive statue of King George III. I stayed at the edge of the crowd, hoping for a glimpse of Curzon or a soldier familiar from my visit to the Battery.

The King was mounted on his horse, and the horse mounted on a white marble pedestal that rose to the height of three men standing one atop the other. Both the horse and the man were fashioned larger than could be possible, but I supposed that was the way of kings. They were both made of gold that sometimes glittered in the sunlight but dulled when the clouds interfered.

Ropes appeared as if conjured, thick ropes used for tying ships to the docks. The men cheered louder and worked together to throw the ropes over the King and his horse and tie them tightly.

"One, two, three, heave! One, two, three, heave!"

The men strained their arms and backs. Boys on the edge of the crowd jumped up and down. Common folk stood froze at the sight of a king being pulled down by the strength of the men working together.

"One, two, three, HEAVE!"

The statue toppled, slowly at first, then gaining speed as the weight fell from the sky to the ground. The men scrambled out the way, no one wishing to be crushed by a fallen king. As it crashed, they shouted even louder and swarmed over the thing. Axes were called for and rushed out of workshops and up from the barracks. A half-dozen men took to chopping the King and his steed to bits.

I inched closer. How could they be chopping through a statue with simple axes? A piece of tail broke off, and a soldier held it up for all to see. The King was not made of gold, but of soft lead, covered with gilt paint. The crowd shouted again as another soldier lifted the King's head freshly removed from his neck. A fife-and-drum corps started playing just beyond the mob, piping out the song usually heard during a tar-and-feathering party.

The men made short work of King George. When the statue was reduced into pieces that could be easily carted off, they did just that. The plan was to melt down all the lead into bullets.

"We'll fire Majesty at the redcoats!" joked a man with a booming voice.

"Aye," said his companion, shouldering an axe. "Emanations from Leaden George will make deep impressions on the enemy!"

As the crowd marched off to make bullets and celebrate liberty and independence in the taverns, I realized dark was fast falling, and I had tarried overly long. I picked up a sliver of lead that lay in the street. It was fringed with gilt; my own piece of majesty. *Tyrants beware,* I thought as I put it in my pocket.

I was surprised to see the front parlor windows alight when I walked down Wall Street.

"Is the master back?" I asked Becky. She was dozing in the chair by the kitchen fire with a red-checked shawl around her shoulders, still worn down from her illness.

Becky yawned and stretched. "Far from it. Madam paid a call on the reverend's wife after supper. Came home with high color in her cheeks and a bee in her bonnet. 'Dress the child,' she says. 'Make sure both of the girls eat something nourishing and sweet.'"

"Did she fall and hit her head?" I asked, setting down the basket of eggs.

Becky laughed. "I think the Missus Reverend served her a dose of Scripture, the hard kind. Madam says, 'I've been too harsh on my servants. I must mend my ways or the Lord will punish me.'"

I was confuddled. "She's being kind to Ruth again?"

Becky stood slowly, wincing from the aches in her bones. "Surely so. Ruth lit up like a lantern when she saw them fancy clothes again. Promised to be quiet as ever. Made short work of the gingerbread Madam baked, too."

This was too much. I sat down at the table. "Madam baked?"

"She's a fair hand in the kitchen when she puts her mind to it. Left the dishes for yours truly, but the cake was tasty. Those two pieces are for you. She was most firm about it." She stopped to cough up what sounded like a large, wet worm from her throat. "She cooked up sweet milk for you, too, with nutmeg, cinnamon, and sugar. Said you was to have some with your gingerbread."

I sniffed the pitcher. It smelled good enough. "Did you have any?"

"Not with this cough. Milk would stop up my lungs."

I looked around the kitchen. "Where's Ruth now?"

Becky unpinned her apron and folded it, then tied on her bonnet, preparing to go home. "Madam got it in her head to play cards this eve. Has two companions in with her, the missus Drinkwater and her daughter, the one who's to marry some sort of lord or duke or somesuch. Ruth is in with them. She was right cheered after the cake and milk."

"Should I take anything in?"

"I just come from there. Madam was most definite: 'Tell Sal to enjoy her cake and a night off. She has worked hard these weeks and could do with a good night's sleep.'"

"She called me Sal instead of Girl?" I asked. "And you are full certain she didn't hit her head today."

Becky laughed, and the laugh caught in her throat and bubbled into a cough. "Look here. She's likely to turn back into a sour old cow by breakfast, so I say have a good sit-down and enjoy a little peace."

I poured a mug of the milk. "Huzzah for the reverend's wife."

I wanted to savor the gingerbread bite by bite and sip the milk slowly, but I couldn't help myself. The mug was drained and the plate empty soon after Becky left. The milk was the sweetest thing I had ever tasted, the spices so thick I could near chew them. No wonder Ruth was cheered by it.

I washed up my dishes, tidied the kitchen, and found myself with idle hands. A rare event, indeed. I might could sneak into the library and borrow that *Crusoe* book. I could read by the fire with a mending basket nearby to slip the book into should Madam approach.

That seemed a fine plan. But first I wanted to shed my bodice; it pinched something awful under my arms. I felt my way down the cellar stairs with my toes and heard the sound of laughter from Madam's company. I yawned. When would they leave? And what sort of ladies came to call this late?

I removed my bodice and hung it on a nail. The pallet looked soothing and cool, and the thought of climbing the stairs again made me weary. But I would like to read a few more pages . . . but I was overly fatigued . . . but Mr. Crusoe was facing all sorts of dangers . . . but . . .

Inbetwixt one thought and the next, I fell asleep.

For that, I shall never forgive myself.

CHAPTER XXI

Wednesday, July 10, 1776

To be sold at the office of William Tongue,
Broker, at the house of the late Mr. Waldron
near the Exchange (lower end of Broad street)
the following goods and merchandise, viz.:
One Negro Wench, 22 years old, has had
smallpox, is a useful domestic, price 80 £, . . .
one Negro Boy, 16 years old, price 90 £, . . .
one Negro Wench, 30 years old, with or
without her son 5 years old price 60 or 80 £.
–Advertisement in the *New York Gazette
and Weekly Mercury* newspaper

In my dream I stood on a sandy beach, my back to the sea, the moon over my left shoulder. An enormous map was unrolled at my feet. The roads on it were marked with velvet black ink, rivers a pearly blue, mountains a speckled green. It was a map of a country I had never before seen.

Just as I opened my mouth to call for Ruth, who always tagged along in my dreams, a thick mist blew over the beach. The roads on the map twined and twisted round each other, hesitating, then they rose up off the paper, no longer roads, but thick eels with amber eyes. They crawled out of the map, and I feared they would bite me. They pondered me a moment, then slithered down the beach and into the water.

I awoke with a start and flung aside the blanket, looking for the eels. There were none there, nor in the potato bin. Ruth wasn't there, neither, and her side of our pallet was cold. She was gone to the privy, no doubt. I needed to visit the same place.

The sun was already in the trees when I stepped outside. How had I slept so late?

"Ruth?" I called, walking toward the little building. My nose wrinkled. The Locktons would soon need to dig a new privy hole.

"Ruth?" I knocked on the door and it swung open.

The seat was empty, with a few flies buzzing in the stench. Two blue jays in the sycamore tree called loudly. There was the distant sound of officers shouting orders on Broadway and the clatter of cart wheels. But no Ruth.

I made quick work of looking in the yard. The back entry to the stables was locked, she could not have gone out that way. The gate to the street was closed, too, and the latch too high for Ruth to reach. Had Madam already dressed her, taken her on a call?

A thought slid through me, quick and slimy as a cold eel.

I ran for the kitchen door. "Becky? Becky!"

She came out of the pantry as I flew through the door.

"Where's Ruth?"

"Oh." Becky looked down at the worn tips of her shoes, then turned away from me. Her eyes were puddled up and red rimmed.

"I can't find her," I said. "She was gone when I woke. Have you seen her?"

Becky took the jar of flour down from the shelf.

"You know where she is, don't you?"

She removed the lid and stuck the scoop into the flour.

"Tell me!"

Becky shook her head from side to side. "I should have started this bread earlier," she said, pouring the flour into the bowl. "The wet air will ruin the loaves, that's my concern. I should have stayed and baked in the cool of the night." She dabbed her eyes on her sleeve and measured out another scoop of flour. "But Madam sent me home. Said she wanted a quiet house last night. No baking."

She looked at me over her shoulder. The eel squeezed out all my air.

"No," I said.

"I wouldn't have gone if I'd known—"

"No, no, no." I backed away, shaking my head. "She didn't. She wouldn't. No."

"Isabel, don't." Becky followed me down the hall, trying to control her voice. "It won't change anything. What's done is done."

"Ruth!" I screamed up the staircase.

"Stop, Isabel!" Becky grabbed my arm and pulled me backward, clamping a flour-covered hand over my mouth. "You can't storm around here like a banshee. Madam will beat you bloody. Me too."

I pushed her hand away and wiped off the flour. "Where is she? What did they do to her?"

"She's gone," Becky said.

"Gone?" I repeated. "Gone where?"

Becky studied her shoes again. "Sold."

I stopped hearing right. No more birds or buzzing flies or grandfather clock marking time.

"Sold?" I repeated. "No, she's not. They didn't."

Becky's eyes filled again. "Yes," she said quietly. "She did."

I paced the hall. "No. I slept too heavy last night. Didn't notice when she woke. She wandered outside. We need to find her. She could be lost, could have taken ill and fallen."

Becky watched me go to and fro. "The sweet milk Madam made up? I figure it contained a sleep potion, knocked you out cold so they could spirit her away. I am dreadful, powerful sorry, but they sold her away from you."

It made no sense. I would have known. I would have woken up, fought them off, killed whoever tried to take her from me. I took care of Ruth. I promised Momma I always would.

Becky's face shrank down to the size of a coin. It sounded like she spoke through a long wooden pipe. "Madam was returning in the carriage when I arrived this morn," she said. "Told me not to worry about the milk spoiling no more, that Ruth was headed to Nevis, sold to a physician's family."

I shook my head, trying to clear my brainpan. "Where's Nevis? How do I get there?"

Becky's face grew larger. "You need to sit down. I'll get a cloth for your head. This has been a right shock to you."

"Where's Nevis?" My voice echoed off the walls.

"West Indies," Becky muttered.

"The islands?" All of Momma's terrible stories of slave life in the islands flooded back. "Ruth can't cut cane! She'll die! She'll die in a day!" My feet started for the front door.

"Wait!" Becky grabbed my arm to prevent me from

running off. "I questioned Madam about that very fact, questioned her right close, I did. 'Not to cut cane,' said she, 'but to be a house maid, in a fine house. A physician's house, so they'll care for her should she fall.'"

"She's lying," I said. "She's a spiteful, hateful liar."

A door opened on the second floor. "Becky?" Madam asked. "Has someone come to call?"

"No, ma'am," Becky said in a false, high voice.

Madam came down the stairs, one hand on the railing, the other holding a sheet of paper, half-covered with writing. The paintings of her dead ancestors on the wall watched her. "I do not appreciate interruptions when I am communicating with my husband," she said. "What is the matter here?"

"Nothing, m-ma'am," Becky stuttered. "I was giving the girl her directions for the morning."

Madam looked down without seeing me; she looked at my face, my kerchief, my shift neatly tucked into my skirt, looked at my shoes pinching my feet, looked at my hands that were stronger than hers. She did not look into my eyes, did not see the lion inside. She did not see the me of me, the Isabel.

I saw her. I saw all the way down to her withered soul.

I walked up two steps. "Did you sell Ruth?"

"You will not address me in that insolent manner." Her voice shook a little.

Becky wrung her hands. "Come, Isabel. You need to peel the potatoes. Would Madam like some tea or coffee?"

I took another step up. "Answer me, you miserable cow. Did you sell my sister?"

Madam backed up a step. Her letter fluttered to the bottom of the stairs. Her ancestors hung silent. "Stay away from me," she said. "Get back to the kitchen."

"She is five years old." I rose another step. "She is a baby, and you sold her away from me."

She swallowed hard. Her hands quivered.

I wanted to grab her by the hair and throw her down the stairs, throw her out a window, beat her face with my fists. I wanted her blood to splash the paintings, soak the wall and the wooden stairs.

"Isabel," Becky warned.

The sunlight coming through the window was rosy red. I took the next step. I was almost close enough to reach her.

"Isabel," Becky tried again.

"One more step and I can have you hung," Madam whispered.

I held my breath. There was a click of metal on metal.

Becky had opened the front door wide. A hot wind from the street rose up the stairs, fluttering our skirts and causing me to turn. Madam grabbed a painting from the wall and threw it down on my head. I raised my arm too late and the frame crashed into me. The blow made me addlepated and weakened my knees. Madam ran upstairs, screaming like a house afire.

Becky dragged me down the steps and shoved me toward the open door. "Run!" she screamed.

I ran out the front door for the first time.

People walking under the shade of the sycamores across the street paused at the sight of a slave running away from a mansion where a woman was screaming. A man called after me, "You there! Girl!"

I ran straight down Wall. Didn't worry about escaping notice of soldiers or strangers, just flew over the cobblestones as fast as I could. The red fog slowly rolled out of my mind. There were more shouts behind me, and people turning to stare at the cause of the commotion. I didn't dare take the time to turn around. Past City Hall, cross Broadway. I leapt over the remains of a sentry fire, bumped into a gray-bearded soldier wearing a homespun shirt, and startled a man carrying two live hens by the feet. One of the hens broke free in an explosion of feathers. The man shook his fist and called out for someone to stop me. I ducked down one street after another, trying to find a way to the river, but the army had erected barricades at the ends of most of the roads to keep out the British.

I was penned in.

The shouts behind me grew louder and closer.

I darted down an alley, turned blindly toward the right, and ran smack into the barrel chest of a giant.

"Whoa there, young filly," a deep voice boomed. "Don't want to go swimming in the river, do you?"

I had run straight into a blacksmith.

"Please, sir," I said.

His enormous hands released me and I looked over my shoulder.

"Looking to get away from someone, I suspect," the blacksmith said. Behind him billowed the coal smoke from the forge. The air was filled with the hot tang of metal and sweat.

"You're hurt, child," the blacksmith said. "In need of some help?"

I wanted to spill out my story and to trust he could advise me, but he was a stranger, they were all strangers and Ruth was gone and there was blood on my forehead from the painting Madam threw at me and she was going to see me hung and I'd never be able to rescue Ruth and she would be all alone and . . .

"Tell them I went north," I gasped as I picked up my skirts and darted around the forge to the south.

The blacksmith called after me, but his words were lost in the din of the soldiers and the sailors who cluttered my path. The wind off the river cooled my face and helped with my decision. I would turn myself over to the rebels. I had helped them fair and square. Now it was their turn.

We were all fighting for liberty.

"Ad astra!" I shouted. The words were not as magic as I had hoped, but the door eventually opened.

Colonel Regan was sitting in a chair, a white cloth around his neck, his face covered with foamy soap and his eyes closed. Behind him stood a barber, a slave, I assumed because of his African skin, with grizzled hair and an apron. On the table beside him stood a bowl of steaming water, a leather strop for blades, and a cup of lather with a brush in it. He turned the colonel's chin with one finger, then delicately shaved away a stripe of soap with a razor.

"By your leave, sir," said the sentry.

"I am busy," the colonel said, without opening his eyes.

"This girl knew the password, insisted on seeing you," the sentry continued.

The barber scraped off another stripe of soap and whiskers. "Take her to Jamison," the colonel said.

"No," I said.

The barber froze in midshave, and the colonel opened his eyes.

"Please, sir, you must help me," I said quickly. "As I once

helped you. She sold my sister. Please, sir, I'll do anything, just find Ruth, she's so small and–"

The door behind us opened. Two more sentries filed in, followed by Madam Lockton, breathing hard, and a tall gentleman I'd not seen before. My sentry waved me farther into the room so that the newcomers might all fit. I worked my way toward an open window.

"What is the meaning of this?" the colonel asked wearily.

Madam's voice cracked across the room. "Are you the man in charge?"

The colonel sighed deeply, waved off the barber, and stood up, his face still half-covered with soap. "Colonel Thomas Regan at your service, ma'am." He bowed stiffly from the waist. "How can I be of service?"

"You have stolen my property," Madam announced.

"We have several clerks assigned to record civilian concerns. My sergeant will show you–"

"I will not speak with subordinates or grubby clerks. That chit of a girl belongs to me, Colonel. She has committed terrible crimes and must be punished. I demand you return her to me."

The barber rinsed the razor in the water bowl.

Regan looked from Madam to me and back again. "What did she do?"

"She abused me most violently, sir."

The colonel put out his hand and the barber placed a clean towel in it. "Yet it is the girl with blood on her face," the colonel said, wiping away the soap from his chin and cheeks.

Madam's eyes narrowed. "Give her to me."

The sentries shifted their boots on the floor; one cleared

his throat. The gentleman who accompanied Madam stepped forward. "The law is quite clear on this matter, sir. None of us want to live in a world where servants rule their masters. Both the Parliament and the Congress give Madam Lockton rule over her slave."

A flock of crows swooped past the window. A three-masted ship, sails unfurled, pushed down the river. Ruth could be on it. Or she was already at sea, in a dark hold with no candles. Who would feed her? Who would hold her when she shook?

"The girl says you've sold her sister," Colonel Regan said.

"Do you mean to purchase Sal for the army?" Madam asked. "I'm sure she'd make a passing fine washwoman. I shall expect full payment, in cash."

He handed the towel back to the barber. "A washwoman is the one thing I don't need right now. If you had any manservants capable of ditch digging, I'd take you up on the offer, but . . ." He paused and shook his head.

I looked out the window again. One crow had come back. It landed on a carcass near the water's edge—a dead dog or a rat. The crow pecked at the meat of the thing, snatched a pink strip in his beak, and tugged until the piece broke away. He beat his wings once, twice, and flew up in the air high enough to catch a breeze that rode him out over the water.

Another man had entered the room. The night of my first visit to the fort he had worn his uniform coat over his nightshirt. Now his coat was properly buttoned and his breeches tucked into his boots.

"Thomas, we cannot interfere," he said. "This girl is not our concern. And you are late. We dare not keep him waiting."

I looked out the window at the carcass. "Please, sir," I said in a quiet voice. "Let me stay."

Colonel Regan fastened his collar without looking at me. "The law binds my hands and my actions. You must return with your mistress," he said, concentrating on his task. "Even during time of war, we must follow the rules of propriety and civilization."

With that, the matter was concluded. Madam turned to thank the man who aided her. The sentries slipped into the hall. Colonel Regan picked up his hat from the table and set it on his head.

As I stepped toward the window, the barber studied me close. He shook his head once from side to side, just as Jenny had back in Rhode Island, one hundred years ago. Bad advice on both occasions.

I bolted for the open window.

I almost made it.

CHAPTER XXII

Wednesday, July 10–Monday, July 15, 1776

BUT AS IT IS, WE HAVE THE WOLF BY THE EAR, AND WE CAN NEITHER HOLD HIM, NOR SAFELY LET HIM GO. JUSTICE IS IN ONE SCALE, AND SELF-PRESERVATION IN THE OTHER.
—THOMAS JEFFERSON, WRITING ABOUT SLAVERY

WHEN I WOKE, THE BARREL OF A GUN was stuck up underneath my chin.

Men-voices shouted. Boots stomped. A rain of hands grabbed at me, countless bodies, smelly breath, unwashed feet. My head felt cracked in three pieces.

A woman shrieked and shrieked; she was a crow shattering the air with her harsh calls. I moved, not by my own devices. My toes dragged in the dirt. They tried to pull my arms from my body, ripping the arms off a cloth doll. They dragged me from one place to a second place.

More shouts. More shrieks and whistles and calls, rumbling thundervoices.

They dragged me from the second place to the third place, every voice sowing the wind, all things summoning the whirlwind that would sweep us all away to drown in the deepest sea.

My thoughts would not line up like good soldiers. They

swarmed afield and fled, chasing the blood that dripped from my head and stained my shift. My eyes were swold up and hard to see through. Someone had stolen a tooth or two.

They tied my hands together with prickly rope. They tied the rope to the back of a cart. They tied a horse to the front of the cart. The horse lifted one tired hoof after another and dragged the cart, and the cart dragged me up the broad street where people smiled and laughed and pointed. My eyes cast down. The cobblestones mocked too.

I tried to figure the whos and the whys of the matter, but my own name escaped me, and I knew only the pain in my head and the iron taste of lost teeth. My remembery broke into bits when they beat my head.

They took me to the dungeon under City Hall to await my trial. The jailer locked me in a cell with a toothless madwoman who huddled in the corner and spat at me. She pulled the hairs from her head and dropped them to the mud. She was near bald.

At sunset, the jailer came back with a cup of water and a piece of foul pork half the size of my hand. Dirty men in the other cells fought each other all night long.

On the second day we heard shouts and screams from the world above us, then came the boom and roar of cannons, followed by the crack of musket fire, and the sounds of hundreds of boots shaking the earth. Some prisoners hollered in panic and tried to pull their chains from the stone walls. The madwoman in my cell laughed and laughed, slapping her skirts.

At last the noise above ceased. The jailers threw buckets of cold water on the men who had lost their senses in fear.

They said for us to shut our gobs. The British had sailed their war ships up the North River and had fired on the town, but now all danger was past. Anyone who continued to blubber would feel the lash.

I said not a word.

The second night was same as the first, filled with moans and muttering, scratching, and the sound of teeth and claw. It rained. Water pooled on the floor and soaked through my shoes. Rats wandered in and out of the cells, squeezing their fat bottoms through the bars. I dared not sleep for fear they would bite me. The madwoman and the rats stayed in the corner, red eyes waiting for me all night long.

On the third morning, the jailer unlocked my cell and motioned for me to follow him. The madwoman laughed again.

He took me up the stairs to the courtroom. It was as big as the inside of a church, with the same white walls and dark wood. The windows were of clear glass, grimy with neglect. They stood me behind a rail. Kept my hands tied. I shook with fever and hunger.

"Oyez, oyez, oyez," called a man in the shadows. He said more, but his words slurred together.

A tall man wearing black robes and a long wig sat at a table that was raised on a platform. He was a judge. This was a court. My head was broke and my sister was stole and I was lost.

The woman with the crow voice, her that threw the picture at me, stood up. I raised my head to look at her. Someone poked a stick into my ribs, hard, and hissed at me. I lowered my eyes.

Voices buzzed and blurred into words I did not understand. Lockton, I finally remembered. Lockton, Madam Lockton, her that bought us, her that stole Ruth away. I kept my head down, but lifted my eyes, tho' they pained me. The pain was good. It drew back the curtains of my mind and forced me to pay attention.

Madam was pretending to cry into her lace handkerchief. ". . . and I am but a poor woman, alone, my husband having fled for reasons I cannot comprehend. I plead with Your Honor to assist me in the correct punishment of this girl."

The judge frowned and asked questions of two officers who stood near Madam. I wanted to ask about Ruth, and where the blood on my shift came from, and who broke my teeth, but I was the only person in the room whose hands were tied, so I kept silent. Questions were asked of the incident. Lies were given as answers.

Finally the judge said, "Where is the housekeeper who saw this crime, Missus Lockton?"

"Becky is indisposed, sir," Madam answered. "She suffers the ague."

"Are there no other witnesses to the events you describe?"

A stranger stood up in the back of the room. "I was passing in the street, Your Honor," he said. "I heard the commotion, saw the girl fleeing, and observed the destruction myself."

"There are several other people of standing willing to testify, Your Honor," Madam added. Her tears had mysteriously vanished.

The judge used the end of his quill to scratch at an itch under his wig. "It is clear that this slave has violated the person of her master, destroyed valuable property, and attempted to run away, all contrary to the laws of our colony."

"State, Your Honor," reminded the lawyer. "We are a state, now. Independence and all that."

The judge rolled his eyes. "Colony. State. Who knows what we will be next?" He sighed deeply. "No matter. This girl's crimes of insolence, property destruction, and running away from her rightful owner are not devious enough to warrant a sentence of death. Do you have any wishes as to the punishment that I should consider, Missus Lockton?"

Madam sighed deeply, like my behavior caused her great sadness. "She is a willful girl, Your Honor, with numerous character defects. I believe a permanent reminder of this day might prove the appropriate remedy."

Her words stuck in the air, like flies caught in a spider's web. I could make no sense of them. I could make no sense of anything.

The judge scratched at his wig with fresh vigor. "You wanted her branded then? Twenty strokes of the lash would be more in keeping with her crimes."

"We are now led by men from Virginia, I am told," she said, "land of my birth. I assure Your Honor that in Virginia, we do not tolerate the rebellion of slaves."

The judge nodded. "Once kindled, rebellion can spread like wildfire. Do you want your husband's initials used?"

Madam shot a sideways glance at me. "I prefer the girl branded with the letter *I* for 'Insolence.' It will alert people to her tendencies and serve as a reminder of her weakness."

The judge picked up his gavel. "So be it. Sal Lockton, it is the order of this court that you be branded on your right cheek with the letter of *I* in punishment for your crimes against your lady mistress."

Crack! The gavel cracked on the block of wood. "Next case."

CHAPTER XXIII

Monday, July 15, 1776

I ALSO HAVE BEEN WHIPPED MANY A TIME ON MY NAKED SKIN, AND SOMETIMES TILL THE BLOOD HAS RUN DOWN OVER MY WAISTBAND; BUT THE GREATEST GRIEF I THEN HAD WAS TO SEE THEM WHIP MY MOTHER, AND TO HEAR HER, ON HER KNEES, BEGGING FOR MERCY . . .
—REV. DAVID GEORGE, ON HIS CHILDHOOD AS A SLAVE

A MAN PULLED ME BY MY ROPE outside to the courtyard. After two days in the dungeon, the noonday sun scalded my eyes. I stumbled but did not fall. The man led me to the stocks, then untied my hands and pointed. I laid my head and hands in the crescents carved into the wood. He lowered the top board, pinning me in place, and secured the two pieces together with a large padlock.

A brazier filled with hot coals set on the ground a few lengths in front of me. A second man stuck two branding irons into the metal basket to heat them up.

My knees turned to water. I sagged against the wood.

"Stand up, girl, or you'll choke yourself," growled the man locked into the stocks to my left. I couldn't turn my head enough to see him, but his voice was rough and scarred. "Whatever you do, don't scream," he continued. "That's what they want to hear."

I did not answer him but forced my knees to hold me up.

The wood locked around my neck was rough and splintering. My hands were soon without sensation, my neck and arms pricked a hundredfold by pitchforks. Two men were housed in the iron cage next to City Hall. One lay on the ground, asleep or dead. The second, his skin burned by the sun and peeling and missing his left ear, stared back at me blankly.

A court official, his coat covered with yellow dust, arrived with a man who wore a leather apron. He set to work pumping a hand-bellows to increase the heat under the branding irons. The bellows wheezed in and out while the sun rose higher in the sky.

It had rained in the night. The mud puddles scattered around the yard gave off steam like cauldrons coming to boil.

Sweat rolled off my face and fell in great drops to the dirt below. The wind shifted and blew the smoke from the brazier into our faces. I held my breath. In betwixt me and the brazier, dandelions grew in the mud.

The man in the dusty coat pulled one of the branding irons out of the fire. He brought it close to his face and spit on it. The iron sizzled. My companion coughed and cursed the court officials and the judge who had sentenced him.

A crowd had gathered a few lengths on the other side of the brazier, mostly soldiers and tradesmen, with a few women, one carrying a babe in her arms. I thought I saw a boy in a red hat, but when I blinked, he was gone. Men at the front of the crowd called us names and jeered. The sunburned man in the cage yelled back, and soon the courtyard was filled with shouts and filthy language, the kinds of words my mother never wanted me to say or hear. I fought against tears and lost; they fell to the dust in big drops too. If I cried a river, maybe I could swim away, or slip under the water to freedom.

The man in the dusty coat said something to the man in the leather apron. I could not hear him because of the noise of the crowd and the crackling coals and the beat of my heart in my ears. The men walked toward me. The dandelions were lemon yellow with bright green leaves and thick stalks pointing at the sky.

At home in Rhode Island, the corn was tall as Ruth now. The spring lambs would be too heavy to pick up. The new goat, he'd be running headfirst into every fence post. This was a good day to bleach the wool.

The man with the leather apron pinned my head against the wood. He stank of charcoal. I tried to pull away, but my hands and head were locked fast. The splinters chewed on me. Dandelions grew in the mud.

The glowing iron streaked in front of my face like a comet.

The crowd roared.

The man pushed the hot metal against my cheek. It hissed and bubbled. Smoke curled under my nose.

They cooked me.

The man stepped back and pulled the iron away. The fire in my face burned on and on, deep through my flesh, searing my soul. Stars exploded out the top of my head and all of my words and all of my rememberies followed them up to the sun, burning to ash that floated back and settled in the mud.

A few people at the edge of the crowd had fallen silent. They walked away with their heads down.

My momma and poppa appeared from the shadows. They flew to me and wrapped their arms around me and cooled my face with their ghost tears.

Night crept into my soul.

CHAPTER XXIV

Monday, July 15–
Sunday, July 21, 1776

THE TIME IS NOW NEAR AT HAND WHICH MUST PROBABLY DETERMINE, WHETHER AMERICANS ARE TO BE, FREEMEN, OR SLAVES; . . . THE FATE OF UNBORN MILLIONS WILL NOW DEPEND, UNDER GOD, ON THE COURAGE AND CONDUCT OF THIS ARMY. . . . WE HAVE THEREFORE TO RESOLVE TO CONQUER OR DIE.
–MESSAGE ISSUED TO CONTINENTAL TROOPS FROM NEW YORK MILITARY HEADQUARTERS, JULY 1776

THE SPARK KINDLED ON MY CHEEK flared and spread through my entire body. First my eyes, then hair, then down my limbs, until even my toes and fingers felt they were aflame.

Strange scenes swam before me, first in light, then darkness, then light again. I saw Poppa, but no, not truly him; another son of Africa, brow furrowed, his voice deep and strong as a church bell. Momma hovered over me, but her face faded into a woman I did not know, older than Momma, with strands of white in her hair. She talked Jamaica, more song than words, and brought bitter tea to my mouth and made the world smell of lemons and told me to sleep. I asked about Ruth over and over again and tried to apologize for letting her get stole, but the words were sawdust in my mouth.

Curzon's face floated up in front of me. He told me to shake my lazy bones and get out of bed. He did not turn into a dead person from when I was little. This was a strange comfort.

I blinked and he was gone.

The room was dark again, with starlight in the windows and the sounds of a baby crying, and farther away, the barking of a lonely dog.

Strangest of all was the hive of bees that had taken up residence inside of me. They swarmed under my skin and gave off peculiar vibrations. The buzzing echoed in my brainpan and crowded out my thoughts.

The fire in me burned on and on.

I woke.

I did not know where I was.

This was not Rhode Island, or the hold of a ship, or the Locktons' cellar or any other room in their house. It certainly was not the dungeon under City Hall.

Was this a dream? Had I passed over to the land of the dead? Did ghosts sleep on clean sheets that smelled of mint?

I sat up. The room was warm and quite small but entirely free of dirt, vermin, and mice. The walls were freshly whitewashed and the floor polished. Lace curtains fluttered in the window. Through it I saw the tops of trees. This was an attic room, then. The bed was softer than anything I had ever lain in, properly made up with linens, two pillows, and a coverlet of deep blue. A chair was positioned next to the bed, and a chamber pot, empty, rested under that.

I tried to stand, but the room spun around me and I

plopped back down. I was wearing my shift, still stained with blood at the neckline, but my skirt, stockings, and bodice were not to be seen. Or my shoes. I closed my eyes tight, then opened them again. Same room. Still no shoes.

The door opened and in stepped the funny-talking Dutch maid of Lady Seymour. Her eyes flew open wide, then she slammed the door shut and ran away. A moment later, the door opened again and in walked the Lady herself.

"Ah," she said with faint surprise. "You've come back to us." She poured water from the jug into a mug, handed it to me, and sat on the chair.

I drank down a gulp. My lips were dried and cracked. When I swallowed, it caused my burned cheek to ache. My fingers flew up to check the wound. There was a cloth stuck to my face, with ointment oozing out from the edges.

Lady Seymour leaned forward and gently removed my hand. "Best not to touch it yet," she said. "The healer woman put a comfrey salve on it to draw out the pestilence."

"Beg pardon, ma'am," I croaked. My voice was raspy with lack of use. "But where am I? And why?"

She glanced out the window before she spoke, her mouth set in a grim line. "How best to say this?" she began.

I waited, not sure how to answer.

"You have lain here, near insensible, for six days."

"Six?"

"Do you remember what happened?"

The bees threatened to overtake my mind again, their wings beating quickly. I took another drink of water. "I remember some. The rest is a jumble, ma'am."

"You tried to run away and were beaten in the attempt. You passed two days under City Hall and emerged gravely ill with fever and heaven knows what else. After your trial, you were branded. I was not aware of these events until after they occurred. Your friend with the red hat came to the door with the news that you were near-dead in the stocks. After consulting with Anne, I arranged to have you transported here."

She looked directly at me. "I further questioned Anne and discovered her version of the events. I find the buying and selling of children most repugnant. Your reaction to the news of your sister, while unfortunate, was understandable, in my view."

Ruth, Ruth, Ruth, buzzed the bees. I blinked back tears. "Do you know who bought my sister, ma'am?"

"I have so far failed to uncover that fact." She stood up and walked to the window. "My nephew's wife is stubborn as well as intemperate."

I clutched at the bedcovers. *I will find her.*

She pulled the lace curtain aside and studied something passing in the street below.

I thought through what she said and found a slim thread of hope to grasp hold of. "Begging pardon again, ma'am, but do I work for you now?"

She let the curtain fall. "I am afraid not. Anne insists that you be returned to her household as soon as you are able. The law supports her position, I fear, and in these unsettled times, there is little remedy."

A wave of weariness crashed over me at the thought of serving Madam again, of allowing her to see her mark upon my face every day.

"I expect you'd like to bathe," Lady Seymour said. "Angelika is preparing the water for you as we speak. You'll find the rest of your clothes in the kitchen." She paused in the doorway. "You miss your parents terribly, don't you?"

"Pardon, ma'am?"

"While you lay in the fever, you spoke of them with great affection, as if they were in the room with us." She hesitated for a moment, then picked up her skirts. "No matter. I will escort you back to Anne's once you've bathed and eaten."

Angelika took the trouble to make the tub full and the water warm and sweet-smelling. I thanked her and she gave me a little smile. She said something in the Dutch speech, which I did not understand. We must have looked two fools, me speaking English, her talking Dutch, both nodding our heads and wishing we had the right words.

My clothes had been washed and ironed, my shoes wiped clean of mud and muck. Even better was the meal of fried eggs, toasted bread, and a fruit compote of pears and apples topped with strawberries and cream. When Angelika set the food in front of me, her eyes went to the fresh scar on my face, rinsed clean of salve and patted dry. She winced at the sight.

As I wiped up the last of my egg with the bread, Lady Seymour entered, followed by her cat. She had changed into a peach-colored crinoline gown and was pulling on lace gloves.

"It is time," she said.

I walked two steps behind her, carrying a basket of daisies and a heart filled with dread. When we arrived at the Locktons' she walked up the front steps without ever looking back at me. She paused before she lifted the door knocker.

"Go on," she said.

I opened the side gate to the garden, entered, and closed it behind me. I heard the knocker booming under Lady Seymour's hand as I walked, slowly, to the back door.

Part II

CHAPTER XXV

Sunday, July 21–
Tuesday, August 20, 1776

OUR SLAVES, SIR, COST US MONEY, AND WE BUY THEM TO MAKE MONEY BY THEIR LABOUR. IF THEY ARE SICK, THEY ARE NOT ONLY UNPROFITABLE, BUT EXPENSIVE.
—BENJAMIN FRANKLIN, THE *GAZETTEER AND NEW DAILY ADVERTISER*

MELANCHOLY HELD ME HOSTAGE, and the bees built a hive of sadness in my soul. Dark honey filled up inside me, drowning my thoughts and making it hard to move my eyes and hands. I worked as a puppet trained to scrub and carry, curtsy and nod.

Madam would not look at me. When she had an order to give, it went through Becky, even if we all stood in the same room.

"Tell the girl the hearth needs sweeping."

"Sal," Becky would say, "please sweep the hearth."

"Tell the girl to fetch my fan."

"Sal," Becky would say, "please fetch Madam's ivory fan."

"The library needs dusting. Tell the girl."

"Sal–"

I swept the hearth and fetched the fan. I dusted the library without looking at the books on the shelves or the horse on the wall. I preferred the chores that took me out of the kitchen, for it was there the bees tricked me into seeing Ruth's ghost playing on the floor, churning butter, or counting out kernels of corn. When her voice whispered to me, I caught fire again, from my toes to my face, and I burned slow, like damp wood.

Becky watched me careful when I turned inside myself like that. She once tried to apologize for what happened. The instant she stopped talking, I forgot what she said.

"Tell the girl there are bedbugs in my chamber."

"Tell the girl to wash the steps."

Curzon came around day after day and talked to me through the boards of the fence.

I did not answer him.

July marched out and August sailed in on a suffocating tide.

British ships continued to land at Staten Island, hundreds of them carrying thousands of soldiers armed with countless guns and bullets. We went two weeks without rain. There were outbreaks of camp fever, smallpox, and dysentery amongst the rebel troops. They turned King's College into a hospital to care for thousands of sick men.

I prayed that Colonel Regan was there. I prayed he would fall ill and die a terrible death for lying to me and betraying me and letting them break my body. Whenever I heard the words "liberty" or "freedom," I wanted to spit in the dust.

The air was steeped in evil during those muggy, pestilent days.

"Tell the girl to sweep the cellar."

When I swept it I found the cobwebs I had saved for Ruth. I threw them into the kitchen fire, along with the mouse carcasses and rotted potatoes.

"Tell the girl the milk has soured."

'Twas left in the sun on purpose.

The British finally made a move toward the end of August, rowing half their army across to the Long Island in flat-bottomed boats. Becky convinced Madam to send me to market on my own again because she was afraid to go, what with battle due to break out any minute.

Madam agreed. She said my mark would ensure I stayed out of trouble.

As commanded, I purchased two packets of straight pins, a piece of lace, and a basket of turnip greens. The shopkeepers and other folks looked at my face and saw only the angry red scar, just starting to fade at the edges. They did not see the girl hidden behind it.

Curzon approached me on Pearl Street and tried to talk.

I walked away from him and carried the purchases back to Madam's house, wings abuzz in my ears.

Hours later, as I ate my dinner of greens and cornbread with molasses, Becky entered the kitchen with a scowl.

"That Curzon boy, the one with the hat, he's in front of the house again," she said. "You must tell him to leave."

I lifted my eyes from my plate. "Why?"

"Because Madam wants him arrested, and I don't want trouble, that's why," Becky snapped.

I did not move.

"Do you want his beating on your conscience?" she continued.

I chewed the last of the cornbread, then wiped my fingers and stood up.

"Tell him to stay away," she said as I set my plate in the washing-up tub. "Blasted fool doesn't know what's good for him."

When I lifted the latch of the garden gate, Curzon appeared, mouth a'flapping. "Finally! We've much to talk about."

"Go away," I said.

He glanced up and down the empty street. "Look, I'm sorry. The colonel . . . I thought sure he would help." He stopped and leaned close to my face. "You don't look right. Camp fever?"

My tongue felt the ragged edge of a broken tooth. "I'm fine."

He dropped his eyes to the ground. "Sorry's not enough, but . . . I am. Sorry. About all of it."

I picked at a splinter of wood on the gate. There was something changed about him, but I could not figure it. Many things looked different since they burned me up. "Not your concern," I said.

"'Tis so," he said. "I've asked about your sister. A sailor I know thinks she was put on a ship to Halifax."

"No. They sent her to Nevis."

He opened his mouth but could not find any words.

"Go away," I said, "or they'll arrest you. Madam said."

"Has she received any letters from Lockton?"

The question hit me like a bucket of cold water. "You asking me to spy again?"

"Listen," he started. "Our freedom–"

I did not let him continue. "You are blind. They don't want us free. They just want liberty for themselves."

"You don't understand."

"Oh, no. I understand right good," I countered. "I shouldn't have believed your rebel lies. I should have taken Ruth and run the night we landed. Even if we drowned, we would have been together."

He reached out and grabbed my arm. "Don't say that."

His hand was strong, but so was mine. I grabbed his thumb and twisted it backward. "Turn me loose." My body and voice shook as if trapped in one of Ruth's fits.

"Sorry." He released me, and I released him. "I'm sorry for your sister and your face and your broken head." He wiggled his thumb. "A hundred times as sorry as the hills."

I moved to shut the gate in his face.

He held it open. "We all have scars, Isabel."

"I'll never talk to you again." I threw myself against the gate, shut it, and threw home the latch.

CHAPTER XXVI

Wednesday, August 21–
Sunday, August 25, 1776

We have our coach standing before our door every night, and the horses are harnassed ready to make our escape, if we have time. . . . Poor New York! I long to have the battle over, and yet I dread the consequences.
—Letter written by Mary, daughter of Patriot Brigadier General John Morin Scott, as her family prepared to flee New York

The storm that hit the city the next night was the worst I had ever seen.

A thundercloud big as a mountain swept up the river just before sunset. Lightning danced at its edges like horses at a mad gallop, then the sky turned ink black and the storm crashed over us. The wind blew signs off buildings, overturned soldiers' tents, and stripped the clean clothes that had been pegged out to dry. Thunder boomed like a thousand cannons. A house three blocks over was struck by a lightning bolt and burned to the ground. Thirteen soldiers were killed by lightning, too, the coins in their pockets melted and their flesh roasted. One lightning-struck soldier survived but was turned deaf, blind, and unable to speak.

We were forced to concern ourselves with more domestic

matters. The window frames in the front parlor leaked terrible during the storm. Rain soaked the drapes and rugs and left the wall plaster soft and spongy.

"Tell the girl to clean up this mess."

Becky asked around for days, but there were no spare carpenters to be found, no matter how much coin was offered. The men were all getting ready for war. The British had set up a new camp in Brooklyn on Long Island, and Washington was moving his troops around like pieces on a checkerboard. He sent most of his men across to face the British and others north to defend Fort Washington and Harlem.

The front windows continued to leak.

Becky began to talk of leaving for her uncle's house in Jersey. I pretended to listen to her. The streets were filled with the hurry-scurry of a moving army, splashing through mud puddles. Madam called for tea.

I left to fetch fresh water.

A few bees flew out of my head as I walked north with my buckets, blown out by the strong east wind. The pain helped, too. I had cut the palm of my left hand on a dull blade at breakfast. Becky wrapped it for me, but it stung to carry even an empty bucket.

Nassau Street was fair deserted all the way up to the Commons. Most folks had fled, afeard to be caught between two angry armies. That's why I was surprised to see a crowd at the water pump, a dozen or so men and boys—slaves who had been hired by the army to build barricades—and a few women fetching water, like me. Beyond the men I could see the pile of paving stones that had been pulled up for the barricade. It was midday and the folks were gathered for a cool drink, a bite to eat, and some conversating.

The talk stopped as I approached. All eyes went to my face.

I had not been to the pump since my branding. I gripped the buckets tight, holding in the pain. Most in the crowd were strangers to me.

"Mercy," muttered one woman as she studied my scar.

"Pain you much?" asked another, her hair wrapped in a worn yellow cloth.

"It tugs some, ma'am," I said. "Not as much as it did."

One man spat over his shoulder and said something in a language I did not understand.

The other men turned their eyes from me back to Grandfather, the old man who sat by the pump, and went back to their argument. I was grateful to have the attention leave me.

"You're not looking at the facts," a bald man said to Grandfather. "The British Lord Dunmore in Virginia offered freedom–total freedom–to any slave who escapes to his camp." He shook his fist in the air when he said "freedom." "Thousands have run away and joined up already."

Grandfather simply nodded his head. "With more behind them, I expect."

A second man, this one with neatly trimmed hair, leaned on his shovel. "Dunmore freed the Virginia slaves so the crops would go unharvested and ruin the planters. The British care not for us, they care only for victory. Some Patriots own slaves, yes, but you must listen to their words: 'all men, created equal.' The words come first. They'll pull the deeds and the justice behind them."

"You're a fool," the bald man said. He motioned to the piles of paving stones and the logs waiting to be dragged into position. "We should sabotage the barricades. If the British win, we'll all be free."

"Shhh!" several people scolded.

I blinked. The bees in my head fell silent and hugged their wings tight to their bodies. The British would free us? All of us?

The men fell to arguing with each other, the women chiming in occasionally. Finally the bald man raised his hands. "One of us here was privy to the rebel plans, worked with one of the bosses there. Tell us, Curzon boy, what do you think of the rebel lies?"

At the sound of his name, Curzon stepped forward from the side of the building where he had been sitting in the shade. He looked even more changed than he had the week before. What was different?

"What say you?" Grandfather asked.

"I say I'm an American," Curzon said. "An American soldier."

It was his clothes. When I first met him, he was dressed like the house servant of a wealthy man, which he was. Now the tailored waistcoat was gone and his shirt was dirty with sweat and mud. It hung over a pair of working man's breeches that were cut off below his knee. He did not have on stockings or shoes. Even his fancy red hat was flecked with mud.

The wind caught at my skirts and swirled them around my ankles. Did he say *soldier*?

The first man laughed. "You are an American slave." He untied the cloth around his neck and rinsed it in the pump water before adding in a lower voice, "As are we all."

Curzon shook his head. He was still stubborn as ever, if a bit worn. "Not me. Not for long. Master Bellingham promised me freedom for enlisting in his place."

"And you believe him?" The man laughed louder. "He's feeding you to the cannons so he can be safe! If you don't die, he'll stick your neck under his boot again."

"Lower your voices." Grandfather held up a shaky hand and motioned to me. "Come, child. Get your water."

I walked to him and set my buckets on the ground.

The woman in the yellow head cloth worked the pump for Grandfather. "The British promise freedom to slaves but won't give it to the white rebels," she said as she pushed the handle up and down. "The rebels want to take freedom, but they won't share it with us."

She set down the first bucket and picked up the second. "Both sides say one thing and do the other."

"The British act on their promises," insisted the bald man.

"No!" The man with the shovel drove it into the ground with frustration. "They lie. When the British fled Boston, back in the spring, they took escaping slaves with them. They promised them freeeeeeedom." He stretched out the word until it sounded ugly. "Where are those slaves now?"

No one answered him.

"I'll tell you," he continued. "Forced into the Louisbourg coal mines in Canada. They work and die under the ground. They never see the sun, and they'll never taste your freeeeeedom."

We stood in silence as the pump handle creaked. At last, Grandfather chuckled.

"This is not funny, old man," said the fellow with the shovel.

"Young people are always funny," he said. "Funny and foolish."

The woman in the yellow head cloth finished filling the second bucket. "What do you mean, Grandfather?"

"This is not our fight," the old man said. "British or American, that is not the choice. You must choose your own side, find your road through the valley of darkness that will lead you to the river Jordan."

"We don't have the river Jordan, here, Grandfather," the bald man said as he retied the wet cloth around his neck. "We have the East River, with currents fast enough to kill a man, and the North River, two miles wide. Both are mighty hard to cross."

Grandfather chuckled again. "You don't understand. Everything that stands between you and freedom is the river Jordan. Come closer, child."

This last he said to me. I stepped in front of him and reached for my buckets, but he took my hands in his.

I stopped, unsure what to do next.

"Look at me," he said.

I bent down a little, bringing my face level with his. He tilted my chin to the side so he could examine the brand on my cheek. I tried to pull away, but he held fast.

"A scar is a sign of strength," he said quietly. "The sign of a survivor." He leaned forward and lightly kissed my cheek, right on the branding mark. His lips felt like a tired butterfly that landed once, then fluttered away.

I stepped back and touched the cheek. The men were returning to the barricades. Other servants had formed a line for the pump.

Grandfather winked and handed me the buckets. "Look hard for your river Jordan, my child. You'll find it."

Carrying those full buckets back to the Locktons' was powerful hard. The cut on my left hand pained me too much to use it, and my right hand was not big enough, my arm not strong enough, to carry two buckets at once. I journeyed in a crow-hop fashion–carrying one bucket for twenty strides, setting it down, then returning to fetch the second bucket and carrying it forward to meet its partner.

I made slow progress in this manner for two blocks when Curzon joined me.

He would not look at me. Didn't say a word, neither. He simply carried the buckets to the Locktons' gate for me, then walked away.

CHAPTER XXVII

Monday, August 26–Saturday, September 14, 1776

PERSONS EXPOSED TO GREAT DANGER AND HAZARD . . . REMOVE WITH ALL EXPEDITION OUT OF THE SAID TOWN [NEW YORK] . . . WHEREAS A BOMBARDMENT AND ATTACK, MAY BE HOURLY EXPECTED—
—GENERAL GEORGE WASHINGTON, OFFICIAL HANDBILL ISSUED TO NEW YORKERS, IN AUGUST 1776

THE BRITISH THRASHED THE PATRIOTS in a big battle in Brooklyn. Thrashed them but good. They killed or captured near a thousand rebels and sent the rest scurrying away. After the worst of the battle, the skies opened up again and we all waited—us in a house with leaking windows and a damp parlor, the soldiers in open fields and muddy ditches—for the rain to stop.

Madam wore a groove in the floor pacing back and forth awaiting news of the final British victory, her footsteps tipping and tapping in measure with the ticking of the clock. I poked at the logs in the kitchen hearth, trying to summon back the bees so they would chase out the thoughts invading my brainpan.

But the words of the bald man echoed.

Would the British truly free me? Should I flee to them? What about Ruth; would they help me find her?

The firewood was wet and green and would not catch. It smoldered and smoked and made a terrible stink.

When morning came, a thick fog smothered New York; the kind Momma called a "pea-souper." When the fog finally lifted, the American army was not to be found. Washington's men had spent the dark night and foggy morning rowing all of the troops back to New York Island—some nine thousand men, folks said. That Washington was a conjure man, for sure.

Madam took to her bed when Becky brought back the news. I muttered a quiet "Blast" and continued to eat my dinner, porridge with dried apple.

Becky didn't hear me. She was going on and on about the nasty things she'd passed by at the campgrounds. "—and there was this one lad, ooh, he'd had his hand blown clean off and a grubby bandage wrapped round his wrist, and I looked at that and I said to myself, 'That arm's coming off next, young man, and maybe your leg for good measure' on account of a noxious pestilence that filled the air. The stench of the place! And the groans and moans!"

She shivered with gruesome delight. "If I had a stronger stomach, I'd take a nurse job and help a bit with the washing of the wounds and the like. But with this heat and the flies, you just know the wounds will be maggoty by morning, and if there's one thing I can't abide, it's the sight of maggots in living flesh."

I looked in my bowl. The dried apple bits curled like fresh-hatched maggots.

I stopped eating.

Becky ladled out her own meal. "They's all saying that this proves the Lord Himself is on the side of the Rebellion, on account of that fog He created. Did the same thing for them back in Boston; blew in a thick mist so the American army could win the day."

It seemed to me that if God really wanted the Americans to win, He would have sent sea monsters to devour the fleet when it left Boston. As I went to empty my porridge into the scraps bucket, Becky pointed to her own bowl. I filled it with my leftovers and commanded my belly to stop flopping so at the sight of the curly apples.

Becky paused with her spoon in the air. "Makes a body wonder, though . . ."

"What?" I asked.

"Washington had them melt down the church bells and remake them into cannons. That will surely displease the Lord, I say. If God switches sides and allows the British to take New York, you'll see me headed for Jersey, back pay or no back pay. I'm not sitting here waiting to get carved into pieces by them beastly redcoats."

It took me eight days of slow trips to the market and the water pump before I finally spied Curzon working with other men to set up a filthy tent in the mud of the Battery campgrounds. It was good to see him not dead nor chopped up.

CHAPTER XXVIII

Sunday, September 15, 1776

THE CLOUDS GROW VERY DARK.
—DIARY OF WILLIAM SMITH, CHIEF JUSTICE
OF THE PROVINCE OF NEW YORK

THE TRUE INVASION OF NEW YORK started with the firing of a hundred ships' cannons when we were at church Sunday morning. The first blast made the women shriek. The second blast made me wonder if God Himself was fixing to blow the island apart.

The third blast caused us to run for the door.

Rebel soldiers were dashing everywhich direction on the street, muskets in their hands, officers bellowing loud. The horses pulling carts and carriages whinnied nervously, bobbing their heads up and down and rolling their eyes in fear of the commotion and noise.

The cannons roared again. The sound was coming from the East River side of the island, to the north. I searched the skies for flaming comets, for that was how I pictured a cannonball would look. All I saw were startled birds and campfire smoke. The city itself seemed unharmed, though fear ran neck-deep.

Madam reached out and grabbed at the coat of an officer striding toward the Battery fort. He whirled, a curse on his lips, but caught himself when he realized he was speaking to a lady.

"Does this unholy racket mean the arrival of the war?" Madam asked.

"Yes, ma'am," the officer said. "But you need not be afraid. The generals have the matter well in hand." He hesitated as the cannons roared again. "Civilians should go home and lock your doors. Do not peer out of windows."

Madam contemplated him coolly. "What are those men doing?" she asked, pointing to the campground. The soldiers were quickly assembling their guns, ammunition, and whatever they could stuff into their sacks. They moved so fast you'd have thought the ground was afire.

"We are preparing to meet the enemy," he said.

"You are running away," she said.

"No, ma'am," he said as he started to move away from her. "We're moving up to Fort Washington, to guard the King's Bridge." He shouted to be heard as a wagon pulled by four horses raced by. "We must follow orders!"

"Indeed," Madam said.

Becky had the Sabbath off, so I served Madam her meal of cold pork, peas, and onions cooked with sage. She was calm about finally having war at her doorstep and thousands of riled-up menfolk marching with guns. In fact, as she ate, she kept a sheet of paper, a quill, and an ink bottle by the side of her plate and would from time to time jot down a word or two.

When her plate was empty, she spoke to me direct. "I am

preparing a list of items for you to purchase. You may leave as soon as the dishes are washed."

"Beg pardon, ma'am?"

"I need you to go down to the shops. I've no doubt Elihu will soon return home, and I'd like to celebrate with a suitable meal. It's a shame that turtles are so hard to come by here. Elihu loves turtle soup."

Had she lost her mind?

"But the cannons, ma'am," I started. "The battle. Surely it will be a few days before–"

"Most of the items can be purchased at Mr. Mason's." She dipped the quill and scratched out another item. "He's a thieving rat of a man, but he's loyal to the King. I know he's been hoarding his best wares." She paused as cannon fire boomed again from the north. "I don't know why the rebels don't just surrender. They cannot win."

I froze at the sideboard. The words of the bald-headed man came to me: "If the British win, we'll all be free."

Could it be so simple? Might the invaders liberate me from this nightmare? Was this my chance?

Madam said something, but I couldn't make out her words. "Yes, ma'am," I mumbled, my hands doing the work of a slave, my mind racing free.

I will run and join the British.

The thought washed over me like a river, sweeping away the dead bees that had filled my brainpan with confusion. The answers tumbled one after another. They'd grant me freedom and give me work. I'd save my money and make my way to Nevis and rescue Ruth. Plain, simple, and true.

"Are you deaf?" Madam scolded me.

I had been staring at the door and not minding her words.

She shook the paper in her hand. "I said take this to Mason. If he can't supply you with everything, he'll direct you where to go."

I'll be going home, I thought. And you can fetch your own food and empty your own chamberpot and carry your own blasted firewood from this day forward.

"Girl?" Madam squinted at me and tilted her head to one side. "Are you feverish?"

I gave thanks that she could not hear my thoughts. "No, ma'am." I put the list in my pocket and set the last knife on the tray. "I'm strong as can be. I'll go to Mr. Mason's directly."

I paused at the parlor door. "I may be delayed a wee bit, ma'am," I said with care. "What with the commotion and all."

A dozen or so soldiers dashed down the middle of the street, their boots thudding.

"It cannot be helped," Madam said with a sigh.

Walking down Broadway I was a fish swimming in the wrong direction. Everyone else in New York flowed north and fought against my progress: Continental troops in ragged formation, militia units carrying packs and haversacks, small artillery pieces pulled by horses, and carts weighed down with women and children. The noise was deafening. Along with the shouts of men and women, every dog in the city was barking alarm, pigs squealed underfoot, and occasionally a musket would fire, which led to shouted oaths and yelps. Drums beat and fifes blew and beneath everything was the steady clockwork blast of the British cannons firing at the troops stationed north of us.

I kept to the fronts of buildings, ducking into doorways when necessary, until I finally took refuge in the abandoned chandler's shop. The door was locked, but the front windows had been smashed to bits when the owner was tarred and feathered some weeks previous.

I crawled through the window, taking care not to cut myself on the glass shards jutting out of the frame. I set my basket on the floor. Ruth's doll rested inside it under a rag. That was the one thing I could not leave behind.

The shop smelled musty and damp and the shelves stood empty. All the candles and other goods were stolen the day they ran the chandler out of town. It was a gloomy place but would serve well as a temporary shelter.

I stood by the window and watched the tide of people roll out of the city.

Hurry, I silently urged them.

Hurry, I also urged the British army. I did not want them to land right away, not until the last of the crowd had fled. But it would be nice if they arrived right quick after that, before Madam could hire someone to seek me out.

Finally the crowd thinned and cart wheels could be heard echoing up the road. I waited a little longer, just to be sure. A few Continentals dashed by, their hands holding their hats on their heads, and canteens and cartridge cases banging against their backsides. They were followed by a rough-looking militia unit that was trailed by a group of slaves carrying shovels and pickaxes. I searched for a familiar red hat but did not find it.

When the air fell still, with just a few voices calling orders in the distance, I hiked up my skirts and crawled out through the window.

CHAPTER XXIX

Sunday, September 15, 1776

. . . THE DEMONS OF FEAR AND DISORDER SEEMED TO TAKE FULL POSSESSION OF ALL AND EVERYTHING UPON THAT DAY.
—JOURNAL OF PRIVATE JOSEPH PLUMB MARTIN,
FIFTEEN-YEAR-OLD PATRIOT SOLDIER

I WAS THE ONLY PERSON ON THE STREET. The army was gone and the city abandoned. I shivered, though the day was still warm. Had I made a mistake? Should I run after the rebels and join them? Should I go back to the Locktons'?

A cannon boomed to the north.

No, I chose the right course. At least, I hoped I had.

I headed for the waterfront. Several of the grand mansions of lower Broadway stood with their doors ajar. A fire burned at the edge of the street, heaped with books and scads of papers. The smoke rose up into the air, drifting toward the masts of the few ships at anchor. Cannons boomed again.

What if they didn't arrive right away? How long did I have before Madam grew suspicious?

A gust of wind blew and carried with it the first hint of fall: canoe-shaped chestnut leaves, turned yellow round the edges.

The leaves caught and piled up against the soldiers' tents left behind at the Battery campground.

I walked over and pulled back the flap of a tent. Inside lay two bedrolls, a pipe and tobacco pouch, and a shirt dropped in the middle of mending, the needle still threaded and stuck in the fabric. I closed the flap. They left near everything—tents, blankets, extra clothing, cook pots, and food. It would be a cold night for Curzon and his companions.

Voices came from the waterfront, military voices shouting orders. I hurried away from the Barracks, dashed down Water Street, and hid behind a rain barrel at the corner of the joiner's workshop.

A half-dozen flat-bottomed boats were being rowed to the docks. Two were already tied up, and tall soldiers wearing the red uniform of King George were striding down the street. Lobsterbacks, folks called them. They fanned out across the waterfront, their muskets primed and held at the ready position. As I watched, a third boat floated to the wharf. The soldiers on it jumped out and marched in formation to the Battery, in search of rebel soldiers.

A woman carrying a baby fled, screaming loudly. A few of the redcoats chuckled and stabbed at the air with their bayonets. My throat went dry.

As the fourth boat landed, an officer stepped off and barked a command at the laughing men. They lined up and stood at attention. The officer gave another command, and the men marched off, splitting into three groups to investigate the Battery and waterfront buildings.

The officer stood alone at the foot of the dock, surveying the deserted town as more boats splashed toward the landing spot. This was my chance. I forced myself out of my hiding place and walked toward him, my back ramrod straight.

"Begging your pardon, sir," I said boldly.

"What is it, girl?" he asked.

Before I could answer, a soldier dashed up to him. "Captain Campbell, sir. The campground appears deserted. The rebels left behind their tents and bedrolls."

"Secure the tent flaps open and check every one," the captain commanded. "It could be a trap."

"Yessir," came the crisp reply before the man ran off.

I prayed I would not faint from fear and tried again for the captain's attention. "I can cook, sir," I said. "I can wash, sew, even doctor the sick a little."

"Don't bother me, child."

I trailed after him as he walked toward the campground. "Please, sir," I insisted. "I'm all kinds of useful. I can chop wood and carry water or messages."

I was interrupted by another soldier, who approached us and saluted.

"Report," Captain Campbell said.

"The spies were correct, sir. The rebels have retreated. The Battery is empty of men but filled with the provisions and weapons they left behind, including several cannons. They even left a tea kettle bubbling over the fire. Civilians in the first three streets north of here all attest to their haste. Putnam's unit was the last one out. They're on their way up the island, by way of the Greenwich Road. Do we pursue, sir?"

The captain fought the smile that played at the corner of his lips. "Our task is to occupy the city. We'll let the Highlanders hunt them down. Tell the men to take over the barracks and prepare Washington's headquarters for Major General Robertson."

"Yessir." The soldier saluted again but did not move.

"What is it now, Jennings?" asked the captain.

"Begging pardon, sir, but I've not been informed as to the whereabouts of Washington's headquarters. If I was to be given that information, I could pursue my obligations with greater speed."

"I don't know where it is," Captain Campbell said with irritation. "Use your noggin, man. Ask the tavern keeper."

"You want the Kennedy mansion, sir," I said. "Just beyond the end of Battery, facing the Bowling Green."

"What did you say?" the captain fired at me.

My knees were shaking under my skirt. "The Kennedy mansion, sir, that was General Washington's main headquarters. Number 1, Broadway. His wife stayed up at the Mortier House. But he kept headquarters straight thataway"–I pointed west–"and more army offices were in City Hall." I pointed north, up Broad Street.

"Very good," he said. "There you have it, Sergeant. Proceed."

The sergeant yelled to his unit as he walked away from us. The waterfront was awash in red now as boatloads of soldiers disembarked. Shouted orders filled the air, along with nervous laughter and the sound of British boots on the cobblestones. A few more boats were on their way in, with the first boats headed back for more. The occupation was well and truly begun.

"You are correct, young miss," Captain Campbell said to me. "You are useful. But we do not want troublemakers in camp. What is the meaning of the mark on your face?"

I touched the raised scar and decided that honesty was

my only course. "This stands for Insolence, sir. When my mistress sold my little sister, I tried to run away. She is five years old, sir. My sister, not my mistress."

He blinked and cleared his throat. "Regrettable. And understandable. I have a younger sister myself. Your mistress, am I to assume she supports the rebel cause?"

"No, sir," I answered. "Our house is Tory. My master was driven out of town by the Patriot leaders. My mistress is much cheered by your arrival. She wants to hire a proper staff so she can entertain again. She'll not miss my services one bit."

The words tumbled out before I measured them. The captain's mouth hardened, and I knew I had stepped wrong.

He tugged on his sash. "I cannot accept your service, child. We only employ slaves run away from rebel owners."

I did not hear him right. "Pardon me?"

"Gentlemen docking, sir!" cried a soldier on the wharf.

Captain Campbell turned as the men tossed thick ropes from the dock to the occupants of the next boat. It contained only four soldiers, each manning an oar. The rest of the passengers were men dressed in expensive civilian clothes.

"When they're ashore, escort them into the tavern for a celebration," the captain said loudly. "Issue the tavern keeper an Office of Forage certificate. Warn him, Sergeant, he is not to ask the gentlemen for payment, unless he wants to spend this night in irons. They are our guests."

"Yes, sir!" came the enthusiastic response.

As we had been talking, ordinary city folk had begun to creep out of their houses. Now there was a full crowd gathered, the Tories of New York who had been awaiting this day for months, years. Cheers were heard in the distance. The arriving soldiers were greeted by townsmen who shook their hands and patted them heartily on the back. I recognized a few faces—the reverend and his wife and a few people who had called at the Lockton home.

Captain Campbell bent toward me. He spoke quickly and quietly. "I do not hold with slavery, but I cannot help you. We do not interfere with Loyalist property. Return to your mistress."

A loud "Huzzah!" from hundreds of throats came from the Battery as the American flag was pulled down. A drummer started beating time, and the Union Jack rose to the top of the flagpole, accompanied by whistles and shouts from the lobsterbacks and Loyalist New Yorkers, who took off their hats in respect. A woman in the crowd snatched the American flag out of the hands of the British soldiers and stomped it under her boots. The men laughed.

The *ratatatat*ing of the drumsticks rattled through me, setting my teeth to shaking and waking the bees who had lately gone to sleep in my brainpan.

He couldn't take me. He would not.

I was chained between two nations.

The bees swarmed again behind my eyes, making the scene grow dim and distant. The sun was nearing the horizon, casting long shadows across the wharf. I was a ghost tied to the ground, not a living soul.

"All ashore, sir," called the soldier tying up the last boat.

"All ashore, Corporal," the captain acknowledged. "I want patrols assembled immediately to keep watch in the streets, and sentry fires built on every corner."

"Yes, sir!"

The gentlemen who had arrived in the boat walked toward us, talking with great excitement. One of them was painfully familiar. He called to me before I could flee.

"Sal?" called Master Elihu Lockton, thinner from his exile, eyes bloodshot and wary. "Is that you?"

I dropped into a curtsy and dared not say a word.

He studied on me with suspicion. "What are you doing here?"

Sergeant Jennings approached. "The tavern is open if the gentlemen would care to drink to victory."

Lockton waved to his companions. "I shall join you shortly." As the gentlemen hurried to the tavern, his eyes traveled from my head down to my shoes and back. "What news, Sal?" he asked. "How do you come to be here?"

I pulled Madam's list from my pocket and prayed he would not look inside my basket. "Come to market, sir," I whispered.

"Ah. What is this?" He took my chin in his fingers, turning it so that the last rays of the sunset fell on my scar. "Is the *I* for 'illustrious' or perhaps 'impertinent'?"

My face burned both in the scar and where his lavender-smelling fingers pinched my skin. The bees flew through me and told me to grab Campbell's sword and run it through Lockton's belly.

And then what? And then what?

"I suspect it stands for Insolence," Captain Campbell said calmly. "'Tis a common brand among the people of Boston."

Lockton laughed at the small joke and released me. "Now we'll call her Insolent Sal, a very saucy gal."

The captain smiled and put his hand on the hilt of his sword. "I should have known she was attached to your household, sir. She greeted me in the name of the King and thanked me for rescuing the city from the rebels."

They both looked at me.

"We prayed for liberation," I said.

"Even our slaves have become political," Lockton said. "How quaint."

"Do you wish to accompany your servant home to greet your mistress?" the captain asked.

Lockton shook his head. "Not at the moment. Go on home, Sal. Tell Anne I shall be along after I've lifted a few glasses in celebration."

The two men headed for the tavern as the sun finally dropped out of sight.

I must have gone to Mason's and bought the items on Madam's list, tho' I remember it not. My body moved through the streets, past sentry fires and redcoats carrying torches down suspicious alleys and into abandoned houses. Around me was the sound of the victors celebrating and the smell of meat they roasted for their supper.

Around me, all was darkness.

CHAPTER XXX

Monday, September 16–
Saturday, September 21, 1776

OH, THE HOUSES IN NEW YORK, IF YOU COULD BUT SEE THE INSIDES OF THEM! OCCUPIED BY THE DIRTIEST PEOPLE ON A CONTINENT . . . IF THE OWNERS EVER GET POSSESSION AGAIN, I AM SURE THEY WILL BE YEARS IN CLEANING THEM.
–A LETTER FROM NEW YORK IN THE *MORNING CHRONICLE AND LONDON ADVERTISER* NEWSPAPER

THE BRITISH ARMY PARADED UP Broadway the next day, cheered by Loyalists all wearing a red ribbon or flower in their hats in support of the King. I did not see this, of course. I overheard the report that Madam gave the master as they ate supper that eve with their houseguests, the two officers who had moved into the bedchambers on the top floor.

The highest-ranking men of the British army had taken over the empty rebel mansions. Lower-grade officers had moved in with Loyalist families who had suitable furniture and staff, such as the Locktons. Only we didn't have a staff. Becky had vanished, her rooms at the Oliver Street boardinghouse abandoned. I was the only servant in the house.

It mattered not. My bones were hollow sticks; my brainpan empty.

I cooked a chicken and roasted potatoes and carrots. I left the chicken over the fire too long because Madam ordered the silver polished and the table linens ironed in honor of her guests. The bird was so dry it near splintered the tongues of the officers. Madam let loose on me in the kitchen after the gentlemen had taken Master Lockton to Ashley's Tavern for a night of beer drinking and pipe smoking.

It mattered not.

When Madam finished scolding me, I set to my evening chores; cleaning out the ashes from the bedchamber fireplaces and carrying them outside, bringing in the firewood and laying the fires in case the night turned cold, turning down the beds, cleaning up from supper, and sweeping the floor.

When I finally laid down to sleep, I set Ruth's doll beside my head. I had stopped kissing it good night. I did not say prayers.

My bones were hollow and my brainpan empty.

Madam ran me like a donkey all the next day, then demanded that I stay awake all night to make rolls for breakfast because the bakers in town were rebels, and they had fled. I did as she ordered and ruined two perfectly fine batches of dough. I threw them down the privy and baked cornbread deep in the night for that was one thing my hands knew how to bake.

The cornbread burned to charcoal when I fell asleep, head on the table.

It mattered not.

Three mornings after the invasion, a message was delivered to the master as I served the coffee. I set the note on a small silver tray and carried it into the drawing room.

The officers were in the middle of excusing themselves from the table, buttoning up their coats and putting on their hats. After the master said his "good days" to them, he opened the note.

"A social invitation?" Madam asked. "Or business?"

"Neither," Lockton said. "It's a desperate plea." He handed the note across to his wife. "Aunt Seymour is in need of our Sal. All of her Dutch girls fled, and she is without servants."

Madam snatched the paper from his hand. "Surely she can do for herself. We have company. Why should we go without a servant?"

"We have only two men lodging here. Somehow Aunt has managed to take on a dozen Hessian brutes. She requires our assistance."

Madam gave a little shudder. "Hessians." The hired soldiers from Germany had a fearsome reputation. She crumpled the paper. "I will not perform housework like a common wench. Tell her to hire someone."

"The times demand sacrifices, Anne. Just for a week or so. Women will soon come to the city looking for work, and you and our aunt will be able to hire a full staff."

Madam scowled into her cup. "You favor her over me, Elihu. It's unseemly."

Lockton wiped his mouth with his serviette. "The loan of the girl is the least we owe her. I hope you regret your decision to send away the sister. Even small hands would be helpful now."

His mention of Ruth so startled me I near dropped the tray.

Madam bit back the hot words in her mouth, picked up her serviette, and cleaned off her chin. "You will clean the kitchen and prepare the dinner, girl, then you will take yourself to the house of Lady Seymour and do what she requires of you."

Lockton shook his head. "No, Sal. You will leave immediately."

I took a clean apron and Ruth's doll with me to Lady Seymour's house. In truth, I did not walk there quickly. In truth, I dawdled something fierce. Folks said that Hessian soldiers were fire-breathing monsters who walked about with swords drawn and blood on their chins. I figured that would be as bad as Madam.

I was near correct.

They did not breathe fire, tho' they spat when they talked. Nor did they walk about waving their swords, tho' some sported knives in their boots. None had blood on their chins, except when they ate rare-cooked meat. I found it hard not to stare at the enormous mustachios that sprouted under their noses, especially when the men combed and waxed them, and twirled the ends.

Their speech sounded like they were swallowing rocks, but Lady Seymour understood them. She learned the German from her husband, she said, same way she learned the Dutch. There were all manner of secrets locked in that old skull.

When I served them supper my first night, a couple of them said *"Danke"* to me. Lady Seymour explained that *danke* is German-talk for "thank you." She told me not to be afeard, that they were just soldiers far away from home. A couple of them were fond of her cat, she pointed out. How could men who liked cats be bad? She tolerated them fair enough, except for the muddy boots on the furniture and when they spread butter on their bread with their thumbs. That made her gasp and go pink in the face.

I practiced saying *"danke"* when alone.

The work at the Seymour house was every bit as tiring as it had been at Madam's, more so because there were more mouths to feed and boots to clean and basins to fill and linens to wash and coats to beat free of dust. Lady Seymour made sure I et a proper meal three times a day and let me sleep in the tiny attic bedchamber on the bed where I laid after my time in the stocks. It was hot up there, but there were no mice nor worms on the floor when it rained.

The city swelled by the hour with Loyalist refugees who wanted to live under the protection of British cannons. Some of the folk returning from exile were surprised to find strangers had taken over their houses and were sleeping in their beds and wearing the clothes they left behind. There were many fistfights, a great deal of name-calling, and threats of duels.

The British didn't mix in with the arguments. They had war on the brain, drilling their soldiers from sunup to sundown. At the Middle Dutch Church they pulled out the pulpit, the pews, and the floorboards and let the horses of the Light Dragoons practice. Horses in a house of the Lord made some folks grumble, including Lady Seymour.

Up to the Tea Water Pump, I found only unfamiliar faces, slaves who had freed themselves by joining the British. I could not bring myself to speak to them. The old man we called Grandfather had vanished. Maybe he had started his own revolution and led Curzon and the other slaves over the river Jordan to freedom.

A fanciful notion. 'Twas useless to ponder such things.

Friday stretched long and longer because the Hessians had moved in five more of their countrymen. I heard Lady Seymour arguing with the fellow in charge, but he would not listen to her pleas. I spent the afternoon chopping a field's worth of cabbage while a half pig roasted in the pit dug by the men in the flower garden. The soldiers ate their supper and drank more beer than I thought a body could hold. They lost the few manners they possessed and used the table linens for blowing their noses.

It was a relief when they finally left for merrymaking elsewhere.

I prepared a tray of supper and served it to Lady Seymour in her bedchamber, the one room where she could find peace. When my chores were done, I climbed to my attic room, kicked off my shoes, and laid down on the bed without even removing my skirt or bodice. Ruth's doll lay next to my head, her eyes staring up at the ceiling. I knew I ought pray for Ruth, or for Momma, or for anything; I ought just pray, but the words would not come. I feared the Spirit had left me.

I slept.

When I woke, the city of New York was consumed with burning hellfire.

CHAPTER XXXI

Saturday, September 21–Sunday, September 22, 1776

The Fire raged with Inconceivable Violence and in its destructive Progress swept away all the Buildings between Broad Street and the North River . . . Several Women and Children perished in the Fire; their Shrieks joined to the roaring of the Flames, the Crash of falling Houses, and the widespread Ruin which everywhere appeared, formed a Scene of Horror great beyond Description, and which was still heightened by the Darkness of the Night.
—*New York Mercury* newspaper

I awoke coughing so hard I near brought up my supper. When I finally caught my breath, I smelled the smoke and saw the light, bright as day, outside my window. I jumped from the bed and peered out.

It was not morning; it was an inferno.

Flames curled out of all the windows next door. The rooftop beyond that was a lake of fire. Every building in sight was burning. The air was filled with crackling and popping sounds, with shrieks and screams coming from the street below.

A hot gust of wind blew the curtains back and sent the

fire straight at me. Fiery shingles floated from the roof and caught in the branches of the tree outside my window, setting the bark ablaze. A burning leaf drifted to the sill. I quickly brushed it off, my hands quivering.

Get out!

Seized again by coughing, I fell to the ground where the smoke was not so heavy. I pulled my shoes toward me and quickly buckled them on, then took a deep breath, rose to my feet, grabbed Ruth's doll off my bed, and opened the door.

Smoke filled the hall, curling down from the ceiling along with fingers of fire.

Get out now!

I clattered down the stairs, screaming, "Fire! Fire!"

The door to Lady Seymour's bedchamber was just opening. As I went to pass by, she grabbed my arm.

"Quick, child," she cried. "Help me!"

Her chamber was even brighter than the attic, but the windows were closed and the smoke thinner. She bent over an enormous trunk by the wall. "It contains my valuables." She pulled at a handle. "Please, Isabel!"

I reached for the handle and tugged. The trunk did not move. "It's too heavy, ma'am. Leave it. The roof is afire."

"No, wait." She flung open the top. The trunk was filled with a silver tea set, a small portrait of a yellow-haired man, something wrapped in velvet cloth, dusty sacks, small wooden boxes, and packets of letters tied in a ribbon.

There was another crash outside and screams. I grabbed her arm. "We'll die if we stay!"

She pulled out the letters and two small boxes and thrust them at me along with the portrait. "Take these!"

I stuck the portrait and letters in my pocket, and balanced

Ruth's doll on top of the boxes in my arms. The room was so hot I thought the cornhusks might explode into flames.

Lady Seymour grabbed two of the sacks; the coins within clinked together as she rose to her feet, coughing. "Hurry!" she gasped.

The smoke in the hall was thicker than it had been moments before. We felt our way, one step at a time, to the staircase. I went down first, with the Lady behind me, her frail hand on my shoulder. My eyes watered. My lungs felt like they were pulling in the flames. I thought for a moment we were trapped; the thick haze tricked my mind and I knew not if we should proceed down or up. My ears filled with the crackle of burning wood.

"Help me!" Lady Seymour cried. Her hand vanished.

"Ma'am? Ma'am?" The smoke stopped up my throat. There was a thunderous crash overhead, a ceiling giving way or a piece of the roof collapsing.

The old woman had crumpled to the stairs. *Is she dead?* I put my hand on her chest. Her heartbeat was light and fast as bird's wings beating against a cage. I put my face close to hers and screamed, "Get up!"

She moaned once and tried to move her hand.

I pulled her arm. She moaned again, but I could not be gentle. I dropped the boxes and doll, draped her arm around me, and half fell down the rest of the stairs. Once on the ground floor, she tried to walk, but one of her legs was failing her. I opened the front door and dragged the two of us out to the street.

The air was aswirl with flame, soot, and burning shingles, each caught in a devilish whirlwind. The cries and screams of men and women mixed with the terror of the horses burning alive in locked stables. Windows exploded, beams crashed, and trees split, their crowns ablaze like torches in the hand of a cruel giant. I felt the clothes on my back ready to ignite. The brand on my cheek scorched, as if the fire within me called to the fire in the air.

Move or die, whispered the flames.

I dragged Lady Seymour north, then east, away from the course of the wind, which blew like a bellows and fanned the flames. British soldiers looted a burning house, running out with arms full of silver, and forks and spoons sticking out of their pockets. A dog ran by howling, its tail on fire. We passed a family, all in their nightclothes, throwing buckets of water against the wall of their house, as the fire chewed through the wood. A group of men had harnessed themselves to a fire wagon that held a large tank of water, but one of the wheels broke and it proved too heavy to drag.

One more block, and we could go no farther. Lady Seymour and me collapsed in a heap on the edge of a graveyard.

Time burned up while we lay there, caught in the sparks that flew overhead, swallowed by the noise of a city ablaze.

When I finally came to my senses, I sat up, coughed at length, and breathed in slow. It hurt, but it would not be the death of me. Lady Seymour still lay beside me, shaking her head from side to side in the dirt and muttering. I bent my ear close to hear.

"The bells, where are the bells?" she asked.

Had the fire ruined her mind? Why worry about bells?

"You're safe, ma'am," I said, patting her hand.

She frowned. "Why don't the bells ring alarm?"

Her words were garbled, like she was talking underwater, but I finally understood. Every bell in every church steeple should have been ringing loud and fiercesome. But they were all gone, melted and reformed into cannons.

I stood up. Over the rooftops I could see men pouring water on the flattish roof of St. Paul's, the buckets handed to them from a long line of people that stretched to a backyard pump. To the south, Trinity Church was not as lucky. Its tall steeple was a pyramid of fire, the flames licking the undersides of the clouds that scuttled above.

"What shall we do, ma'am?" I asked.

Her tears turned black as they rolled through the soot on her face. Her left arm and leg lay limp as if some cog within her had snapped. She did not make a sound.

'Twas up to me to make the decisions.

"Come." I helped her to sit. "We need to make our way to safety."

I stood to her left, draped the useless arm over my neck, and held her body tight to mine. In that manner, step by slow step, we staggered on. We passed countless people standing in the streets like statues, their toes bare on the stones, nightclothes blowing in the unnatural breeze, mouths agape. Carts rolled by carrying half-naked people, bleeding and dazed. A collection of charred bodies had been stacked on a corner, not fully covered by a blanket. A child's boot and stocking lay in the gutter, next to an overturned rain barrel.

Step by slow step we made our way to Wall Street, then down to the seventh house on the left. She was near insensible by the time we reached it. In truth, I pinched her as hard as I could. It roused her some, and she lifted her working leg. Thus we mounted the steps of the Lockton house and entered the front door.

CHAPTER XXXII

Sunday, September 22–Thursday, September 26, 1776

OUR DISTRESSES WERE VERY GREAT INDEED BEFORE; BUT THIS DISASTER HAS INCREASED THEM TENFOLD. MANY HUNDREDS OF FAMILIES HAVE LOST THEIR ALL; AND ARE REDUCED FROM A STATE OF AFFLUENCE TO THE LOWEST EBB OF WANT AND WRETCHEDNESS—DESTITUTE OF SHELTER, FOOD OR CLOTHING.
—*NEW YORK MERCURY* NEWSPAPER

NEAR FIVE HUNDRED HOMES WERE destroyed that night, plus shops, churches, and stables. Thousands of people were homeless, without even a change of underclothes or clean stockings. Many did not eat meat for weeks on account of the death smell that poisoned the air. The job of finding bodies was so gruesome it caused grown men to scream out loud.

They buried the dead quickly.

Folks said the fire started in a low groggery near the Whitehall Slip. From there it burned uptown, pushed by a strong wind, devouring Bridge Street, Dock, Stone, Marketfield, and Beaver, then it ran up both sides of Broadway. Almost every building from Broadway to the edge of the North River was in ruins, all the way up to the open field below King's College. They called it "the burned-over district."

"God's judgment on the British," whispered the Patriots.

"Rebel sabotage," shouted the Loyalists.

Most figured the Americans wanted New York burned to the ground to leave the British without shelter. While the fires still raged, groups of soldiers searched for arsonists. One man, found with rosin and brimstone-tipped slivers of wood in his pocket, was tossed into a burning cobbler shop, another was quickly executed with a bayonet through the chest. Half a dozen people were hung while the fire still raged, one from the sign post of a tavern. Another was hung from his heels and had his throat slashed.

The day after the fire, they captured a schoolteacher, name of Nathan Hale, up island near the Dove Tavern. He admitted he was a spy but said he did not set the fire. There was no trial, nor proof of his guilt. They put a rope around his neck and hung him high.

Folks talked about a pretty speech he gave afore they kicked the stool away from his feet. He said he was sorry that he could die only one time for his country.

The lobsterbacks laughed at that.

I coughed up mouthfuls of soot for days. My eyes felt crusted with embers. No matter how much I rubbed them or rinsed them with clean water, they remained swole up, red, and hard to see out of. I was lucky. I was not killt nor burnt; I had not even twisted an ankle running from the flames.

All I lost in the confusion was Ruth's doll. All I had lost was everything.

My bees a'swarmed back into my brainpan. They hummed

loud so I need not ponder on the baby doll. The burned-over district looked like the inside of me. It was hard to tell where one stopped and the other started. I feared my wits had been melted by the flames, twisted and charred.

Doctor Dastuge came to examine Lady Seymour. The left side of her body had gone to sleep and would not wake. The doctor said it was an apoplexy brought on by the fire. He bled her twice and prescribed Maredant's Drops to cleanse her blood.

Master Lockton insisted his aunt should recover in the bedchamber he shared with his wife. Madam was not pleased with the arrangement but said nothing, for a change. She visited the ruins of the Seymour house daily, waiting for them to cool enough so that she could poke through the ash with a hoe, in search of coin or melted silver.

Lady Seymour called me to her bedside when she regained her senses. She tried to thank me, but the affliction pulled at her mouth and made it hard to figure her words. I gave her the portrait of the yellow-haired man and the letters that I had stuffed in my pocket as we fled. She studied them close with her good eye, then she sobbed and both her eyes overran with tears. Madam bade me leave the room.

By the third day after the fire, the Lockton house was packed tighter than a barrel of salt cod and smelled worse. We had been invaded again. Many of the rebel houses that were occupied by the British army had burned to the ground. Soldiers found themselves as homeless as regular folk, so their commanders ordered that anyone with an undamaged home share it with the men.

We wound up with eleven fellows from Kent sleeping three to a bedchamber and using the second-floor drawing room as their common area for dining and conversating.

The master and Madam moved their bedchamber to the downstairs front parlor and gave the library over to Colonel Hawkins, a high-ranking officer whose favor Lockton sought.

The cellar was turned into a barracks for five soldiers who had their wives with them. This was the Lord's blessing on me because the women were used to cooking and cleaning for their men's regiment. The new bosslady in the kitchen was named Sarah, a black-haired gal with a baby in her belly. She was not a friendly sort—none of them were—but she did not call me names nor seem inclined to hand out beatings.

I did miss Becky Berry, more than I thought possible.

It was odd sleeping in the cellar with strangers. They sure did snore, the women as bad as the men. Their bodies gave off noxious odors, too, gases so strong they made my eyes water. The night of the first frost, I woke up to a soldier pulling off my blanket. I lay in the dark, fists clenched and teeth sharp, thinking he meant to do me harm.

He did not. He was simply cold and in need of another layer of cloth.

Next morning, Sarah agreed I could move my pallet up to the kitchen hearth.

It was lonely sleeping without that fool doll.

CHAPTER XXXIII

Friday, September 27–Saturday, November 16, 1776

MANY OF THE INHABITANTS ARE COME INTO TOWN; AND MANY OTHERS WHO WERE OBLIGED TO FLY FOR THEIR LOYALTY ARE COMING IN DAILY.
—*NEW YORK MERCURY* NEWSPAPER

THE AUTUMN PASSED IN A DOGWEARY haze for me, with much work and little time left to ponder or breathe. Everything was cloaked in gray: oyster gray, charcoal gray, pewter gray, mold gray, storm gray, and ash. Scraps of ash floated through the air for weeks and found their way into everything, from the butter to the tea. The rains turned the ash to mud. Frost painted the ground the color of a gravestone, ashes trapped in ice.

I flaked ashy too. Momma used to rub a salve of bear fat and mint on us as winter approached so our skin would not dry and crack.

Was Ruth's skin dry? Did anyone notice?

Ashes drifted into the hollow places in my bones and silted up my brainpan. I had the fanciful notion that perhaps we had died in the fire, that we were all lost souls, forbidden to enter heaven. When I had low thoughts like that, Curzon's voice would call from my remembery and tell me to join him, to become a rebel.

I told that voice to hush.

With the ash so thick inside and out, I had few thoughts to spare for that fool. I figured he was dug in with the troops at Fort Washington, which seemed a good place, what with the strong walls and the cannons protecting it. Folks said the British wouldn't attack the fort until spring.

The men drilled and patrolled. Sarah and the other soldierwives spent most of their days down at the campground doing the chores for the regiment—washing clothes in big iron pots and cooking whatever could be found to roast or stew. They did some tidying at the Lockton house and kept the officers fed too. The dirtiest jobs fell to me: water hauling, wood chopping, and chamber-pot emptying. On top of that, Colonel Hawkins claimed me for his errand girl, sending me out with messages for this captain or that sergeant or in search of snuff or hair powder or almonds. He was terrible fond of almonds.

By the time the apples were harvested, hundreds of ships crammed with expensive British goods crowded the docks. The price of food doubled and doubled again. This did not affect the Locktons nor the rich Loyalist refugees who streamed into the city toting bags of gold. We took delivery of enough potatoes to fill the bin in the cellar and had no trouble buying meat. But regular folks burnt out of their homes and penniless Loyalist refugees on the run from the rebels, they were forced to shelter in Canvastown, the new name for the burned-over district. They used tent canvas to make huts against the standing chimneys and half-crumbled brick walls. They ate beans and rice when they were lucky and begged on the streets when they were not.

One day I noticed that the plants grown from Momma's seeds had been killed by the frost, the stalks dead on the ground, with shriveled paper leaves. A lump of mud stuck in my throat. I had forgotten to care for them. I collected the few seeds left from the flower heads and wrapped them in a scrap of cloth that I laid under the loose board in the pantry, where I had hidden my sliver of lead from the King's statue.

As the weather turned colder, Lady Seymour's mind cleared and her body strengthened. She could walk with help and move the crippled arm some, but her mouth still dragged at the corner and her speech was hard to follow. Madam was not entirely pleased that her husband's aunt was mending. I heard her grumble to Lockton that "the old biddy will never die, just to spite us."

A month or so after the fire, I was setting down a clean pitcher of water in Lady Seymour's bedchamber whilst Madam read the newspaper aloud to her. I thought the Lady was dozing, but her eyes snapped open when Madam described how British soldiers had looted the City Hall library. They stole books, ruined paintings, and broke scientifical equipment stored there by the professors of King's College.

Lady Seymour made Madam repeat the entire story, then demanded pen and ink and paper, fighting her way out from the blankets with her good arm. Once dressed warmly and settled at the writing table, she composed a strongly worded letter about the library destruction to General Howe, supreme commander of the Royal forces, and called for a glass of brandy and a bowl of soup.

After that it fell to me to walk with Lady Seymour along Wall Street on days when the sun was strong. She hired three seamstresses to sew her a new wardrobe and included a heavy skirt and thick woolen cloak for me in the order. I protested that I could not pay for the clothes, but Lady Seymour simply pointed to the portrait of the yellow-haired man, her husband, on the mantel and his letters stacked next to it.

"We'll not discuss payment again," she said slowly.

"Thank you, ma'am," I said.

After the pigs had been slaughtered and fresh pork was for sale in the market, another wave of British officers moved in and set up their camp beds in the second-floor drawing room. The long dining table was covered end to end with maps. The men would stand over them, chins in their hands, trying to figure out how to finish off the rebels. They were now scheming to finish the war in time for the New Year. Battles and skirmishes were fought on the north part of New York Island, though the city was safe.

Whilst they plotted Washington's downfall, I dozed in a chair in the hallway in case they needed victuals or a bottle of port. Sleep was a rare and precious thing to me in those days.

The next day I was yawning hard as I trudged up to the Tea Water Pump. The November wind carried the promise of snow, and I was glad for the new cloak Lady Seymour had given me. Soon I would need rags to wrap round my hands.

My muddled head did not register the great hullabaloo at first, but then my ears awoke. Folks were shouting and hurrying toward the Greenwich Road where it dumped out onto the Commons. I was not sure what the race was for, but I lifted my skirts and joined along with it.

"They got them!" cheered a red-faced man, throwing both of his arms into the air. "They got them all."

By the time I made it to the Commons, I had to fight my way to the front of the cheering mob. The end of the Greenwich Road was lined with British soldiers, relaxed and laughing as their prisoners—captured American soldiers—walked three to a row between their enemies through the doors of the Bridewell Prison.

"Was there a battle?" I asked a serving girl next to me.

"Up the fort," she answered. "Them Hessians killt lots. Blood was running like water, they say. They fired them cannons from the ships. Blew arms and legs everywhere. Heads, too."

I nodded, unable to think what I should say. A chant started in the crowd, and singing. I did not join in, nor did I throw clods of mud as many did, including the bloodthirsty girl next to me.

The rebels kept coming in, row after filthy row, most with their heads down, some limping with a crutch or an arm in a sling. Their uniforms were torn and tattered. A few walked barefooted over the icy cobblestones, flinching when hit square with mud or a rock. They carried neither flag nor weapons. Their breath billowed like they were hard-ridden horses. It hung around their heads like smoke.

He was toward the end of the line, with the other enlisted slaves, his head bent forward, his face invisible. A bloody bandage was tied above his right knee, and it looked painful to step with his right foot.

The only way I knew him was that hat, nearer brown

than red now, with a rip through the brim, and the ring in his ear.

The guards shoved the last of the prisoners, including the boy with the red-brown hat, through the doors of the prison and closed them with a loud metal *clang*.

CHAPTER XXXIV

Sunday, November 17–
Sunday, November 24, 1776

WE HAVE NOW GOT NEAR 5000 PRISONERS IN NEW-YORK AND MANY OF THEM ARE SUCH RAGAMUFFINS, AS YOU NEVER SAW IN YOUR LIFE . . .
—LETTER OF A BRITISH OFFICER, PUBLISHED IN THE *LONDON PACKET* NEWSPAPER

I HAD NO TIME TO PONDER CURZON'S fate. Madam commanded that a supper be thrown to celebrate the capture of Fort Washington, complete with turtle soup.

The house fair exploded with dust and activity. The junior officers cleared out their cots, clothing, and maps from the second-floor drawing room so we could scrub and polish it from ceiling to floor. The kitchen hearth was crowded with irons heating to press the tablecloths and serviettes.

Madam hired the cook from the City Tavern to prepare the meal. Folks said he had a way with turtles. She then chose the prettiest of the soldierwives to wait at the tables. The ugly ones and Sarah with her big belly were to stay in the kitchen to assist the cook, and wash up. My job was to ferry the food up the stairs and the dirty crockery down.

The food began arriving long before sunup, packed into crates and hauled by sleepy-eyed boys. Three turtles each the size of a footstool came in a wooden pen. The sound of their flippers scratching made Sarah yelp in fright. Two of the turtles kept their heads tight against their shells. The third stretched out his neck and watched the commotion with wet, solemn eyes.

While we scurried to finish the house, and the cook butchered the turtles and plucked the pheasants, the hairdresser arrived to tend to Madam. He spent hours applying pomantum wax, padding, and lengths of brick-colored hair to fashion a high roll on Madam's head. The hair swept off her brow and soared into the air like a wave curling before a ship's prow. I thought the wave might crumble, but Madam did not ask my opinion. She wanted a pot of hot chocolate made with two handfuls of sugar, which was a shocking amount.

Sarah and the cook were exchanging heated words in the kitchen. Empty turtle shells stood drying in the corner, and the cook's assistant stirred the thick soup bubbling over the fire. I grabbed the chocolate pot and left, not wanting to see what became of the poor creatures' heads.

As I served the hot chocolate and tidied the chamber, Madam rubbed her face with Venetian Bloom Water beauty wash, said to remove wrinkles. After that came a layer of Molyneux's Italian Paste to make her skin white as bleached linen. It made her resemble a corpse.

And then, the final triumph. She used a tiny brush to paint a thin line of glue above each eye. Madam opened an envelope and shook out two gray strips of mouse fur, each cut into an arch. Leaning toward the mirror, she glued the mouse fur onto her own eyebrows, making them bushy and thick as the fashion required.

It truth, she looked like a woman with two lumps of mouse fur stuck on her face.

A delicate bell sounded overhead–Lady Seymour summoning help.

"The guests will be arriving soon," Madam said, admiring her reflection. "Aunt Seymour wishes to be seated in advance of them. You may assist her."

After I helped the Lady limp from her chamber to her place near the head of the long table, I placed a foot warmer filled with hot coals under her chair and spread a woolen blanket on her lap. She thanked me kindly and looked about.

"When I was young, we dined thus every night," she said with a sigh.

I could scarce credit it. The table was covered by the finest linen tablecloth I'd ever seen. Each place had china plates, crystal glasses, and ivory-handled knives and forks. Candles were positioned every three hands. Saltcellars, each with a tiny spoon, and pepper mills were set in easy arm's reach of each place. Smaller tables and sideboards were positioned at the edges of the room to hold trays and dishes. One table was covered with wine bottles.

Candlelight reflected back and back again in the polished mirrors that hung from the walls. I caught a glimpse in the hearth mirror of a girl with a mark on her cheek that trumpeted her shame. I quickly turned my eyes away.

There was a heavy knock on the front door.

"It begins," Lady Seymour said. "Go below, child."

I set the tray loaded with the turtle soup bowls on the table by the door. Three more trays needed to be brought up the stairs, but I allowed myself a quick peek at the company before I fetched them.

The table was crowded with officers wearing splendid uniforms and perfectly powdered wigs along with several of Master Lockton's business companions. Lockton wore a cardinal red satin waistcoat, black satin coat and breeches, and shoes with silver buckles. The new clothes could not hide the fact that the master was grinding himself down with work. Long hours serving the British commandant had melted off the fat from his second and third chins and created heavy black circles under his eyes. But his bags of gold grew fatter, and that was what he cared for the most.

Madam reigned over her end of the table with the occasional flutter of her fan, the wave of hair above her brow threatening to crash at any moment. Lady Seymour, the only other woman present, looked like an elegant spider wrapped in her black lace shawl. Her eyes were lively in the candlelight and her cheeks had color in them for the first time in weeks. The officer next to her was the size and shape of Edward, the shaggy bull who lived down the road from us in Rhode Island. The man did not have a ring in his nose, but he laughed with an impatient snorting sound.

I hurried up and down the stairs with the remaining trays of soup, then the roasted tongue and mushrooms. The serving girl cut the meat on Lady Seymour's plate before setting it down so that the weakness of her arm would not hinder her. The young soldier who was appointed wine steward danced around the backs of the guests, keeping their glasses full. The conversating flowed as fast as the wine—the taking of Fort Washington, news from London, plans for a fox hunt. At this last, an officer joked that the next fox would be a tall sort from Virginia, by the name of

George Washington. That caused hearty laughter all around and glasses raised.

A serving girl hissed at me to go back to the kitchen.

When I entered the room a half hour later, my arms shook under the weight of the tray. The cook had prepared enough to feed a battalion: pheasant stuffed with figs, stewed oysters, potted larks, greens cooked with bacon, pickled watermelon rind, and buttered parsnips. The pheasant smelled good. I had hopes that some might find its way into the scraps bucket.

By the time I lugged in the dessert tray–rice pudding, lemon biscuits, two creamed pear tarts, and an iced cake– the fire was blazing and the room much warmer. Lockton had freed the top buttons of his waistcoat, and two of the officers had loosened their lace neck cloths. The heat had softened the glue of Madam's left mousy eyebrow, and it had begun to free itself from her face. She did not notice this. The serving girls and wine steward watched the progress of the eyebrow and fought to keep the smiles from their faces.

The voices of the men were loud and booming, as if the wine they drank affected their hearing. I handed a plate of tart to one of the serving women, who carried it to the table and set it in front of Colonel Hawkins.

"So how many rebel prisoners did your men bag, Colonel?" asked Master Lockton.

I passed another dish of tart.

The colonel shook his head. "Near three thousand of the devils. Wish we could have shot them all."

My hand shook as I reached for the third.

"Why so?" Lockton asked.

"We've no place to put them." The colonel pushed the

tart to the side and reached into the bowl of shelled almonds in the middle of the table. He tossed a few into his mouth and crunched loudly.

"I thought you were using the Bridewell," Lockton said. "That should provide ample space."

The colonel snorted and shook his head. "The prison is so stuffed, the walls are ready to burst. We've had to pack them into the sugarhouses and the confiscated churches, too." He reached for more nuts. "It's a right nuisance. Never thought we'd have so many."

"I'd say so many prisoners are a badge of honor for your men and the King," Lockton said.

The colonel raised an eyebrow. "We do not need a badge of honor. We need a decent plague to take them off our hands." The men around the table chuckled. "The expense of feeding them will be staggering."

"The rebels planted the seeds of war, let them enjoy their harvest." Lockton ate a forkful of tart. "Force the local Patriots to feed them."

"I say shoot 'em," growled the man who looked like Edward the bull. "'Course then we have to dispose of the bodies. Messy work, that."

"Waste of ammunition," the colonel said. "And some members of Parliament would fuss like wet hens. No, I predict a cold winter will dispatch most of them in a natural way."

Lady Seymour spoke up. "What if the rebels decide that turnabout is fair play? We need to care for them so they do not harm their British captives."

"With all due respect, ma'am," the man said with a smile, "the rebels would first have to capture a prisoner. Given their blunders, it is an unlikely prospect."

Lady Seymour nodded gravely. "What of the prisoners they took after their victory at Breed's Hill?"

The table fell very still at that. Talk of what happened at Breed's Hill in Boston was as rude as stating that Madam's false eyebrow was about to fall off. But Lady Seymour was the wealthy, elderly widow of a British lord, incapable of social error, so all pretended she had not said a word.

Several men cleared their throats and reached for their wine. Madam lifted her goblet.

"I am told there are plans to reopen the John Street theater," she said loudly. "This heralds a return to civilization and order."

Her eyebrow flopped into the rice pudding. The man seated to her right coughed loudly into his napkin. The wine steward's face turned the color of a plum, and a serving girl bit down on her lip to prevent a laugh.

Madam avoided looking at her pudding. "A toast," she said with a wobbling voice.

"A toast to civilization!" Lockton added. "I've heard plans for a cricket club, too."

As the men roared in approval, I carried the tray loaded with the dirty supper dishes down the stairs. On my return trip upstairs I carried two pots of coffee. My trips up and down the stairs continued until my knees threatened to fold up and quit, bringing dishes down, carrying more delicacies and hot drinks up. Down, up, down, up, a hundred miles of stairs in one night.

As the candles guttered out and were replaced with new, Madam and Lady Seymour retired to their bedchambers and Lockton's business companions left to play billiards at the King's Head tavern. The officers requested more coffee, lit their pipes, and unrolled their maps across the tablecloth, stained now with splashes of turtle soup, butter, wine, and candle wax.

The serving girls moved down to the kitchen, where kettles of water were put on to boil for the washing of the dishes. The cook was long departed, and Sarah dozed on a kitchen chair, her swollen feet propped up on a pillow.

I picked up the enormous bowl of table scraps and headed out the back door. Miss Mary Finch always mixed table scraps with muck and spread the smelly mess on her garden come spring, but the Locktons weren't much for growing things, not when the markets were so close to hand. Scraps here were dumped down the privy.

I closed the door behind me and stopped. The cold air took my breath away. The sky was a black curtain; the stars, ice chips whittled by an old knife. I wrapped the shawl tighter across my shoulders and pulled it high to protect my neck.

Through the kitchen window I could see two of the women squabbling about who would wash and who would dry. The second floor windows glowed with candlelight shadowed by the shapes of the officers circling around the map.

I shuddered and my teeth banged together. Water would turn solid tonight. It was a bad night to be without a blanket.

Would they truly allow prisoners to freeze to death?

The soldierwives stopped arguing, and the men lit fresh candles. The stars wheeled above me and inside, deep inside, something turned. I could not name it nor recognize its form. I drew in a cold breath and blew it skyward. The air came out of me in the shape of a cloud. It drifted above the rooftop and dissolved into the stars.

Would they let him starve?

The stars said not a word.

The back door banged open and I jumped. "Don't tarry," said Sarah. "You need to dry the last of them glasses afore you lay yourself to sleep."

"Yes, ma'am. As soon as I finish this."

I quickly carried the scraps bowl out into the yard, walking past the privy, all the way back to the stable wall where straggly holly bushes grew. I glanced quick at the house to make sure no one was watching, then pulled aside the prickly branches of the bush and set the bowl down within it. I covered the bowl with my apron. On my way back to the house, I loaded my arms with firewood. I doubted she'd notice that I left the bowl outside, not with me bringing in extra wood.

I took another deep breath of the frozen air before I opened the door, confused that I should be so awake after such a long day. I frowned as my thoughts tumbled and multiplied.

I had been invaded. A dim plan had hatched itself in my brainpan without my consent, and I did not much like it.

CHAPTER XXXV

Monday, December 2, 1776

YOUNG MEN, YE SHOULD NEVER
AGAIN FIGHT AGAINST YER KING!
—SCOTTISH SERGEANT SCOLDING REBEL TROOPS
AFTER THE DEFEAT OF FORT WASHINGTON

I HAD TO WAIT THREE DAYS TO SNEAK up to the prison.

My chance came when Madam received an invitation from a friend who had moved into an abandoned rebel mansion in Greenwich Village, north of the city line. Madam smiled in triumph as she read the note, then told me to clean her best shoes. After the midday meal, the soldierwives helped Lady Seymour and Madam into the carriage. I brought out foot warmers filled with hot coals and heavy blankets to lay over the women for the air was crackling and cold.

The driver snapped the whip above the heads of the horses, and the carriage rolled away. The soldierwives waited until it was out of sight, then dashed off to visit their own friends. When they were gone, the house stood empty for the first time in months.

I lined my shoes and cap with newspaper to keep out the wind and emptied the leftovers hiding under the holly bush into a bucket that I covered with an old rag.

I stood across the street from the Bridewell Prison and pondered hard.

Don't do this. Don't do this.

All around the Commons folks went on their business, soldiers rubbing the cold out of their fingers, women wrapped in long cloaks and thick shawls. They walked over the ground where the gallows had been built last summer, where they hung the traitor Hickey. Back in August the Patriots had torn it down to use the wood for the barricades. The British had built their own hangman's platform at the opposite end of the Commons. It could kill three people at a time.

The ashes in my soul stirred.

Don't do this.

Men stood at the windows of the prison, calling out to those who passed by. Few folk looked in their direction, pretending that the noise came from the throats of the crows circling overhead.

Go back. 'Tis not your affair.

The whispers in my brainpan grew louder as I crossed the street.

Madam will beat you bloody, he's not your concern, it's not your place. Go back, go back before it's too late.

The crows cawed and wheeled and beat their shiny black wings against the wind-whipped clouds. They saw everything. I stopped in front of the iron-studded oak door and frowned.

He freed me from the stocks. He is my friend. My only friend.

With that, the ashes settled and shushed. My arm lifted light as a feather and pounded the door knocker.

A giant guard opened up. "Wot do ye want?" he growled. He looked like he had been fashioned by setting boulders atop boulders; his hands were iron mallets and his face rough-carved out of granite. He was a mountain clothed in a lobsterback uniform.

"'Nother do-gooder," he grunted, when I explained my mission. He lifted the corner of the rag that covered my bucket and sniffed. "You got anyfink tasty in there?"

"Scraps, sir. The mistress normally feeds them to the pigs, but she's a good soul and told me to bring them for the prisoners," I lied.

He grunted, peered into the bucket, and poked through it with a finger. "Rice pudding?"

"Yes, sir."

The guard crossed the room, took a bowl down from a shelf, and used a spoon to dish the rice pudding from the bucket. "And you're kin to this boy you seek?" he asked.

"My older brother, sir," I lied. "Always was a stubborn cuss. Made Momma cry herself to sleep at night."

"Why ain't yer mother here then?"

"She's dead, sir." That much was true.

The guard was more interested in rice pudding than my patchwork story. He shoveled several spoonfuls in his mouth and chewed while looking me over.

"Come on then," he said, taking a ring of keys from a hook on the wall. "I'll give ye a little time."

The sound of his key turning in the lock brought back my time in the City Hall dungeon with the madwoman and the rats. Despite the cold, a trickle of sweat inched down my backbone. We walked down a hall lined with four doors on each side and at the end, a staircase. He stopped at the last door on the right and unlocked it.

"'Ere we go," he said.

The cell was little bigger than the one I had been confined in. It was filled with men and boys milling around like nervous cattle herded into a goat pen. There was no fire burning, nay, not even a hearth where it could burn. A short man dressed in black peered out of the cell's one window, stuck in the middle of the outside wall. The man's collar was flipped up to protect his neck, his hat was pulled down, and his hands were stuck in his armpits for warmth. The window had bars across it, but no glass. It was an empty hole open to the rain, wind, and snow.

All turned to stare as we entered.

"Girl come to see her brother," the guard said.

"Excuse me, sir," I said as he started to close the door. "What about my bucket?"

He smiled. "Needs further inspection."

No one said anything nor moved until the guard finished relocking the door and his footsteps echoed down the hall.

"You'll be wanting him in the corner," said the short man by the window. "Show her."

A few of the prisoners stepped to the side so I could see a bundle of rags on the floor. Curzon was lying on the stones, with no blankets covering him nor a pallet under him, not even straw. His leg was still wrapped in the bloody bandage, his lips were dry and cracked. He clutched his hat in one hand.

I crouched next to him, unsure what to do. The soldiers around us grew tired of staring and returned to their low conversating. I leaned close to figure if he was breathing. Finally, I put my lips to his ear.

"Are you dead?" I whispered.

He answered without moving. "No, Country. Are you?"

I near jumped out of my skin. "Curzon?"

His eyes opened slow, bloodshot and bleary.

"Can you sit up?" I asked.

"Suppose so."

I helped pull him upright. He winced and leaned against the wall, shaking with chills.

"Here." I untied my heavy cloak and laid it over him.

He protested. "You don't have to—"

I interrupted him. "Hush. Did you get shot?"

He pulled the cloak up under his chin and shivered again. "In the leg. My luck held, though; bullet went in and out fair clean. Didn't break the bone." He stopped as a man nearby broke into a fit of coughing.

I sat next to him. "Was it awful?" I asked.

He closed his eyes and shook his head. "You don't want to know."

"Yes, I do."

"When the redcoats invaded," he started, "we raced up the island to the fort. Figured we'd hold there for months, then drive them from the city come spring when our forces would be stronger."

"Ha!" spat the man closest to us. He rolled over to face the wall.

"Did you shoot a gun?" I asked.

"Mostly dug ditches and carried rocks. The soldiers, they worked alongside us, and they drilled to get ready. When the battle finally started, the men fired their guns so fast the barrels grew hot. The cannon smoke was thick as fog. I saw the most horrid sights, Country, not fit for the eyes of any person."

He swallowed hard. "I wound up next to a militia boy

from Connecticut. He'd just learned to shave and was a poor hand at it, razor cuts all over his chin. Said he was worried his pa was mad at him on account of he didn't make it home for the apple harvest like he promised."

He fell silent for a moment, then continued. "So this boy, he had two muskets, one his own, the other from a fella who died on Long Island. When the Hessians came at us, the boy would shoot one gun, whilst I reloaded the other. We continued thus, loading and shooting, loading and shooting half the day.

"The British moved their small cannons up the hill and took aim, but I loaded. He shot." He paused to wipe his eyes on his sleeve. "As I handed him his gun, a cannonball ripped his head from his body."

We sat without a word. The ashes within me swirled and filled up my throat again. Around us men muttered low and coughed.

Curzon let his tears run. "After that, I shot the guns for myself. Took the bullet in my leg, but kept firing. An hour or so later, Colonel Magaw surrendered the fort. We laid down our weapons and walked out. The British called for our officers to walk forward, and we feared they'd be shot."

"Were they?" I asked.

"Not hardly." He sat up a little straighter. "Officers get special treatment on account of they're considered gentlemen. They have parole to walk around the city. They live in boardinghouses and eat regular."

The man who faced the wall muttered a string of curses that echoed against the stones. He said every kind of bad word imaginable about officers, gentlemen, the war, the British, and the Congress, and he cursed himself for leaving his wife and farm in Maryland.

Curzon's tears dried, leaving a thin trail of salt down his cheeks. "You should go home now."

Before I could ask one of a hundred questions, the key turned in the lock and the guard appeared. He stuck out my bucket. "Inspection complete," he said, wiping a smear of butter off the side of his face.

I stood, walked to the door, and looked in the bucket. Half of the food was gone.

"May I stay a while longer?" I asked.

"Sing out when you need me," the guard said with an unsettling wink.

As soon as the door was relocked, a man with powder burns on his face snatched the bucket from my hands. "I'll take that," he snarled.

I held tight to the handle and shouted, "Give it back!"

The man grabbed my arm, his fingers like the claws of a panther.

"Enough!" shouted a powerful voice.

The cell fell silent as a tomb.

The short man dressed in black limped over to us from his post by the window. "Release that bucket, Private Dibdin," he ordered.

The thief did as he was asked but crossed his arms over his chest and stood his ground. "She brought food for the black boy, Sergeant," he complained. "T'aint right for the slave to eat while we starve."

The tiny sergeant stood motionless. Somewhere water was dripping. "No one here will starve long as I have breath." He turned to me. "Excuse the poor manners, miss, but we've not eaten for three days. Hungry men are sometimes rude."

"I understand," I said.

"Would you be willing to share what you've brought?" he asked. "We would all be most grateful."

I looked the sergeant in the eye. He wasn't much taller than me. "There's not enough to feed everyone."

"I know that, miss. But we're all equal hungry."

"Don't fuss, Country," Curzon asked. "We fought together, we'll eat together."

Outside a heavy cart rolled down Broadway, the driver calling to his horses. There was an argument from the cell on the other side of the wall and a thump from the one above.

I handed the bucket to Curzon.

The nasty man dug his claws into my shoulder. "The sergeant goes first."

I waited for him to release me, fighting the urge to bite his wrist down to the bone. Once he let go, I gave the bucket to the sergeant. He looked inside and pulled out a piece of pie crust the length of my finger. He handed the bucket to Curzon, who removed a long parsnip peel.

The bucket made its way around the room at a snail's pace as each man studied the contents and chose a small portion of discarded potato or bread or gristle. When it was returned to me I was confuddled.

"There's still food in here," I said.

"These are fine men," the sergeant said with pride. "Each took his portion without stealing from the next. Mind if we send it round again?"

"No, sir."

As the bucket went down the line again, the sergeant motioned for me to stand with him close to the wall.

"I wonder if I might ask a favor."

"What kind of favor?" I asked.

"We need to pass messages on to our captain. He'll be able to get word out of the city. Some of the other womenfolk who bring food to the prisoners are helping in this manner."

"I can't spy for you."

"No, no, not a spy. Simply a message carrier. You come by here, I drop a word or two in your ear, and you pass it along."

"It will put me in danger."

"It's a way for you to continue our fight for freedom."

The bucket was moving more quickly the second time around.

"I cannot, sir." I was not fool enough to let the Patriots hurt me again.

The key sounded in the lock as the bucket returned to my hands, wiped empty this time. The guard entered. Curzon struggle to his feet and handed me my cloak. "Here."

"No," I said. "You keep it."

"As soon as I fell asleep, it would be . . . borrowed, little sister. Bring it the next time you come."

I wrapped the warm cloak around my shoulders and was struck with a sudden notion. I pulled the newspaper out from my cap and quickly removed the pages lining my shoes. "Can you use this?"

"Hurry up," said the guard.

Curzon smiled. "Just what I need for a bed," he said. "Go on home now."

I nodded, grateful to be leaving and heavy with guilt. "You'll be here when I return?"

"Don't plan on leaving anytime soon," he said.

CHAPTER XXXVI

*Tuesday, December 3–
Friday, December 13, 1776*

. . . OUR PRIVATE SOLDIERS IN YOUR HANDS,
ARE TREATED IN A MANNER SHOCKING TO HUMANITY,
AND THAT MANY OF THEM MUST HAVE PERISHED THRO'
HUNGER, HAD IT NOT BEEN FOR THE CHARITABLE
CONTRIBUTIONS OF THE INHABITANTS.
—GENERAL GEORGE WASHINGTON COMPLAINING
TO BRITISH GENERAL WILLIAM HOWE

LADY SEYMOUR WAS STRUCK BY A FEVER whilst visiting up in Greenwich. She had to be carried to her chamber, her skin the color of an old beeswax candle. Doctor Dastuge came to bleed her so that her bodily humors would go back into balance.

When the bleeding was over, Madam saw the doctor to the door. I was dusting the grandfather clock in the front hall.

"Good sir," Madam said in a low voice. "I wonder . . . I believe our aunt would recover faster at our estate in Charleston. She could sit in the sun for hours and breathe the healthful air. Don't you agree?"

The doctor's bushy eyebrows flew up in alarm. "South Carolina is hundreds of miles from here—over bad roads. Lady Seymour would be dead by Philadelphia."

Which was likely Madam's intention, I thought.

The doctor pulled on his gloves and picked up his bag. "I doubt she'll be well enough to travel until spring. I will call again tomorrow." He tipped his hat. "Good day, Madam."

Lady Seymour's bell rang upstairs as the door closed behind him. Madam squeezed her lips together so tight I thought she had bit them off.

"Girl," she spat. "Go see what she wants."

By supper it had been decided that I would tend Lady Seymour whilst she was bedridden. The master used his connections in the British high command to secure extra firewood for the house, declaring that his aunt's bedchamber be kept as warm as the month of June. The heat of the room helped to bake out the fever in Lady Seymour's blood and ease her cough. 'Twas warm enough that I could go about in stocking feet which was a comfort for my shoes had taken to pinching my toes something wicked.

As she recovered, the Lady took to reading all of the newspapers printed in the city. Whenever she dropped off to sleep, I would steal as many sentences as I could. Thusly I followed the progress of the war, what was left of it. The flame of independence was sputtering and expected to burn out any day. The rebels had run out of ammunition, soldiers, and money. Mayor Matthews, him who plotted to kill General Washington, escaped from the rebel prison and returned to New York in triumph. The American Congress, frightened by the marching British, fled Philadelphia and ran to Baltimore. Newport, in my home state of Rhode Island, fell to the British too.

When I read that last bit of news I was stunned. I had not

spared a thought for Rhode Island for months.

'Twas several days before I could again sneak up to the Bridewell, toting sausages, crusts, and cheese rinds. The guard stole a few of the sausages and gave me only a few moments to conversate. It mattered not. Curzon was not feeling up to much talk. I sat on the stone floor and checked the hole in his leg. It was hot but free of yellow pus.

Conditions in the prison had eased some. Folk in town had donated enough blankets that there was one to be shared between every two or three men. The British promised each prisoner would receive two pounds of pork and hardtack biscuit every week. They did not announce that the pork was often spoiled, nor that the men had to eat it raw for there was no fire to cook it over.

For my next visit I saved my own helping of mince pie. I filled the bucket with potato scraps and mutton fat, and put the pie on top. The guard took the pie, as I had hoped.

"I loves a good mince pie," he said as he unlocked the door to the prison, pie crumbs spilling from his mouth. Frozen bodies were stacked in the hall waiting to be buried in the pits. The clothes had been taken from the bodies to keep the living soldiers warmer. I kept my eyes on the ground out of modesty.

Curzon was still not in the mood for conversating, not even a little bit. I thought he looked feverish but when I went to feel his forehead, he pushed my hand away. The men snickered at that. I took my empty bucket and left.

Snow fell all that night.

Lady Seymour prepared an errand list for me the next afternoon. She had spent the morning gazing into the fire and had not taken any food. I made bold and suggested that she eat a biscuit with honey, for her own good.

"You need strength to get through the winter," I added.

She set down her pen, picked up her teacup, and sipped the hot cinnamon water. "I thought it pleased you when I left so much on my plate."

"Ma'am?"

"The more I leave behind, the more there is for you to take to the prison." She studied me so close I thought she could see my thoughts. "That is where you've been taking the table scraps, isn't it?"

My head bobbed once, like a puppet's.

"Am I to assume you know someone confined there?"

I found my voice. "Yes, ma'am."

She sipped again and looked at me over the rim of her teacup. "It is honorable to help a friend in need."

"How did you know?" I blurted out.

She folded the sheet of paper on the table. "These are the items I would like you to fetch for me. Purchase the ink and newspaper at Rivington's, but not the books. He overcharges. Go to that shop near the baker on Hanover Square. Elihu said they haven't closed."

I bobbed once and took the paper. "Please, ma'am," I tried again. "How did you know?"

Her gaze returned to the logs in the hearth. "Take care how you go, Isabel. Many people think it is a fine and Christian thing to help the prisoners. I do not think my niece is one of them."

"Yes, ma'am," I whispered.

It started to snow whilst I was in Rivington's. The wind blew the snow direct into my face as I crossed the square, and I was grateful to step into the shelter of the stationer's store for 'twas warm and dry inside, near peaceful, if such a word can be used to describe a shop.

A jelly-bellied officer with thick spectacles was purchasing a tall stack of books from the man behind the counter. They were deep in their talk and appeared not to notice me. I took a slow turn around the shop, admiring the shelves heavy with books, business forms, proclamations from Parliament and General Howe, slates, thick paper, quills, and sealing wax.

The books called to me. My fingers itched to touch them. It had been months since I dug into the story of Robinson Crusoe.

I glanced toward the counter. The men were arguing friendly-like about a fellow named Hume. They both had their faces planted in the same pamphlet. When I trod on a squeaky board, they did not even look up.

I reached up to a bookshelf and flipped my way through the books standing at attention. The titles were near as long as books themselves: *Treatise on the Propagation of Sheep, the Manufacture of Wool, and the Cultivation and Manufacture of Flax*, by John Wily, or *Cato Major, Or His Discourse of Old-Age: With Explanatory Notes,* by M. T. Cicero, or *Poems on Various Subjects, Religious and Moral*, by Phillis Wheatley, and countless tracts containing sermons and advice.

My fingers backed up.

Momma told me about Miss Wheatley. She was kidnapped in Africa, sold in Boston, and wrote fancy poetry that smart people liked. She had visited London in England. She had been an enslaved girl but was a free woman.

I took the slim book off the shelf and opened the cover. I had never read a poem. What if I lacked the skill? What if I were caught?

Might as well throw myself in the river.

Bang!

The closing door startled me so I near dropped the volume. I quickly set it back on the shelf and approached the counter.

"Can I help you?" asked the young man who stood behind it.

"Yes, please, sir." I handed him the list. "From the Lady Seymour."

"I hear she's been poorly," he said as he looked over the list.

"Yessir, but she is strong enough to sit by the fire now and has a powerful urge to read."

He nodded. "She's a good customer. I am glad she's on the mend."

He quickly assembled everything on the list—*The Letters of Lady Mary Wortley Montagu*, *History of the Roman Republic, Volume One*, and *The Expedition of Humphry Clinker*—and pulled out a large sheet of paper to wrap them in.

As he worked the scissors, he paused. "You knew that boy, didn't you?"

"Pardon me?"

He continued cutting. "Bellingham's boy, red hat. Quick talker." He creased the paper with his finger. "He brought you here once, in May. Pointed to you out the window. Convinced me to hand over two fresh-baked rolls. Told me you were like to die from hunger if I didn't help."

He smiled at the memory.

"I'm sorry, sir," I said. "I didn't mean to take your food."

He pulled off a length of twine. "You didn't. One of the advantages of courting the baker's daughter is all the bread a man can eat."

He had not yet commented on my looking at the books. I feared he might try and trip me up, get me to say something

I ought not, but saw no other choice than to be polite. "I hope your lady is well, sir," I said.

He concentrated on tying a bow. "So do I. She fled with her father to a village in Pennsylvania. Place called Hatboro. They make hats there. Clever, don't you think?"

He tried to smile, but his eyes were downcast and melancholy.

"Perhaps 'tis safer there," I said.

"Aye," he said, finishing the bow, "with plenty of young men eager to protect her. But that's a tale for another day."

He kept the package in his hands, lost in thought.

"Master Lockton will settle his aunt's account at the end of the week," I said.

"Oh, aye." He gave me the package and waited as I settled it in my basket. "I hear tell you're one of them who feeds the lads in the Bridewell."

A sizzling log in the hearth popped suddenly and I jumped. "Not me, sir. Begging pardon, but someone is mistaken."

He crossed his arms over his chest and shook his head. "That there mark on your face makes you hard to forget, lass."

The heat from the hearth filled the room and made it hard to breathe. My eyes darted to the windows and I fought the urge to run. It felt like all of New York was watching me.

He leaned forward, put his elbows on the counter, and lowered his voice tho' we were the only people in the shop. "You tell them boys in the jail to hang on. There's plenty of us out here trying to help."

"Sir?"

He removed a slim volume from under the counter. "This is for you. Don't let your mistress see it."

"I cannot read, sir," I lied.

He snorted once as he quickly wrapped the book. "Of course you can't." He pushed the package to my side of the counter. "All who love liberty should commit the words to heart."

"I can't take it," I started. "I cannot pay—"

"I only have a few left and those I should burn," he said with a wave of his hand. "Read it. Pass it on. And keep feeding the lads."

I bobbed once and hid the parcel in my pocket under my apron. As soon as I could stand close enough to a fire, I'd get rid of it. The last thing I needed was more trouble on account of independence.

"Yes, sir," I said, hurrying for the door. "Thank you, sir."

He raised his finger to his lips in a last warning. "Shhhhhh!"

CHAPTER XXXVII

Saturday, December 14–Monday, December 23, 1776

THE DISTRESS OF THE PRISONERS CANNOT BE COMMUNICATED IN WORDS. TWENTY OR THIRTY DIE EVERY DAY; THEY LIE IN HEAPS UNBURIED; WHAT NUMBERS OF MY COUNTRYMEN HAVE DIED BY COLD AND HUNGER, PERISHED FOR WANT OF THE COMMON NECESSARIES OF LIFE! I HAVE SEEN IT! THIS, SIR, IS THE BOASTED BRITISH CLEMENCY!
—LETTER WRITTEN FROM NEW YORK DESCRIBING PRISONERS CAPTURED AT FORT WASHINGTON

LADY SEYMOUR REGAINED HER strength by the day. I was no longer allowed to spend warm hours in her bedchamber. She took her breakfast and dinner alone but joined the rest of the company for supper each night. Madam was saddened by her husband's aunt's return to health.

The next week passed in a kitchenstorm of flour and sugar, for Christmas was fast approaching. Madam's list of required delicacies was endless: gingerbread, pies of brandied peaches and preserved cherries and mincemeat, macaroons, blancmange, Jordan almonds, sugar candy, as many kinds of cake as there were fingers on both hands. I was the dogsbody in charge of keeping the oven stoked with wood and the ashes cleared out, fetching forgotten ingredients from the market, and beating eggs, ten at a time, till my arm was near to fall off.

Two of the soldierwives got into a terrible squabble the day the woodpile froze. Hannah told Mary it was her turn to fetch home the buckets from the Tea Water Pump and Mary said, no, 'twas Hannah's turn. Back and forth they went, the words getting hotter as their tempers grew shorter.

"I went yesterday," Mary said loudly as she poured boiling water into a basin. "You know that for a fact because you told me my nose was the color of a cherry when I came in."

Hannah shook her head as she scrubbed the floor. "No, no, no, that was two days ago. Yesterday I slipped on the ice and fell on my backside. Near broke my tailbone, I did. Could barely come up the steps this morning."

"Yer a lying codface, you are," Mary said.

Hannah threw the brush in the bucket and water splashed on the floor. "Who you calling a liar?"

Sarah, the bosslady, came through the door just as Mary rounded the table, her hands balled up into fists. Sarah was getting close to her time and had a bit of a temper herself. She slammed the door so hard the whole house shook. "Shut yer gobs!" she shouted. "I'll report the pair of you to the colonel if you don't straighten up. There'll be no more brawling or caterwauling in this kitchen."

"But–," they both said.

Sarah leveled such a glare at the pair of them I thought their hair would catch fire. And I suddenly saw a way clear to my own purposes.

"Begging pardon, Miss Sarah, ma'am," I said meekly.

"What do you want?" she said, her eyes still on the other women.

"I can fetch the tea water," I volunteered.

Mary shook her head back and forth. "Oh, no, she won't. She'll tarry at the shops to get out of her own chores. Make one of the men do it, I say."

"I'm the first one awake to build up the fires," I explained. "The shops are still closed then. I'll dash up to the pump and be back before the sun comes up."

Sarah gave me a suspicious look. "Why would you take on extra work, special with it being so cold and dark in the morning?"

"I was raised in the country, miss. Too much time inside makes me feel poorly. I like walking in the fresh air, even if it is cold."

'Twas mostly a lie, but the Tea Water Pump was right close to the prison. Fetching water would give me a chance to check on Curzon every day.

Hannah picked up her scrub brush and knelt on the floor again. "Let her go, I say. Saves us the trouble of freezing our tails off." She dipped the brush in the bucket. "Don't know what possessed me to follow my Jimmy to this godforsaken colony."

The next morning found me headed up island long before the sun rose. When I knocked on the guardhouse door of the prison, it was opened by a soldier I'd never seen before, a short man with black hair, sky blue eyes, and a scowl.

"You can't come in," he said after I explained my errand. "Regulations been changed."

"Tell her 'bout the windows," called another soldier warming himself by the fire.

"The regulations permit civilians to deliver food and sundry provisions."

"But not firewood," added the man at the hearth, yawning.

"But not firewood," repeated the first man. "There will be regular patrols round the perimeter of the building to ensure that civilians do not tarry overlong in conversation with the prisoners."

"And we'll be checking on the grub you give 'em," said his companion.

"Guards will inspect all civilian donations," the first man said formally. "If you deliver contraband items, you will be imprisoned yourself."

I shivered once. "Are scones and jam contraband?"

"Not yet."

Back outside, I walked around the front of the building, trying to figure where Curzon's cell lay. Some prisoners were already awake, their hands and arms wrapped in rags sticking through the bars of the window.

Curzon's cell lay to the back of the building. I rounded the corner and stopped. This was where the burial pits were dug. The pits were just a little smaller than the cells, dug down the height of a grown man. One of them had already been filled with bodies and covered again with dark mud. Two lay open and empty, sprinkled with snow like sugar on a cake. I did not know how many bodies would fit in each.

I shivered again and pulled my cloak tight, then turned my back to the graves and counted the windows, *two, three, four,* until I came to the window I hoped led to Curzon's cell. The eastern sky had brightened enough for me to see all around, but the inside of the prison was dark.

I stepped up to the building. The bottom of the window was just above the top of my head. I stood on tiptoe and stretched my hands up to the bars. "Hello?" I called in a hushed voice. "Curzon? Anyone?"

The nasty fellow who had tried to steal my bucket on my first visit, Dibdin, leaned his face against the bars. He had a blanket around his shoulders and Curzon's hat upon his head. "Won't let you in no more, eh?"

"They changed the rules. Can you fetch my brother, please? Sir?"

"He's sleepin'."

I wanted to pull the bars apart, snatch the hat from his head, and thrash him with my fists and shoes, but that was impossible. I forced honey into my voice, and a humble tone. "Well, then, may I please speak to your sergeant?"

"Sarge is dead." He turned his head and spat. "I'm in charge now. I'll take the victuals you brought."

I started to reach into the bucket to hand the scones through the bars, but stopped. "How do I know my brother's not dead, too? Wake him up, please."

Dibdin opened his mouth but closed it without a word. His hunger was stronger than his temper, it seemed. He turned to someone in the cell. "Get the black boy over here."

A moment later, Curzon appeared at the window. He was shaking so badly he could barely stand, his eyes half-closed, teeth chattering. He had no blanket around him and there were puke stains on the front of his shirt. His gold earring was missing, too.

"Curzon! Curzon!" I hissed. "What ails you? What can I do?"

He did not hear me, or could not. He was insensible of his own name and where he was.

Dibdin joined Curzon at the window. "Terrible, ain't it, how fevers and pox tear through this place?"

There was hollow laughter in the cell.

"Give him his hat back," I said. "And a blanket. Is he getting his rations?"

He did not answer me. That was an answer in itself. The prison was not a place of shared hardship anymore; it was a hole of desperation.

"You bloody beast," I swore. "How dare you let him starve?" The words flew out of my mouth without pause.

"Who are you to reprimand me, girl?" he snarled, putting his face up to the bars. His breath stank of rotting teeth, and snot pooled at the edge of his nostrils. "He's a slave. He will not be treated same as free men." He wiped his nose with the back of his hand. "But you can remedy that," he said. "With ease."

I tried to keep my voice steady. "How so?"

Curzon was seized by a fit of coughing so violent I feared his ribs would crack. He choked on his spittle and fought for breath, then finally relaxed back into his stupor, leaning against the window.

Dibdin glanced back at the other men in the cell before continuing. "Our Captain Morse is on parole, lodged at the Golden Hill Tavern, we hear. Go there, tell him the men have fever and pox. One of our lads, Bridgebane, has a father in Piscataway with money and influence. If the captain can get word to him, Bridgebane's father could arrange for a proper physician to attend us here."

Curzon coughed again and moaned. Sweat glistened on his forehead.

"And the doctor would see to my brother," I said.

Dibdin hesitated, then gave a nod. "Aye."

"And he gets a blanket and food."

Dibdin said something to a man I couldn't see. A blanket appeared on Curzon's shoulders. Curzon clutched it around himself.

"And his hat." My voice was ice.

Dibdin removed the hat and placed it on Curzon's head. "Lay him down," he instructed. "On the rushes, not the bare floor."

Someone helped Curzon away from the window.

I had no choice.

I handed the jam-covered burnt scones up to the window. Dibdin stuck the first one in his mouth, then passed the others to the men who suddenly crowded the window.

"If he dies, you'll not see me again," I warned.

"Understood," he said.

I found Captain Morse carrying out rubbish for the tavern keeper. He was a well-fed man wearing the brown coat trimmed with white that signified he was a prisoner of war. There was a big gap between his front teeth, but they looked clean enough.

He joined me in the shadows of the alley and listened as I quickly explained my mission.

"I'll try to get word to Bridgebane's family tonight. It is against all the laws of war to treat prisoners so badly." He paced angrily. "How often can you stop here?"

"Every morning."

"Good. Tell Dibdin I'll see what I can do to ease their suffering, though I fear it will not be enough."

"My brother is among the prisoners," I said. "He's ill. Can you . . . ?"

"Can I see to it that he is given his share of whatever Bridgebane provides? I surely will. Your brother was calm and brave during the final battle. He's a true soldier."

The crow of a rooster interrupted him. The sun was fighting through the leaden clouds.

I picked up the buckets. "I have to hurry."

He nodded. "Thank you for your help . . . my apologies, but I do not know your name."

"I am called Sal."

"Do you carry a last name as well, Sal?"

I hesitated. According to Madam, my surname was Lockton, but it tasted foul in my mouth. I shook my head.

He smiled. "Just Sal, then. Good day to you, Just Sal."

Lucky for me the overcast morn caused the other servants to sleep past their normal time. By the time Hannah and Mary staggered up from the cellar, I had the porridge bubbling and the tea steeping.

I could not eat nor drink a thing for my belly was tied up with fear. My thoughts chased round and round my brainpan. I could not visit the prison daily. I was sure to be caught and punished. But I had to visit the prison daily. Curzon's life depended on it. But someone would see me and was sure to remember the mark on my face. Word would get back to Madam, and she would tell Colonel Hawkins and he would set someone to follow me and Captain Morse would be flogged for passing on messages and the prisoners in Curzon's cell would all be hung and buried in the pit.

When I thought what they might do to me, I ran to the necessary and had me a good puking. But the next day, I made my way up there again–food for the prisoners, water for the Locktons, and every once in a while, a message to the gap-toothed man in the brown coat at the Golden Hill Tavern.

A few nights later, there was a terrible hullabaloo between Madam and the master when he announced at supper that he was planning to travel on the next ship to London. He would carry messages to Parliament, conduct his own business, and likely return to New York by the summer.

Madam was not pleased. First she argued that he ought not go, then she argued yes, he should go, and he should take her with him. When he refused, she threw a goblet in the fireplace and carried on so loudly that the Master and Colonel Hawkins finally called for the carriage and left for a tavern.

Madam dosed herself with strong wine after that and went to bed.

That night the temperatures fell so far below freezing that the biggest fire could not keep away the chill. I moved my pallet as close to the hearth as I dared and sat with all my clothes, my cloak, and my blanket wrapped around me. 'Twas so cold, I could not sleep. General Washington and his men were holed up in Morristown. Folks said they were in desperate need of stockings and food. I could scarce credit how hungry men with frozen feet could win a war. They were fools to even try.

I waited as the clock first chimed eleven times, then twelve, watching the firelight and trying not to ponder. When I got up to add wood to the fire, my feet wandered themselves to the pantry, and my hands pulled the loose board there. Under the board were some sheets of newsprint I had saved, the lead piece from the statue of King George, my seeds, and the book given me by the stationer. I carried the book to my warm pallet and quietly untied the twine and removed the paper wrapping.

I opened the cover. A fellow named Thomas Paine wrote the little book. He called it *Common Sense*.

Momma always said that common sense was far from common, that's why it was so special when you found it.

The first sentence in the book did not seem to contain any.

"Some writers have so confounded society with government, as to leave little or no distinction between them; whereas they are not only different, but have different origins. Society is produced by our wants, and government by our wickedness . . ."

It took four readings to figure out the meaning, which I took to be that the life of folks is different than the world what rules over them. Paine sure did dance a long time with the notion before he said it.

I closed the book and longed for Robinson Crusoe, still stranded in the study where Colonel Hawkins was asleep. I dared not rescue him.

I opened the book again and attacked the next sentence.

CHAPTER XXXVIII

Tuesday, December 24–Wednesday, December 25, 1776

CHRISTMAS IS COME, HANG ON THE POT,
LET SPITS TURN ROUND, AND OVENS BE HOT;
BEEF, PORK, AND POULTRY, NOW PROVIDE
TO FEAST THY NEIGHBORS AT THIS TIDE;
THEN WASH ALL DOWN WITH GOOD WINE AND BEER,
AND SO WITH MIRTH CONCLUDE THE YEAR.
—*ROYAL VIRGINIA ALMANAC*

I SPENT THE DAY BEFORE CHRISTMAS fighting a holly bush with a pair of scissors. Madam required its twigs and berries for her decorating schemes. My morning dash to the prison, pump, and tavern had gone wonderful fast. There were no new messages to pass from Curzon's companions to Captain Morse, and the doctor secured by the rich Bridgebane family had delivered potions and bleedings to all, as promised. Curzon was spending most of his days sleeping, but he was not dead.

And it was Christmas Eve day.

The holly bits were tied with pine branches and set on the sills of the street-facing windows. Glass bowls of red berries were set on small tables in the drawing room, library, and the front parlor. Madam had two soldiers hang a ball of mistletoe in the front hall. This provided great merriment amongst the men and some blushing on the part of their wives.

I had never seen a house decorated with tree branches to celebrate the birth of the baby Jesus, but it did pretty up the place. The best was when Madam told us to hang dried rosemary throughout; that cut right through the lingering stench of boots and belchings.

In keeping with tradition, I was to have Christmas Day free from work. I pondered hard on what I should do with so many hours for myself. Christmas at home had meant eating Momma's bread pudding with maple syrup and nutmeg, and reading the Gospel of Matthew out loud whilst Ruth played in Momma's lap. I was miles away from celebrating like that. I tried to bury the remembery, but it kept floating to the top of my mind like a cork in a stormy sea, and foolish tears spilled over.

I finally decided to treat myself to a long stroll through all of New York: from the waterfront north to Chambers Street, and a side-to-side wander from the East River to the North River, which some had taken to calling the Hudson. For one day, my legs would be my own, not at the beck and call of others.

On Christmas morning, Lady Seymour presented me with a new pair of black leather shoes that did not pinch any of my toes. Madam gave the soldierwives each a coin. She gave me nothing.

When we returned home from the service at St. Paul's Chapel, Madam explained that my day off would begin as soon as I had finished serving the midday meal. Sarah had cooked it in advance: a sirloin of beef, smoked ham, onion pie, and a plum pudding for dessert. Master and Madam both filled up on the onion pie and hardly touched the fresh-baked bread. Lady Seymour ate enough for an undersized mouse.

I et porridge and beef for my Christmas dinner, a right curious combination but a tasty one.

As I cleared away the table, Madam informed me that my day off would begin after I brought in wood and washed up the dishes. Lady Seymour fired off a cannonblast of a glare at her, but Madam pretended not to notice, and the master kept his face planted in his newspaper. There had been heat rising between the two women for days. Madam was prepared to row the aunt to Charleston to get rid of her.

After the meal, the master went to order the carriage to take them to some admiral's house for eggnog. Lady Seymour said she was going to rest and required nothing of me. As the lady limped to her chamber and the master disappeared down the stairs, I picked up the tray that held the last of the dishes. Madam poured herself another cup of tea.

"One moment, girl," she said.

I paused. "Yes, ma'am?"

Madam said nothing while she stirred the sugar into her tea. She sipped, wrinkled her nose, added another spoonful, stirred, then sipped again. She set the teacup in the saucer and examined the walnut tarts on the plate before her.

I stood like a statue holding the tray. Would she take away the rest of my day? Force me to wash the table linens or starch the master's shirts?

Madam gave her tea another stir. "You have been idling around the Bridewell prison."

My heart stopped.

She picked up a tart, considered its scorched bottom, and returned it to the plate. "My husband's aunt says that you visit the prison at her direction, bringing tablescraps not good enough for pigs. She declared that forgiving and caring for the enemy is doing the Lord's work."

My heart started up again, racing so fast I thought it might escape my body.

Madam picked up a second tart and scratched off the scorched bits with her knife before taking a bite. She chewed, sipped more tea, and swallowed. "My husband's aunt is a blithering idiot who has completely lost her wits. You should have told me of her requests at once."

She finally looked at me, her eyes cold as frozen coins. "You represent this house, girl. Your visits could put us under suspicion of having rebel tendencies. I will be not ruined by you, be it through innocence, as Aunt proclaims, or insolence, which I suspect. I forbid you to go to the prison."

My arms shook from the weight of the tray as well as her words. She could do anything: order me to the stocks, another branding, or a public whipping of hundreds of lashes. She could beat me herself. She could sell me as she had done Ruth, only place me with the cruelest master, who'd work me to death in days.

A pearl of sweat trickled down my cheek.

Madam finished the tart and wiped the corners of her mouth with her fingertip. "While my husband's aunt lives here, my hands are tied." She reached for another tart. "But she'll be soon gone, one way or another, and Elihu will be in England." She popped the entire tart into her mouth, chewed, then licked her fingers.

"That is the day you should fear, girl."

After the carriage left and dishes were washed and Lady Seymour was sound asleep, I started my free day, still trembling from Madam's threat. How could I get word to Curzon that I couldn't bring food any longer? Would Dibdin let him starve if I stopped being his messenger? What if I ignored Madam's rule and continued to visit the Bridewell?

I walked block after block pondering. I walked past the ropeworks and the brewery, to the orchards on the east side, silent under the snow. I walked past houses that had letters "G R," *George Rex*, carved into the front door, property stolen in the name of the King.

Like Madam had carved her letters into my soul, burned the mark into my skin.

She can do anything. I can do nothing.

The ashes of sadness and the buzzing bees of my melancholy all spun a storm inside of me, and I walked and walked until my new shoes rubbed blisters all over my feet and the blisters popped. I took off the shoes and walked in the snow. Once my feet were froze enough, the blisters didn't hurt.

As the sun ran for the west, rowdy songs started up in the taverns and groggeries. I found myself on the shore of the North River, just above the Battery. Empty rowboats were tied up to a wharf. As the tide pulled out to the ocean, they bobbed and bumped against each other. A few lights twinkled across the water in faraway New Jersey. I thought of all the ancestors waiting at the water's edge for their stolen children to come home. Waiting and waiting and waiting . . .

A thought surfaced through my ashes.

She cannot chain my soul.

Yes, she could hurt me. She'd already done so. But what was one more beating? A flogging, even? I would bleed, or not.

Scar, or not. Live, or not. But she could no longer harm Ruth, and she could not hurt my soul, not unless I gave it to her.

This was a new notion to me and a curious one.

A group of soldiers singing loud as they could swayed down the street, very muddy in drink. I hid in the shadows until they were gone, then headed back to Wall Street. I passed several houses filled with Christmas carols: "Joy to the World" and "I Saw Three Ships" and "The First Noel." A fat candle glowed on a parlor windowsill of a house on a corner, set there to guide someone home.

The Locktons and Lady Seymour were all retired for the night by the time I returned. The house was still empty of soldiers and their wives. I built up the fire in the hearth, set my shoes and damp stockings to dry in front of it, and rubbed a calendula salve on my blisters.

Christmas, Momma's voice reminded. *Keep Christmas.*

For the second time on the very same day, tears threatened. I rubbed them away and vowed not to cry again. 'Twas a nuisance.

I found myself studying the loaf of bread on the table. A sharp knife showed up in my hand and the loaf was soon cut into fat slices. A chipped crockery bowl appeared from the pantry, alongside the butter and eggs and milk and the sugar loaf and the nutmeg grater and the small amber flask.

I baked me a maple syrup bread pudding in the Rhode Island style.

While it cooked, I cleaned myself up good and proper. I thought about stealing a piece of Madam's rose-scented soap, but that would have made me smell like her. I preferred to smell like strong lye. I washed my arms and legs and the back of my neck and my ears and my face and I dried myself with a soft, clean rag. I frowned as I stepped back into my clothes. I'd grown some and they didn't fit proper. I'd let out the seams of the bodice as much as I could and taken out the hem of the skirt. Much more growing and I'd look a right scandal.

But I wouldn't think on that now. I was trying to make a Christmas.

I pulled on my dry stockings and stepped into my new shoes even though they rubbed fierce on the popped blisters. I put the bowl of bread pudding into a basket, tied on my cloak, and wound up my hands in rags to keep the frost from biting.

I walked out the back door. It was not yet midnight, so in truth, 'twas still the day I could call my own. I set my path westward to the burned-over district, to Canvastown.

The line where September's fire had stopped was sharp cut. First a house with no damage, next a house still bearing black streaks of soot and smoke, then a field of ruin, with makeshift hovels crafted from tent, brick, and scorched timbers. Rats nibbled on frozen garbage heaps. The smell of the fire still lingered, tainted with the smell of filth and decay.

But in the bleakness, there were spots of hope. A wreath was stuck on the front of a tent. Children's clothes hung from a clothesline, stiff with ice, but still sweet-looking. A butter churn stood watch over a neat stack of fresh-split wood. Smoke swirled slow from the top of a chimney, dipped at the roof line, then rose up to the stars.

I lifted my face to the sky and for the first time in much too long, I prayed. I prayed as hard as I could, without words or shapes or fancy talking. I just prayed. When I was done, I felt cleaner than I had after my bath.

I walked on until I found a hut built against a lone brick

wall. From inside came sounds of a family, the poppa's low rumble, the momma's bright laugh, and giggling children who had been allowed to stay up much too late and who did not want to fall asleep.

I greeted them through the piece of canvas that served as their front door. The hovel fell silent, then the canvas was pushed aside and the father stepped out, a musket in his hand. His wife came right behind him, though he told her to stay inside.

It took some convincing to explain my mission, but I spoke polite and firm and held out the bread pudding, and the children snuck out in their nightclothes and just about dove into the bowl. The mother took the basket and said "Thank you" and then "Thank you, again," and then "Thank you most, most kindly," and they went back inside.

I hummed a carol as I walked away, finally feeling at peace.

CHAPTER XXXIX

Thursday, December 26– Tuesday, December 31, 1776

IN THE ARMY AT PRESENT, MERIT IS MEASURED ONLY BY RANK. THOSE WHO ARE HIGH IN RANK ARE CLEVER FELLOWS. THE LOW ARE SMALL FOLKS– AND THOSE WHO HAVE NONE AT ALL, LIKE US, ARE POOR DEVILS–WE ARE NOBODYS. WE HAVE NOTHING.
–SAMUEL TENNY WRITING TO HIS FRIEND PETER TURNER, ABOUT HIS FRUSTRATION WITH THE PRIVILEGES OF OFFICERS

TWO DAYS LATER SARAH HAD ME go with her to the fish market. Her back was hurting her fierce, and I was to carry the cod and halibut needed for a fish chowder. The market was crowded with folk whose cupboards had been cleaned out by the Christmas feasting, and Sarah muttered rude things. Her growing discomfort had put her in a constant temper.

The cod was easy enough to purchase, but stall after stall turned up no halibut. Sarah insisted that haddock or catfish would not do, so we marched on. The air was thick with the cries of the stall owners promising the juiciest fish, the freshest fish, and fish fit for the King himself.

Before dawn I had made the trip to the Tea Water Pump, but I had not dared visit the prison or Captain Morse's tavern. I was still confuddled about what to do. My thoughts wandered. I did not realize that Sarah had moved ahead of me in the crowd until a great shout went up. An oyster seller's cart had overturned in front of the carp stall, and the two men were hollering at each other. The crowd halted and I had no place to turn. Sarah's white cloth cap bobbed away in the distance as I looked for a path out of the crowd, but bodies pushed in from all sides to watch the two men arguing.

When a hand grabbed my arm, I gasped.

"Apologies, Just Sal," Captain Morse said as he released me. His eyes were tired, but his cheeks were flushed.

My mouth gaped open like that of a fish breathing its last. I shook my head. He couldn't talk to me in view of all! There was no mistaking what he was, dressed in that brown-and-white coat. I turned first one way, then the other, but bodies were packed around me tight as could be.

Morse kept his eyes on the arguing men but leaned his face close enough to mine that I could hear him whisper, "We must talk."

Sarah had realized I was no longer with her. Her cap stopped, then slowly started back toward us. Her husband was a British gunner. If she saw me talking to a rebel officer . . .

"Go away," I muttered.

"I have news for my men."

The oyster seller picked up a carp and shook it in the other man's face. The crowd laughed. Sarah plowed toward me.

"I beg you," Morse whispered. "Please."

Soldiers appeared on the edge of the crowd to restore order.

"Come up to the tavern."

"Yes, yes," I told the captain. "I'll come this afternoon. Now go away!"

The crowd melted under the eyes of the armed soldiers. The carp seller was explaining the ruckus to a sergeant while the oyster seller reloaded his cart. Sarah kicked oysters out of her way as she approached.

"Where in the name of all that's holy did you get to?" she asked.

"I was trapped in the crowd," I said. "I called but you could not hear me."

She grunted and handed me a small fish with glassy eyes. "This will have to do. Halibut is rare as hen's teeth today."

I settled it in the basket atop the fat cod and followed Sarah as she headed away from the market. We walked in silence for a few blocks, her concentrating on her huffing and puffing, me trying to figure if I dared go up to the tavern. The sky promised more snow. How long would Dibdin wait before reclaiming Curzon's hat and blanket?

We crossed the street. "Miss Sarah, ma'am?" I asked, sweet as honey.

"What is it?"

I chose my words with care. "Has Madam Lockton said anything about me, in your hearing?"

She tilted her head a bit as she looked at me. "Aye, this morn, matter of fact. Said you wasn't allowed to go to that blasted water pump. Said I should send one of the other girls, even tho' the sun not be up at that time of day, even tho' the streets be covered in ice."

Sarah reached for my elbow as we trod upon a slick patch of cobblestones.

"But I like getting out," I said. "And I don't mind the chore."

We reached a stretch where ashes had been thrown onto

the ice and the going was safer. "I don't answer to her," Sarah said as she released my arm. "I answer to the King's army. I'd be right pleased if you kept fetching the water. Makes my life easier."

She stopped and put her hands on her back, breathing heavily. Her baby belly was so big she could have loaded it in a wheelbarrow and pushed it in front of her. She caught me studying her and gave a quick smile.

"The babe will come soon," she said.

"It'll be a joyous day," I said. "I'll keep getting the water, but . . ."

"But what?"

"Could you please not tell Madam?"

Sarah stretched to one side and winced. "What she don't know won't hurt her. It's not like she's up at that hour anyways."

After the midday meal, I contrived to overturn the pitcher that held the tea water, dumping it on the floor.

"Clumsy dolt," Hannah scolded as I knelt to clean the floor with rags.

"Don't be looking at me to trudge up there and get more for Her High Mightiness," Mary said from her chair by the window. She squinted and sewed another stitch. "I've got to hem these breeches before the light fades."

"I'll run up and fetch it," I said. "Double-time, I promise."

Sarah gave me a good hard stare, sensing she did not have the entire picture before her.

"It's your neck," she finally said. "Mind she don't see you leave."

I near ran up to the Golden Hill Tavern, my raw blisters hurting with every step. Captain Morse was idling on the porch, smoking a pipe. He disappeared inside when he saw me and was waiting in the alley when I reached it.

"Here," he handed me a loaf of bread.

"You made me come up here for this?" I asked.

"Take it to Dibdin," he said, fighting a smile. "There's a note baked inside."

"A note?"

"It contains wondrous news." He looked ready to jump out of his skin. "Washington has beaten them!"

"Sir?"

He clenched his fists and unclenched them. "On Christmas night the general led a surprise attack on Trenton. He beat the Hessians–killed a handful and took more than nine hundred prisoner."

"Are you sure?" I thought someone told him a falsehood. The British officers I knew were confident the American army was fallen apart.

"Positively," he said with a grin.

"But won't that make the British mad?" I asked.

"I truly hope so. I hope the King is so upset he jumps up and down on his crown. This war is not over, not by a long shot."

I handed the bread back. "I'll tell them the news, but I cannot pass a note. That could land me in jail."

He shoved the loaf back at me. "You are a serving girl delivering a tavern loaf to the starving prisoners. You don't know about the note."

"But why is it necessary?"

"The men need to see my signature to know this is truth.

They have endured so much, Sal. Don't deprive them of this chance to celebrate. It will strengthen their spirits."

I pulled up the hood of my cloak to hide my face as I approached the prison. The Commons was filled with drilling soldiers, much more than usual. Their officers barked commands with urgency, the men marched grim faced, swords flapping against their legs, rifles bouncing on their shoulders. Perhaps the captain's news was indeed the truth.

I hurried behind the building to the right window. I stood on tiptoe and squished the loaf through the bars.

Dibdin's face appeared at the window.

"There's a note inside," I whispered. "Tear into it carefully." I ran away before he could answer, willing my feet to move faster.

I had walked a block south when an enormous roar erupted from the prison—hundreds of throats cheering, hooting, hollering; hundreds of hands clapping and feet stomping with joy. The noise was such that folks stopped what they were doing and ran out of doors to stare.

The news spread from the prison as fast as it had spread from cell to cell: The rebels had attacked instead of running. The rebels had advanced instead of retreating. The rebels had won a battle.

Folks could scarce credit it.

CHAPTER XL

Wednesday, January 1–Tuesday, January 7, 1777

IT IS WITH MUCH CONCERN THAT I AM TO INFORM YOUR LORDSHIP THE UNFORTUNATE AND UNTIMELY DEFEAT AT TRENTON HAS THROWN US FURTHER BACK, THAN WAS AT FIRST APPREHENDED, FROM THE GREAT ENCOURAGEMENT GIVEN TO THE REBELS.
—BRITISH GENERAL WILLIAM HOWE WRITING TO LORD GEORGE GERMAIN, SECRETARY OF STATE FOR AMERICAN COLONIES AFTER THE AMERICAN VICTORY AT TRENTON

JUST AFTER THE NEW YEAR CAME word of another shocking victory for the rebels, this one at Princeton in New Jersey. Washington's troops chased the British from the battlefield, killed a passel of them, and took a couple of hundred prisoners. Folks could scarce credit this, neither. Colonel Hawkins let out a roar in the study when the news was delivered and hit the unfortunate messenger on the head with a rolled-up map. Then he called for his horse and galloped off to headquarters.

Within a day, the British promised boiled peas and rice with butter twice a week for their American prisoners. But they still did not allow fires in the Bridewell cells. The men had to eat their meat raw. Their chamber pots froze solid at night.

The master's trip to London was moved up so that he could deliver news of the setbacks to the Parliament and King. Madam had finally accommodated herself to the notion of his voyage and had found a way to turn it to her advantage. Whilst we prepared Lockton's clothes for the journey, she wrote out long lists of items she wanted him to buy in England.

I kept to the kitchen and cellar and woodpile when she was awake, but made my trips up island each day before dawn, looking over my shoulder at every sound, choosing a different path daily. The constant worry et a hole in my belly. Curzon was stronger and told me not to fret, for he was not coughing up blood and his bowels were in fine working order. But he always asked me to come back on the morrow.

The day of the master's departure, I roused myself extra early on account of I feared Madam might do the same. I deposited stale rolls and burnt hunks of pork on the windowsill of Curzon's cell, then crossed the Commons on my way to the pump. There were a few folk out on their own early-morning errands, all bundled in cloaks and blanket coats and shawls and scarves wrapped high.

"You there!" a loud voice called out. Everyone stopped to look. "You there, girl!"

Oh, no.

A British soldier hurried toward me. I relaxed some when I saw his face. It was the mountain-sized guard who had let me visit Curzon's cell when he was first imprisoned. The one who liked to eat.

"Haven't seen you round," he said as he neared me.

I bobbed quickly. "The rules don't allow civilians in the cells."

He lowered his rifle to the ground and eyed my bucket. "True enough. Wot you bring him today?"

"Bread crusts and burnt meat, sir."

He wrinkled his nose. "Wot about yesterday?"

"Yesterday was kidney pie and stale almond cake, sir."

He shook his head and licked his lips. "Sorry I missed that, I am. Wouldn't hurt to drop off a bite now and then to one such as myself, would it?"

"No, sir," I answered. "I shall remember that."

He tilted his head to the side. "Your master ever hire you out?"

'Twas common in those days for folks to hire out their slaves to make money. The slaves did not see the money, of course. But if I had the chance to work away from the prying eyes of Madam, I'd be grateful for it.

"Yes, sir," I lied.

"We need a maid to clean out the cells. Dying men do puke out some terrible things, they do. You're a steadfast girl. Tell your mistress we'd pay her the going rate for your services."

"I shall tell her, sir."

He shouldered his rifle. "I'm on the night watch now. The name is Fisher. Bring me round some cake, and I'll keep an eye on your brother."

"Thank you, Mister Fisher, sir. I shall."

"No kidney pie, tho'. Kidneys sour my gut somefink terrible."

The master left for London with much muttering on the part of his wife. She did not take to her bed as I expected but was driven round to the home of Missus Taylor to play cards and, no doubt, complain about her husband.

While she was gone, Sarah birthed her baby boy in the

cellar. I was sore tempted to sneak down the stairs and watch. I'd seen kittens and calves come into the world but not babies. I had a powerful curiosity about it, but I dared not. I kept water boiling for the midwife and stuck cloth in my ears to keep out the noise.

When Sarah stopped hollering, I crept down the stairs to see the babe. He was a round-headed fat fellow with big eyes and bigger ears. "George," Sarah called him.

"You named him after the King?" Hannah asked.

"Perhaps," Sarah said cheerfully. "We never figured the colonists would hold on this long. My man was saying the other night that mebbe the King should stop the war. Mebbe the babe and us might stay here, not sail home. 'Plenty of room here,' he said." She kissed the baby's nose. "A name like George is a good one on either side of the ocean."

"Shhh!" warned Mary.

The next day, Sarah and her George moved to a house set aside for new mothers attached to the army. I was sad to see them go, for I had wanted to hold the little one and make him laugh.

Lady Seymour wanted to hear all of the details about the new baby. I thought maybe I could visit Sarah and ask her to bring the little lad by. Something about a baby always brings old folks back to life.

When I mentioned this notion to the Lady, she just shook her head.

"Not until this pestilence has left my lungs." She coughed into a stained handkerchief. "Heaven knows when that will be."

Her health was changeable and flighty. One day she'd feel

strong and lively and she'd eat three meals and drink a gallon of tea; the next she'd lie abed with fever, looking so poorly it tempted Madam to order the coffin made.

I went to place another log on the fire. Lady Seymour was lying propped up on pillows in her bed. She shook her head. "No more wood, I am warm enough. Please sit down, Isabel."

"Ma'am?"

"I would like you to sit down, either in the chair or on the edge of the bed. I should like to talk to you."

It was improper for a servant to sit with a lady as tho' they were companions, but she asked me direct, so I sat myself in the chair that was close to the fire. I could not figure what we needed to conversate on. She hadn't sent me for a newspaper or sweets for days and days. Had I displeased her?

"Thank you." She sat back and used her right hand to place her left hand in her lap. "I will soon meet my Maker, Isabel. I am a sinner in need of forgiveness."

I relaxed. 'Twas the pull of Death that made old people go funny. Miss Mary Finch went the same way toward the end. Clouds would roll into her eyes, and she would talk nonsense for hours. Me and Ruth just sat polite and listened. The trick with addled old folks was to be agreeable.

"We all seek forgiveness, Lady Seymour."

"I wanted to buy you," she said.

I wasn't sure I heard that right. "Beg pardon, ma'am?"

"I tried to buy you from Anne after I first met you. She refused and we argued like a pair of fishwives. I rather lost my temper." She chuckled. "Hadn't done that for thirty years."

I knew not what to say.

She studied her useless hand. "When Elihu returned from exile, I should have demanded you be placed in my household. I was horrified by your treatment. And, of course, your poor sister. But then the fire . . ." Her gaze returned to the hearth. "I regret I did not force the matter. You would have suited my household."

It would have eased her mind if I thanked her for wanting to buy me away from Madam. I tried to be grateful but could not. A body does not like being bought and sold like a basket of eggs, even if the person who cracks the shells is kind.

"Isabel?"

She awaited some word from me. I did not know how to explain myself. It was like talking to her maid, Angelika, who was so much like me and at the same time so much different. We two had no string of words that could tie us together.

"Yes, ma'am. Thank you for telling me this." That was all I could muster.

"Forgive me," she said. "I am a clumsy old woman."

There was a shout from the drawing room upstairs, where Colonel Hawkins and his men had been meeting. I stood. "The soldierwives are all visiting Sarah . . . I should . . ."

"Go on," she said, closing her eyes.

Colonel Hawkins was in a right foul mood on account of all the forms he had to fill out and reports that were late. The war seemed fought with as much paper as bullets, what with the letters and the passes and permissions piled on the table, orders received and recorded, recordings of conferences noted down.

When I entered, he hollered that the room was colder than a barn and called me all manner of rude names.

I chose the wood for his fire very carefully, the greenest, dampest logs in the entire woodpile, guaranteed to smolder and sputter without giving off any heat and even less light. After a frigid hour, he left for headquarters. It took all my might not to crack a smile.

The grandfather clock ticked off the minutes.

Madam would not return home for a goodly while. She was a terrible card player, but she had loads of money to lose, so her companions would keep her at the faro table as long as possible. I peeked in Lady Seymour's door. She was wrapped up in her coverlet and sleeping; the blankets barely moved when she took breath.

I pulled out *Common Sense* from its hiding place and read by firelight. In truth, there were some pages that I jumped over for I found it hard to figure their meaning. But I gathered many of his thoughts: Americans had good cause to overthrow their British masters, a person born to wealth was not born to rule over others, and 'twas good and proper to fight injustice.

I kept the mending basket close to hand in case I needed to hide my crime.

CHAPTER XLI

Tuesday, January 7–
Wednesday, January 15, 1777

It is not in the power of the Smiles or Frowns of Her Majesty to affect me either by conferring pleasure or giveing Pain—I was wholy incapable of takeing the place She seemed to assign me when I was presented to Her. I suppose She assented to the assertions . . . that there were no People who had so much impudence as the Americans—for there was not any People bred even at Courts who had so much confidence as the Americans—this was because they did not tremble, Cringe, and fear, in the Presence of Majesty.
—Nabby Adams, daughter of Abigail and John Adams, on meeting Queen Charlotte of England

When Madam woke the next morn, her first command was for hot scones. Her second was that the seamstress must be fetched immediately. The British commandant was throwing a ball in honor of Queen Charlotte's birthday in ten days' time. Madam required a new gown for such an occasion. Perhaps two.

I learnt of all this when I returned from the market with a fresh-killt chicken. Hannah, who had taken over the bosslady job from Sarah after the baby was born, was preparing a cherry pie. Mary sat by the window, mending one of Madam's skirts.

The notion of a ball for a queen confuddled me. "That's a long voyage for a celebration," I said.

Hannah laughed. "No, you ninny. The Queen isn't coming. How could she? She's got ten children to take care of, plus all them castles."

"Eleven," added Mary. "She popped out a new one last spring."

"Even tho' the Queen can't come, the officers always hold a ball in her honor," Hannah said as she rolled out the pie dough. "Gives them a good excuse to eat too much, drink too much, and make proper fools of themselves whilst dancing."

I pulled out the feather bag and a basin. "And Madam Lockton is attending?"

"The colonel will be her escort." Mary bit her thread in two. "All the rich folk will be there."

I ripped a handful of feathers from the chicken and stuffed them in the bag. "Does Madam require anything of us?"

"Not yet," Hannah said, carefully laying the dough in the pie plate. "That will change, no doubt."

"I seen the Queen Herself, you know," Mary said, squinting at her stitches.

"With your own eyes?" asked Hannah. "I don't believe you."

"Well, I seen her carriage and she was in it. The backside of the carriage, mind . . . actually the backside of the troops guarding the backside of the carriage. But I saw the wheels. Bent down to do it." She threaded another needle. "Bet you don't know her name."

"Her Majesty," said Hannah.

"Proves you're not a Londoner," Mary said. "Her proper name is Her Majesty, Queen Charlotte of Great Britain, Dutchess Sophia Charlotte of Mecklenburg-Strelitz."

"How do you remember all them names when you can't remember from one minute to the next how much salt goes into the biscuits?" asked Hannah.

"Biscuits are not as important as the Queen. I practiced her name from the time I was a girl, case the day ever come when she saw me on the street and I could call out her entire gracious name. If I did that, her carriage would stop and she'd make me a lady-in-waiting on account of my good manners."

There was a moment of silence while the two women considered this, then a loud outburst as they near fell over themselves in laughter.

After dinner, Lady Seymour had a frightful seizure of the apoplexy. Looked just like one of Ruth's fits, except not with so much shaking. She fell into a sleep so deep I thought she was stone dead, but every so often she'd take a breath and once, she opened her eyes.

When she woke the next morning, she could not speak nor move her legs. Doctor Dastuge arrived and bled her and stuck pins in her limbs and gave her a bitter tea. In truth, there was nothing could make her better. I was told to tend her again, as I had right after the fire. I fed her and held the teacup to her lips and wiped her chin when she dribbled and helped her with the chamber pot business. This last was most distressing for her, and she cried. Then I wiped the tears from her face.

I heard Madam ask the doctor plain when the old lady would die. The doctor could not answer her.

I figured Madam wanted Lady Seymour to die as soon as possible, but not before the Queen's ball. If the house was in mourning, it wouldn't be proper for Madam to dance with the admiral and make merry.

A week before the ball, Madam ordered that Lady Seymour be moved to the parlor bedchamber downstairs so she could reclaim the largest bedchamber for herself. After two privates had carried the Lady down, and she was propped up on her pillows so she could look out the window, Madam called me upstairs.

"I want this room aired and the linens boiled, girl. It smells of decay in here."

The work of the day was simple and heavy: strip the bed, haul down the linens for to wash, clean out the hearth, open the windows and wash them inside and out, take the rugs down and beat them in the yard, sweep and mop the floor, take the rugs back in, close the windows, and give all the wood a polish.

When the chamber was clean, Madam told me to open the windows again and let them stand open all afternoon to make sure there was no lingering pestilence in the air.

I did as I was told. The doctor came right before supper and gave Lady Seymour a potion that would make the night pass quickly for her.

When she was ready for bed, Madam called for me to bring up a warming pan filled with coals and run it between the sheets because they were chilled and still a wee bit damp.

I did what she asked, then returned to the kitchen, dumped the coals in the hearth, and crept under my own blanket.

She called for me again. The sheets were still too cold for her liking.

I refilled the warming pan, carried it up the stairs, and warmed her bed. Then I stoked the fire in her hearth before returning down the stairs.

The third time she called for me, I was sore tempted to dump the glowing coals onto her bed, let it blaze, and ask if that was warm enough. But I did not. I performed the task she gave me. And when she called a quarter hour later, I did it again.

The sun rose bright the next day, catching in the icicles that hung from the eaves and jumping off the snow like a mirror. The linens pegged out on the line were froze stiff as wood and covered in a lacework of ice. The clouds scuttled away and the sun blazed, turning the yard into a garden of jewels.

Ruth would love this. If we were free and at home in Rhode Island and these were our sheets and our laundry lines and our snow, she'd dance like an angel.

The pictures in my brainpan caught me by surprise. I could not clear them away. She'd clap her hands at the sight of the frozen laundry, she'd twirl in the spinning swirls of snow that lifted in the breeze, she'd plunge her hands into the bushes to pluck off the diamonds. She would do all these things and laugh and . . .

The wind tossed a handful of snow in my face and washed it all away.

Ruth would not see this. Never.

I dried my face. Why was I thinking of Ruth? I'd worked hard to pack her away from my mind, along with the thoughts of Momma and Poppa and the life Ruth and I were promised. Didn't help to ponder things that were forever gone. It only made a body restless and fill up with bees all wanting to sting something.

I kicked at the new snow. It rose up, a sparkling diamond breeze fit for a queen.

'Twas Lady Seymour who did it. Her with her begging forgiveness for not buying me and telling me I'd have been a good slave for her. Her with her wet eyes and skeleton hands. Did she never think about setting me free? That would be a fine question to ask. 'Course, there was no sense to asking it because her mouth didn't work anymore.

I carried the big laundry basket out to the sheets. I'd have to hang them in the kitchen else they wouldn't dry till spring.

Another picture hung itself in my mind, the poetry book in the stationer's shop. The one I'd been afraid to read. Miss Phillis Wheatley went free when her master released her. 'Twas on account of her fame, Momma said. Master Wheatley looked the fool for keeping a poetical genius enslaved in his household.

I'd heard of other slaves who bought their freedom, folks who were given their Sunday afternoons to work for themselves, who saved their pennies and farthings for years and years until they had piled up the hundred and fifty or two hundred pounds to buy their body and soul from their master. If I had Sunday afternoons free, I'd figure a way to earn my pennies. I could sew or hire out to scrub stables. I'd even clean the cells of the Bridewell, like that guard asked.

I took a long stick from the pile of kindling wood.

It would never happen. Madam would not allow it.

She was set on keeping my arms and legs dancing to her tune and my soul bound in her chains.

I pulled the stick back and cracked it against the side of the frozen bed linen. The ice shattered and fell to the ground, tinkling like pieces of falling stars.

CHAPTER XLII

Thursday, January 16– Saturday, January 18, 1777

WE HOLD THESE TRUTHS TO BE SELF-EVIDENT, THAT ALL MEN ARE CREATED EQUAL, THAT THEY ARE ENDOWED BY THEIR CREATOR WITH CERTAIN UNALIENABLE RIGHTS, THAT AMONG THESE ARE LIFE, LIBERTY AND THE PURSUIT OF HAPPINESS.
—DECLARATION OF INDEPENDENCE OF THE UNITED STATES OF AMERICA

DOCTOR DASTUGE VISITED LADY Seymour each morning and eve. She could nod her head yes and shake it no to his questions; yes, she knew who she was; no, she had no sensation in her feet nor her hands. She could barely chew milk-soaked bread and sip broth. Her mind had not gone soft, tho'. Her eyes blazed bright in her skull and followed me as I moved around the room, and when the doctor and Madam talked, she listened in right close. Plainly said, she was as much a prisoner in her broken body as Curzon was in his cell.

Madam's seamstress came near as frequent as the doctor. The birthday ball gown had a scarlet red underskirt topped with a short gown of Royal Navy blue, embroidered with gold. The hairdresser and Madam spent hours consulting prints of fashionable ladies in Paris so that they could design a suitable hairstyle. I was not privy to the details, but I heard Madam talking about jewels made of paste that would sit in her curls. She also wanted a small British flag to fly atop her locks, but the hairdresser talked her out of it.

Hannah and Mary talked about the ball every waking minute. I'm sure even the Queen herself would have grown tired of hearing about it. At noon, the guns at the Battery, which the British had taken to calling Fort George, would fire a royal salute. An hour later, the warships in the harbor would blast a response. At six o'clock, the guests would arrive at the ball, with trumpets playing and drums beating a welcome. The dancing would last until midnight, when the fireworks would explode over the harbor. After that, the banquet would begin.

There was no way under heaven that Madam would survive six hours of dancing without having something to eat.

I finished reading *Common Sense* the night before the ball. The bookseller was right; the words were dangerous, every one of them. I ought throw it in the fire but could not bring myself to do it. Mr. Paine knew how to stir up the pot; he went right after the King and attacked the crown on his head.

I laid down one long road of a sentence in my remembery: "For all men being originally equals, no one by birth could have a right to set up his own family in perpetual preference to all others for ever." Way I saw it, Mr. Paine was saying all people were the same, that no one deserved a crown or was born to be higher than another. That's why America could make its own freedom.

'Twas a wonder the book did not explode into flames in my hands.

I buried it back in its hidey-hole and laid myself down to sleep.

My eyes would not close. My thoughts were churned up like muddy water, with dangerous eels thrashing through it.

If an entire nation could seek its freedom, why not a girl? And if a girl was to seek her freedom, how could she do such a fool-headed thing? Especially a girl trapped in New York? Best thing would be to break into the desk of a British commander, steal a pass and forge her name and his name on it, and act free.

And pigs were likely to fly, too.

Plus, that girl seeking freedom would have to walk.

She could walk the mile from Wall Street to the north edge of the city. But then she'd run into the guards stationed there. She'd have to sneak past them and not get shot. Then she'd have eleven miles of running to the north edge of the island. If she took the Greenwich Road or the Post Road, she'd likely be captured by one in need of a slave or in need of the reward paid for a healthy runaway. If she stuck to the woods that ran up the center of the island, she could be et by a bear or drowned in a swamp. If angels guided her safe through the woods and she made the north edge, she'd have to get past the guards watching over King's Bridge, where New York Island touched the rest of America.

I rolled over, my back to the fire. That girl could more likely grab hold of the feet of a passing crow and bid him fly her to safety. Better yet, sprout her own wings.

The only path left was across the water. A girl like that could not swim and did not own a boat, not to mention the river currents were fast and the crossing would be noted by someone who would raise a ruckus and then the soldiers would line up like a firing squad and shoot that girl dead in the water. They wouldn't even bury her proper, just let the water take the boat and the body and both would be consumed by sea monsters.

I fell asleep cursing them that planted the city of New York on an island.

My dawn visits up the Commons had become the most ordinary of errands. Madam never woke early enough to note my absence, and the soldierwives were so grateful to avoid the chore, they never told. Curzon had grown terrible thin and was still feverish, but his leg had healed up, and he greeted me at the window every day. After I left the prison, I'd fetch the water and head back to Wall Street, passing by the Golden Hill Tavern in case Captain Morse needed me, which he never, ever did.

So when the captain signaled me from the tavern porch the next morning, I was surprised. I had not seen him for weeks, not since the news of the rebel victory at Trenton.

"Good day, Just Sal," he said with a sleepy smile. "How do you fare?"

"Good enough, sir," I said. "Is something amiss?"

He winced and pulled his coat tighter. "Nothing grave, no news of battle or a prisoner exchange."

I waited while he sought the words.

"I'm in need of a favor," he finally said. "It's of no worldly import, but it is a matter of honor for me."

"Sir?"

"I must repay a debt, Just Sal. I wagered Captain William Farrar that the British would not dare hold this ridiculous birthday celebration. It's a slap in the face to the people who are starving."

"Yes, sir."

He frowned and kicked at a stone poking up from the half-frozen mud. "But I'm proven wrong, aren't I? Thousands of pounds are being wasted and so I owe my friend, Captain Farrar, a penny. A gentleman always pays his debts promptly, be they large or small."

I was confuddled. "And you want that I should . . ."

He threw up his hands in frustration. "The British have confined all American officers to their lodging houses today."

"Why?"

"They fear we might mount an insurrection while they are dancing minuets and gorging on stuffed goose. They have a point; the ball would provide the perfect cover for a surprise attack if Washington were nearby. So I am prevented from making good on my bet to William, and he is prevented from coming round to collect his due. 'Tis a small matter of honor, to be sure, but when in reduced circumstances, these things take on greater weight, don't you think?"

Still confuddled, I nodded my head. "Yes, sir."

"Good! Then you'll do it!"

"Do what?"

"Take the penny to William with my salutations. It will give him a good laugh. He lives on Chapel Street, a house with red shutters on the corner of Warren. Say you'll do it for me, Just Sal, and the next penny I earn goes into your pocket, upon my word."

Madam would be wig-deep in preparations for the ball all day. The soldierwives would too, for they belonged to the army of servants who would work at the birthday dinner. Lady Seymour required only a warm fire and occasional help with the teacup. A walk up to Warren Street on a sunny day such as this would be most welcome.

"Happy to help, Captain," I said.

The roar of cannon shook the kitchen just after midday and made me near jump out of my skin. I dropped the turnip I was peeling and it rolled across the floor.

"What was that?" I asked, clutching the table. "Are we under attack?"

Hannah laughed and used the poker to push the logs to the back of the hearth. "No, you goose. That's the royal salute for Her Majesty."

Mary pressed the hot iron against the apron on the table. "Do you figure they might need us early?"

"The major said five o'clock," Hannah said. "Gives us time to finish up here."

"Will you get to see the dancing?" I asked.

"Nah," Mary said. "They'll be too busy running us ragged setting up the dinner. But they've promised to feed us good." She picked up the apron and studied it for wrinkles. "I wish my mother could see this; me, serving at a Queen's Birthday Ball."

"Too bad your mother is on the other side of the globe with Her Majesty," Hannah said.

"They'll both be tragical late to the party." Mary giggled.

Madam sent a note to her friend Jane Drinkwater, who agreed to bring her collection of necklaces and the latest gossip to tea. The news caused Madam to send the soldierwives pawing through the attic for a gown she had not worn yet this year. Hannah sent me to fetch more water, which I did with great pleasure and a short detour.

The houses on Warren Street were a mix; some were modest, two or three were rather grand, with arches over the windows and fancy boot scrapers by the front door. The trees and fences in the neighborhood had all been cut down for firewood. It made the corner of Warren and Chapel looked underdressed.

I went round the back of the house with the red shutters, knocked on the door, and explained my errand to a maid, who fetched Captain Farrar for me, a horse-faced man with an easy laugh.

"Good Captain Morse is indeed a gentleman," he said as I presented him with the coin. "And you're the girl who carries messages to his men in Bridewell?"

"Yes, sir."

"My lads are locked up in the old sugarhouse," he said, his smile fading. "The ones still alive." He stood there caught up in silence and his own thoughts.

I tried to think of a polite way to take my leave but could not find the proper words. The breeze came from the south and carried a salt tang with it. Although snow lay about and everyone was wrapped deep in their clothing, the appearance of the clouds made a body know deep down that spring was stirring.

"Yes, sir," I finally said. "Begging pardon, but I must be on my way."

"Of course, of course," he said, his eyes still distant.

I walked down the path to Warren Street and stopped

when I heard him call me. "Sal, wait there a moment!"

I stood a while longer, watching the clouds and scolding myself for mixing in with the affairs of gentlemen and their honor. Several carriages containing bundled-up ladies and serious-looking officers passed along the street, pulled by shaggy-coated horses. Most folks took no more notice of me than they would a cartman selling oysters or a vagabond from Canvastown.

Just as I set my mind to leave, Captain Farrar came back out. "Give this to Morse, please," he said as he handed me the note. "He'll know what to do."

I studied the folded paper and made bold. "Another wager, sir?"

Another carriage passed on the street, the horses clip-clopping slow.

He shook his head, the laughter gone from his eyes. "No, news from headquarters. Don't tarry with it." He touched his fingertips to the brim of his cap.

I bobbed a curtsy and took my leave, hurrying toward the Tea Water Pump. I should have known I'd be pressed into more message carrying. These soldier types were forever scheming up one thing or another. And it put a girl like me in a rough spot, not that they ever thought about that. I didn't ask to ferry messages across the city for some captain I didn't know. How was that connected to my deal with Dibdin to treat Curzon proper? It wasn't, not one bit.

The good Captains Morse and Farrar would just have to wait till it suited me for this last message to be delivered. If I didn't get back soon, I'd be in for it.

I pushed through the backdoor to the Lockton kitchen, still fussing about selfish captains who only thought of their own skins. When Curzon got out, he'd have a debt of honor the size of a whale to me. I'd make that boy–

I set down the water buckets, removed my cloak, and hung it from a peg near the fire. I stood rubbing my hands together and warming them over the flames. As soon as I could move them, I'd boil up the water.

The door from the front hall slammed open.

"There you are." The words came at me like shards of glass.

I turned. 'Twas Madam Lockton holding a small riding crop in her hand.

"Ma'am?"

She crossed the room and slashed the crop across my face. It hurt fierce, but I knew not to cry out.

"How dare you?" she spat.

CHAPTER XLIII

Saturday, January 18, 1777

THAT EVEN A FAILURE CANNOT BE MORE FATAL
THAN TO REMAIN IN OUR PRESENT SITUATION IN SHORT
SOME ENTERPRIZE MUST BE UNDERTAKEN IN OUR PRESENT
CIRCUMSTANCES OR WE MUST GIVE UP THE CAUSE . . .
OUR AFFAIRS ARE HASTENING FAST TO RUIN IF WE DO
NOT RETRIEVE THEM BY SOME HAPPY EVENT. DELAY
WITH US IS NOW EQUAL TO A TOTAL DEFEAT.
—COLONEL JOSEPH REED IN A LETTER TO
GENERAL GEORGE WASHINGTON

"PLEASE, MA'AM—" I STARTED.

"Silence!" She cracked the crop across my shoulder.

The back door opened and Hannah entered. "Oh, 'scuse me," she said, turning to leave again.

"Stay," Madam ordered.

Hannah let the door close and murmured, "Yes, Madam," her eyes stealing once to me, then quickly away.

I fought the urge to run for the knife drawer.

Madam paced in front of me. "I have never in my entire life been so humiliated." She paused and put on a mimic-face. "I saw your little black girl talking to a rebel officer on Warren Street. Do you allow your slaves to consort with the enemy?"

I could not swallow nor breathe.

She brought the crop down with a crack on the edge of the table. "Jane Drinkwater said this to me. Jane Drinkwater, the biggest gossip in New York." Madam paced again, her hair flying loose, her manner quite unsteady. "I said no, Jane, you must be mistaken, not our Sal. Colonel Hawkins himself uses her for errands."

She stopped suddenly. "And Jane says, 'No, Anne, your girl was speaking to a rebel prisoner on Warren Street. It's hard to miss the mark on her face. From my carriage I saw her take a note from his hand.'"

I opened my mouth to protest, but she slashed at me again. This time the blow opened a cut on my forehead.

"Give me that note," Madam demanded.

"I have no note, ma'am," I said quiet.

She held out her hand. "Liar! Give me that paper or I'll turn you over to the British commander so fast your fool head will spin."

Her voice shook with rage. I reached into my pocket and pulled out the folded note.

Madam looked over to Hannah. "See? You just need to be firm with them."

Hannah said nothing. A drop of blood rolled down the side of my face. I clutched the note in my fist.

"Give it." Madam narrowed her eyes. "Did you hear me, girl?"

Everybody carried a little evil in them, Momma once told me. Madam Lockton had more than her share. The poison had eaten holes through her soul and made room for vermin to nest inside her.

"Girl!" Madam stamped her foot on the floor.

The evil inside of me woke and crackled like lightning. I could wrap my hands around her throat. I could brain her with a poker, thrust her face into the flames. I could beat her senseless with my fists.

I shook from the effort of holding myself still, clutching the crumpled paper. Momma said we had to fight the evil inside us by overcoming it with goodness. She said it was a hard thing to do, but it made us worthy.

I breathed deep to steady myself.

I threw the Captain's note into the fire.

Hannah gasped. Madam shrieked and pushed me out of the way, but the paper was already alight. She dropped the crop and smacked me again in the face with her hand, as she had the day I first landed in New York.

"You foul, bloody wench!" She reached behind her, picked up a bowl, and hurled it at me. I ducked and it crashed against the hearth.

"I will sell you!" she screamed. "I will auction you at dawn on Monday. I'll sell your demon sister, too, to the most cruel, heartless master I can find, the Devil himself if he wants."

She paused to catch her breath.

Ruth?

Hannah stepped forward. "I do believe there was a knock at the front door, Madam," she said.

But she already sold Ruth.

Madam glared at her. "Then answer it, you bloody fool."

Didn't she?

As Hannah left, Madam brushed back her hair, gathering her dignity. I still stood by the fire, where the note had burned to fine ash. I could not think what might happen next.

Madam tugged at her short gown. "What's that stupid look on your face?" she said with a harsh laugh. "You didn't know I still owned her, did you?"

"Ruth?" The name escaped my mouth.

"Brat," Madam spat. "Couldn't find a buyer. Had to ship her down to Charleston. I shall tell the estate manager to get rid of her, toss her in the swamp. Her death will be on your head, you insolent fool."

Hannah came back in from the hall. "The hairdresser, Madam."

"What?" Madam wheeled about. "What did you say?"

"The hairdresser is come to prepare you for the ball. The Queen's ball, ma'am. You must leave in a few hours."

Madam cleared her throat and stood straighter. "Of course. You must first help me into my gown."

Hannah nodded. "Yes, ma'am."

"Lock the girl in the potato bin, then come upstairs."

The bin was more than half-filled with potatoes and smelled of damp earth and worms. There was not enough room to sit up, but lying down was like lying in a bed of rocks. I wanted to scream and pinched myself hard to fight the urge. I did not want to give Madam any satisfaction.

Overhead came the noises of footsteps as the hairdresser performed his job and left, and the colonel returned from headquarters to change into his dress uniform, and Madam sent Hannah running for this folderol and that. There was the sound of horse hooves and the roll of carriage wheels and the front door opened and then closed and the house fell quiet save for Hannah's steps in the kitchen.

A light appeared through the boards of the bin.

"It's me," Hannah said. "She's gone."

The light was set on the ground, then there was a fumbling of a key in the padlock. The bin door opened and Hannah peered in.

"I brought you some things. Here." She handed me a chamber pot, a blanket, and a mug of water. "T'ain't right to lock you away with nothing. You ain't an animal."

"Let me go, please," I pleaded. But before I could say anything further or reach for her, she had slammed down the door and shot home the lock again.

"I'll be back by dawn and check on you then," she said. "Try to sleep."

"Please, Hannah!" I cried. "Please, I beg of you!"

Her footsteps flew up the stairs and the door slammed. I thought I heard a sob, but perhaps I didn't.

The bees overtook me then. As evening moved into night, they ate through me and hived up inside my brainpan with a loud buzz, their wings beating me into submission. Someone whimpered and cried and it must have been me, but it mattered not for I was already dead. It was only a few days, hours perhaps, until my heart would stop beating, in truth, and the bees would fly off to haunt someone else.

And then came the sound of a distant roar, like a lion just sprung from a trap.

The bees paused and I froze, waiting. No one was home except for Lady Seymour, and she was not capable of making noise.

The roar came again. I cocked my head and listened. It did not come from the street nor the house above. It was not cannon fire. 'Twas inside me. A thought, thunderous loud.

Ruth was alive.

Alive, in Charleston. In South Carolina, not on a ship, not on an island.

Alive in a town I can walk to.

My toes wiggled in my sturdy black shoes and my legs itched. I lay flat as I could on the bumpy mound of potatoes and kicked once at the boards of the bin. My heavy shoes made a terrible loud noise on the wood. I stopped, counted to one hundred.

There came no sound from overhead, no commotion out on the street.

I kicked again, at the same spot. The potatoes under me shifted and the mug of water overturned. I kicked a third time. The boards did not move at all. I cursed the carpenter who had built this tomb.

There has to be a way out.

I kicked, stomped, slammed. I raged and screamed and fought. Nothing happened.

I stopped, wiped the sweat from my face, and closed my eyes.

Think.

The bin stood a little taller than Ruth, and was as long in both directions as it was tall. I reached up to touch the boards above my head. They were rough-hewn, put together with cold nails. My fingertips traced the length of each board, feeling along the splinters and the knots in the wood. The top was as solid as a brick wall, each nail fastened tight. I fought back the panic that rose in my throat and tested the strength of each board that ran from the top down the sides. All strong, all sound.

Think. Remember.

When Ruth and I slept down here, the far corner of the cellar went muddy in a heavy rain. Maybe the damp had eaten at the boards. I moved over to that corner of the bin and scooped the potatoes out of the way, heaping them behind me. I sat back and put my feet on each board in turn and pushed.

The third board I tried gave way a little. So did the next two.

I moved the potato heap so I could best lean against it and push with my legs. I kicked. There was a quiet *crack.*

I kicked again and leaned forward to feel the boards. The one had a piece chipped off where the wood was rotted through, the other had a long split in it. I leaned back and took a deep breath, then kicked and kicked with all my strength until the wood broke and flew into the dark.

I took the stairs two at a time and paused before I entered the kitchen. The house was still silent. I hurried down the hall, past the grandfather clock, and up the stairs to the drawing room. I needed a map and had a mind to steal a pass, too, if I could.

I threw some wood on the fire, lit a candle from the flames, and carried it to the long dining table covered with maps and countless papers. I lit the rest of the candles on the table as if preparing for a feast, then searched through the papers, throwing those that were useless to me to the floor.

Finally I found a small map that showed the colonies from Massachusetts down to Georgia. The distance from Rhode Island to New York was the same as the tip of my little finger to the first knuckle under it. From New York to Charleston stretched all the way down my fingers to the palm.

The crackling firewood startled me. I glanced up. There was a movement over the hearth and for an instant, my heart caught in my throat.

A ghost?

The firelight brightened. No, not a ghost. I had caught sight of myself in the large mirror that hung over the mantel.

I could scarce recognize me.

My hands fumbled for a candle. I moved to the mirror,

guarding the flame, and lit the oil lamps that were set into the wall. The mirror caught the light and reflected it back at me.

I leaned in.

In truth, it seemed I was looking at a stranger who lived beyond the glass. My face was thinner than I remembered and longer from brow to chin. My nose and mouth recollected Momma's, but the set of the eyes, those came from Poppa. As I stared, their two faces came forth and drifted back, until I could see only me.

I turned my head to the side a bit and studied the brand on my face; for the first time, studied it hard: the capital *I* that proclaimed my insolent manners and crimes. I leaned closer to the mirror. The letter was a pink ribbon embroidered on my skin.

I touched it, smooth and warm, flesh made into silk.

The scars on Poppa's cheek had been three lines across his cheek, carved with a sharp blade. He was proud of his marks. In the country of his ancestors, they made him into a man.

I traced the *I* with my fingertip.

This is my country mark. I did not ask for it, but I would carry it as Poppa carried his. It made me his daughter. It made me strong.

I took a step back, seeing near my whole self in the mirror. I pushed back my shoulders and raised my chin, my back straight as an arrow.

This mark stands for Isabel.

The clock struck eleven and made me jump. I had much to do and little time.

The fastest way off the island was a boat, much as the thought made me tremble. I searched through the sea of papers on the table until I found a chart of the tides. I ran my finger down the columns. *Huzzah!* The tide would not turn against me for a few hours.

I lacked only a pass. Colonel Hawkins had been in the habit of keeping them locked in the chest in the library, but he had become sloppy and overworked since the rebel victories. I opened the drawers of the secretary table and looked through the large boxes of official papers.

There!

I grabbed the paper and dashed to a small side table for a quill and bottle of ink. I crowded the candles in close together to give me enough light, took a deep breath to steady my hand, and dipped the quill. I took a second breath and bent over to fill in the empty bits of the pass:

New-York, ______________, 1777.

I wrote in *18th, January* in the blank space. It had been some time since I wrote out letters. The *J* wobbled and the *r* appeared to be an *n*. I set down the quill, wiped my damp hands on my skirt, and picked it up again.

*This is to Certify, to whomsoever it may concern, That the Bearer hereof*_______

That was where I had to write my name. I scratched out *Isabel* and stopped.

I was not a Lockton. Nor a Finch. Isabel Rhode Island? That would not do. Isabel Cuffe, after Poppa, or Isabel Dinah, after Momma?

I closed my eyes and thought of home; the smell of fresh-cut hay and the taste of raspberries. Robins chasing bugs in the bean patch. Setting worms to work at the base of the corn plants. Showing Ruth what was weed and what was flower . . .

I opened my eyes, dipped the quill, and wrote out my true name: *Isabel Gardener, being a Free Negro, has the Commandant's Permission to pass from this Garrison to whatever place she may think proper.*

It was signed with lots of fancy titles that belonged to the colonel and the commandant, and the King Himself. I wished that there would have been space for Her Majesty, Queen Charlotte of Great Britain, to sign it too. She and me shared a birthday now, for I was reborn as Isabel Gardener and that paper proved it.

CHAPTER XLIV

Saturday, January 18, 1777

THAT THE QUESTION WAS NOT WHETHER, BY A DECLARATION OF INDEPENDENCE, WE SHOULD MAKE OURSELVES WHAT WE ARE NOT; BUT WHETHER WE SHOULD DECLARE A FACT WHICH ALREADY EXISTS . . .
—THOMAS JEFFERSON ABOUT THE WRITING OF THE DECLARATION OF INDEPENDENCE

I FOLDED THE MAP AND PASS, BLEW out the candles, and crept down the stairs. I took the scissors out of the sewing basket in the kitchen and snipped the threads of the hem of my cloak. I opened the map flat, inserted it between the lining and the woolen layer, then quick resewed the hem.

Next I dressed myself in all of my clothing: two shifts and two skirts, my cloak, shawl, and the blanket from my pallet. I took a basket from a high shelf and loaded it with bread, hard cheese, and a piece of dried beef I cut from the slab that hung in the pantry. As I put the beef back, I studied the loose board in the back of the pantry. I pried it up and removed the lead piece from the king's statue and my cloth packet of seeds. After some consideration, I took out *Common Sense*, too, and stuck all of it in the pocket I wore under my skirt, alongside the false pass.

I walked down the hall, reached for the handle of the front door, and stopped. Lady Seymour lay in the silent parlor. I doubted anyone had thought to put wood on the fire for her. That was my chore.

No, not anymore. I was quit of this place. I reached again for the handle.

But she was alone, old, and maybe freezing.

It would take only an instant.

I stepped into the parlor. Lady Seymour lay in her bed, her eyes closed, the covers barely moving. Her fire was near burned down to ash. I quick added logs and blew on the coals until small flames jumped up and bit into the wood. She wouldn't die of the cold this night, not on my account.

I was halfway to the door when I saw her silk reticule hung from the back of a chair. There were coins in that bag, coins that would help a girl set on walking to South Carolina. But that was stealing from somebody who had showed me kindness. But she stood by when Ruth was taken, and she returned me to Madam. But taking her money was still stealing.

'Twas wrong, but I swallowed hard, opened the bag, and removed the coin purse from the bottom. When I hung it back on the chair, Lady Seymour's eyes were open and following me. The question on her face was plain.

"I'm sorry," I said. "She's made up her mind to sell me."

She nodded once.

"I built up the fire. Would you like some water?"

She nodded again. I poured a cup of water from the pitcher and held it to her dry lips. She swallowed a little, but the rest spilled down her face. I set down the cup and wiped away the water.

"I have to go. Please forgive me."

Lady Seymour cut her eyes at her husband's small portrait on the bedside table, then to the coin purse that weighed down my hand. She gave a sharp nod of the head, one side of her mouth turned up in a smile.

"I'll put the money back," I said. "Forgive me."

She shook her head from side to side, her mouth moving with trapped words.

"I can keep it?"

Another nod and another pointed stare at her husband.

"Because I rescued his picture?"

She nodded again, and a tear slipped down her cheek.

"Well, then, ma'am, I'm happy to take it."

As I set the coin purse in my pocket, she opened her mouth and a small sound escaped.

"Did you say something, Lady Seymour?" I leaned in close, though it scared me, for the smell of death hung over that bed like a fog.

Her lips moved again, forming her last word to me, a whisper almost too faint to hear.

"Run."

I opened the front door of the Lockton mansion and looked up the street and down. Not a soul in sight.

I picked up the basket, tightened the blanket across my shoulders, and stepped over the threshold. I closed the door behind me, walked down the front steps, and turned west.

My plan was simple and foolhardy: steal a rowboat, cross the river to Jersey, and walk to Charleston. I was counting on the commotion of the Queen's ball to distract folks. If I could get to the boat in time, the tide would help pull me away from New York.

At the first corner, my feet stopped. This was where I turned north most mornings to head up to the Bridewell.

I urged my feet west, toward the wharf. They did not listen.

My remembery called up the feel of being locked in the stocks, of my face being burnt, of him watching me from across the courtyard; him watching out for me. 'Twas Curzon who made sure I survived. 'Twas he who had been my steadfast friend since the day they brought me here.

I couldn't. It would be hard enough to sneak past two armies and not get stolen again by someone who would tear up my pass. And I didn't even have a pass for him, how to explain that? No, I couldn't. I looked west, toward the river, then north, then west again. No—not couldn't. I shouldn't. But I had to.

I had a debt to pay.

"Good evening, sir," I said, holding out my basket to the huge soldier, Fisher, who opened the door to the Bridewell guardhouse.

Fisher grunted and yawned. "Wot's your business here? It's going on midnight."

I prayed that the Lord and Momma would forgive the river of lies about to flow from my mouth. "Colonel Hawkins sent me, sir, to clean the cells. As you suggested."

The guard stepped inside and I followed him. He sat heavily in a chair and drank from a mug on the table. "Terrible late to be cleaning cells."

"The colonel got wind of a prison inspector arriving."

"Nobody told me," he growled.

I swallowed hard. Should I flee and give up on this senseless plot?

He spat into the fire. "But they don't tell me nuffink. Wot's in the basket?"

Food to keep me alive for a week, I thought. "Help yourself," I said.

He pawed through it, took out a soft roll and stuffed half of it in his mouth. "Mebbe I should ask the colonel."

I thought quick as I could. "Yessir. Of course. He's at the Queen's ball."

Fisher winced. "Best not disturb that. All right." He stood slow and reached for the key ring and a lantern on the wall. "But don't be asking me to help. Cleaning the cells ain't my job."

I took the key. "Yes, sir."

"Wheelbarrow's in the hall," he said. "Once you've filled it, roll it back here, and I'll let you out so's you can throw the muck and filth in the pit." He yawned. "Mind yer breathing."

I turned. "Pardon?"

"Prisoners been dropping dead like flies. Fever."

The men in the first cell were mostly sleeping, or dying, or dead. None of them had the strength to do more than stare at me in the weak lantern light. I gagged and gagged again as I carried out overflowing chamber pots, and forced myself to take a blanket from a corpse.

Hurry! I screamed inside. *Hurry or it will be too late!*

Fisher looked up and chuckled as I passed back through the guardhouse with the barrow. I pitched the filth into the pit behind the prison and prayed it was not going atop any corpses. Before I went back inside, I cleaned off my hands in a snow bank. My teeth rattled with the cold.

"No fun, is it?" the guard asked as I passed through again. He pulled at the blanket around his shoulders. "Hurry up, now. I need me sleep."

"Yes, sir." I wiped my hands on my skirt. "Almost done, sir."

I did not open the door to the second cell, nor the third. I set the lantern in the wheelbarrow, pushed it down the hall to the fourth door on the right, and held my breath as I unlocked it.

The stench was overpowering—men unwashed for months and puke and muck and rot that was eating living flesh. Two dozen pairs of eyes watched me, burning in skull-like faces. No one spoke. I stepped inside and held the lantern higher. The faces were new to me, men and boys who had been moved in here after Curzon's original companions died.

"Where's Mister Dibdin?" I asked in a small voice.

"Died this morning," croaked a man. "Everyone's dying."

"What about the slave boy?"

He pointed to a corner.

Curzon lay insensible, his skin burning with fever, his eyes rolled up into his head. I called his name and pinched him, but he did not look my way nor speak a word.

He'll be soon dead. Leave him and run.

A weight settled on my shoulders like a cloak of iron. I bent close to his ear. "Shhhh," I whispered.

A blast of cannon fire sounded from the Battery, more royal celebrations. A few men looked to the window.

"He's dead." I stood up. "Can someone help me with the body?"

No one moved.

"Then I shall do it myself."

I grabbed Curzon under his armpits and dragged him across the floor and out the door. It took no effort at all to load him into the wheelbarrow. He weighed hardly more than a large sack of potatoes or a full butter churn. I dashed back into the cell, snatched his hat out of the shaking hands of a man who was putting it on his own head, grabbed the lantern, and closed and locked the cell door.

I could not ponder the fate of the rest of the men. Some things were not to be borne.

Before I pushed him down the hall and into the guardhouse, I covered Curzon with the filthy blanket I'd stolen from the first cell. "You're dead," I hissed to him. "No noise."

In the guardhouse, Fisher was sitting on his bed, leaning against the wall and snoring. He roused some as I shut the door to the cells.

"Got a nasty load here," I said. "Might take a bit to bury it."

He nodded, already half-asleep.

As I pushed the wheelbarrow into the night, my legs shook so hard I thought sure they'd set the earth to trembling and bring the whole building crashing to the ground.

CHAPTER XLV

Saturday, January 18–
Sunday, January 19, 1777

EVERYTHING THAT IS RIGHT OR REASONABLE PLEADS FOR SEPARATION. THE BLOOD OF THE SLAIN, THE WEEPING VOICE OF NATURE CRIES 'TIS TIME TO PART.
—THOMAS PAINE, *COMMON SENSE*

THE PRISON WAS TEN BLOCKS FROM the wharf. I covered the first eight blocks as fast as a girl pushing a near-dead lump of boy could. Then I stopped.

A sentry fire was lit at the corner, burning between us and the last two blocks to the wharf. Six British guards stood warming their hands, their muskets leaning against the small pile of firewood. A dog lay at their feet, head resting on its front paws. One of the men stretched his arms over his head and gave a mighty yawn, and his companions laughed at him. The dog lifted his head once and looked in our direction, but a soldier reached down to scratch his ears and he relaxed.

If I tried to push the wheelbarrow over the cobblestones, we'd be arrested in an instant. If it were half an hour earlier, we could have tracked backward and gone down another street. But the tide wouldn't wait.

I backed up slow as I could, cringing with every creak of

the wheels. Once we were well out of sight of the men, I pulled the blanket off Curzon.

"Get up," I whispered as I helped him from the barrow. "We need to get past those soldiers. After that, it's only two blocks to the river."

"Boat?" he asked, leaning against a wall.

"Of course. Follow me, stay close."

He took one step forward and collapsed against me, the two of us crumpling to the ground.

"No!" I scolded as I stood and pulled him to his feet. "You have to try harder."

"Sorry, Country," he muttered.

He was not strong enough to walk on his own. I was not strong enough to carry him on my back, not after pushing him so far. I pulled his arm across my shoulder and had him lean on me heavily.

"Step quiet," I whispered as we drew close to the corner again.

Twenty paces of open street separated us from the shadows on the other side. One of the soldiers walked to the woodpile, picked up a split log, carried it to the fire, and tossed it on the flames. For the moment, all the men had their backs to us.

"Ready?" I said in Curzon's ear.

He nodded. I drew a deep breath and we started to walk, soft as we could. Twenty paces stretched twenty miles, every faint crunch of our shoes sounding like gunshot.

Five steps, I counted silently. *Six. Seven.*

Curzon had little strength in his legs. He faltered and almost fell again. I wrapped my other arm around him and clutched his shirt. *Eight. Nine. Ten.*

The dog lifted his head. He stared right at me and barked.

One of the soldiers, startled, shouted, "Look at that!" and pointed to the sky.

The heavens exploded into the red glare of rockets and white fountains of light. Curzon and I stood as if planted, amazed at the sight of the fireworks being shot off in honor of Queen Charlotte.

The dog barked furiously in our direction, but the soldiers were all staring at the illuminations above. The noise rolled up, booms that sounded like thunder and cannons. The men all smiled and laughed at the spectacle.

I dragged Curzon across the street and down the last two blocks to the wharf.

It was dark, no watch posted, as I had hoped. "Thank you, Momma," I muttered as we crawled into a rowboat.

Curzon groaned. "What you say?"

I untied us from the wharf. "Never mind."

But he was already insensible again. I picked up the oars.

I rowed that river.

I rowed that river like it was a horse delivering me from the Devil.

My hands blistered, the blisters popped, they re-formed and popped again. I rowed with my hands slick with blood. My back, my shoulders, my arms, they pulled with the strength of a thousand armloads of firewood split and carried, of water buckets toted for miles, of the burdens of every New York day and New York night boiled into two miles of water that I was going to cross.

Set after set of the Queen's fireworks exploded over the roofs of the city, over Canvastown, over the mansions that held the King's subjects in their ball gowns and fancy dress uniforms. Her fireworks blasted off and everybody gazed into the sky and I rowed and rowed and rowed past their homes, aside their warehouses, underneath their cannons, and out into the open harbor betwixt New York Island and Jersey.

My wits wandered some, 'bout the time my hands started bleeding.

Tongues of fog oozed across the water and curled around the bits of ice that floated past. I saw in the fog the forms of people. They never came close enough that I could see their faces. Once, I reached out, feeling a warm presence, but I near tipped the boat over and had to grab for the oar before it slid away. My hands plunged into the icy water. And I rowed and rowed, but it didn't hurt after that because my hands had froze.

I rowed and the tide pulled and the ghosts—who could indeed travel over water—tugged my boat with all their strength. My eyes closed and the moon drew me west, away from the island of my melancholy.

When my eyes opened, I knew I had died and passed onto glory.

Heaven was crystal lit with white angel fire, colored peach at the edges. Heaven smelled of wood smoke.

I blinked.

The Bible did not mention that Heaven smelled of wood smoke.

I blinked again. When I opened my eyes, they watered because of the bright morning light. The rowboat had come ashore in a tangle of bushes that overhung a small bank at the side of the river. The branches overhead were all coated in ice. I was coated in ice, too, that fractured and crackled as I moved.

I looked to the water, then to the rising sun, then to the water again. I looked around me—no houses, no ships, no wharves. The river was narrow and flowing out to sea, south. The sun rose beyond the water, at the other side of the river. I was on the west bank. I was in Jersey.

I had set myself free.

I wiped at the water that flowed down my cheeks and kicked at the stinking bundle at the bottom of the boat.

"You alive?" I asked.

The bundle groaned and pushed aside the shredded blanket. Curzon lifted his head enough to look at me sitting there with a fool grin on my face.

"Where are we?" he asked in a thin voice.

"I think we just crossed the river Jordan." I stood up, steadied myself as the boat rocked a bit, and offered him my hand. "Can you walk?"

RUNAWAYS

NOTICE TO READERS!!!
One & All, Be Hereby Advised
that the Account of Runaways

ISABEL GARDENER

Formerly Sal Lockton

& Companion

CURZON BELLINGHAM

WILL BE CONTINUED
in the Forthcoming Volume

FORGE.

APPENDIX

Was Isabel based on a real person? What about the other characters in the book?

Chains is a work of historical fiction. Most of the characters: Isabel, Ruth, Curzon, the Locktons, Lady Seymour, Bellingham, and various British and Patriot officers, are fictional. The real letters, diaries, newspaper articles, runaway ads, cookbooks, and military reports that I found in my research helped me develop the characters.

There are three "real" people in the book. The mayor of New York, David Matthews, actually did participate in the conspiracy to assassinate Washington. Thomas Hickey was a member of Washington's Life Guards, and was hung for his part in the assassination plot. And Dr. Abraham van Buskirk, the Loyalist sympathizer who sheltered Mr. Lockwood, truly was a doctor in New Jersey.

While the character of Isabel is fictional, her situation is realistic. Child slaves were sold at very young ages and had to work extremely hard. During the war there was an increase in the number of slaves who freed themselves by running away. Most of them ran in search of family members, so they could start their new lives together.

The tension between Patriot and Loyalist New Yorkers, the Tea Water Pump, the taking of lead from houses, the pulling down of King George's statue, the chaos surrounding the British invasion of the city, the fire, prisoners of war, the Queen's Birthday Ball: all of these are historical facts. I wove the fictional characters of Isabel and Curzon into the history to give readers a sense of what life might have been like in those days.

What about the battles? Were they real too?

Yes. There were a number of big battles around New York City in 1776.

In August the British army, with more than 30,000 men, landed at Gravesend in Brooklyn and the Americans prepared to meet them. The two armies clashed on August 27, near the village of Flatbush. The Americans, with only 10,000 troops, were beaten and withdrew to Brooklyn Heights, then across the East River to Manhattan.

This part of the war is sometimes called the Battle of Brooklyn or the Battle of Long Island. It was the first major battle of the Revolution with more than 40,000 men fighting for six hours. The British crushed the Americans, capturing, wounding or killing thousands of men.

A few weeks later the British attacked the Patriots at the northern end of Manhattan, in the battle of Harlem Heights, and later, in the battle of Fort Washington, where thousands of Americans became British prisoners of war. Washington was lucky to escape with the remnants of his army. They marched into New Jersey and headed south to Princeton and Trenton.

Was the Revolution the most important thing that ever happened in America?

That is an interesting question. The American Revolution (also called the War for Independence) was fought for many reasons, but mostly because Americans wanted to be in charge of their own government and have more control over how their taxes were spent.

Most people who lived in the Thirteen Colonies considered themselves British, or at the very least, British colonists. Historians estimate that 40 percent of colonists were firmly dedicated to breaking free from Great Britain, 20 percent wanted to remain a colony, and 40 percent stayed neutral or supported the side that was winning at the moment. After the war, it took a while for Americans to develop their own sense of national identity and pride.

Equally important to the war itself was the establishment of the United States Constitution, which called for a representative government, regular elections, and the checks and balances of the Congress, the President, and the Supreme Court. The Constitution is an amazing document: one that has grown with the evolving perspectives and needs of the country.

The American experiment in democracy, which we are still working on, changed the world forever.

How many slaves lived in America at the time of the Revolution?

When the American Revolution broke out, about 2.5 million people of European and African descent were living in the Thirteen Colonies.

The war came after decades of increased immigration across the Atlantic Ocean. About 150,000 Europeans journeyed to America between 1700 and 1775. About 100,000 more came as indentured servants. In the same time period, nearly 300,000 Africans were kidnapped and shipped to the colonies to work as slaves.

On the eve of the Revolution, one in five colonists—20 percent of the population—was a slave: approximately 500,000 people. Most of them were held in bondage in the southern colonies, but slaves were owned by everyone from farmers in Albany, New York, to shipbuilders in Newport, Rhode Island, to bakers in Philadelphia, Pennsylvania, to merchants in Boston, Massachusetts.

Which side did African Americans fight for during the Revolution?

African Americans fought for both the Patriots and the British, just like members of all other ethnic groups in the country.

Historians estimate that five thousand African American men enlisted on the American side of the war. Free and enslaved black Patriots fought and died at the Boston Massacre, at Lexington and Concord, Bunker Hill, Saratoga, and every other significant battle. Some were Patriots because they believed in the cause of American liberty. Others fought alongside or in place of owners who forced them to take up arms. A few slaves were granted freedom for being soldiers, but not many.

On November 7, 1775, the Royal Governor of Virginia, the Earl of Dunmore, declared that all male slaves and indentured servants owned by Patriots would be freed if they volunteered to work for the British Army. On June 7, 1779, British Commandant David Jones added: "All Negroes that fly from the Enemy's Country are Free–No person whatever can claim a Right to them–."

Tens of thousands of slaves ran away from their owners and fled to the British lines, including slaves owned by George Washington and Thomas Jefferson. Most were used as military laborers digging ditches, building barricades and roads, and driving carts, though some fought as soldiers with Dunmore's Ethiopian Regiment. While the Patriots talked about freedom, the British actually gave it to some slaves.

I'm confused. I thought the British were the bad guys. But if they gave freedom to the slaves, wouldn't that make them the good guys? And does that make the Patriots the bad guys?

It's complicated, and yes, confusing. The situation was too muddy to think about in a "good guy vs. bad guy" way.

Most Americans supported the idea of slavery, though opinions were beginning to change in the late 1700s. Many of the Founding Fathers owned slaves and much of the wealth of America's upper class came from slave labor. Some leaders, like George Washington and Benjamin Franklin, changed the way they felt about slavery as they grew older. Both men freed their slaves in their wills, though all but one of Franklin's slaves died before he did.

Some young American leaders, like John Laurens of South Carolina, saw the immorality of slavery and tried to design plans that would free slaves, including those owned by his father. His plans never gained approval. He died at the end of the war.

To us today, it seems completely hypocritical to fight a war for "liberty and freedom" when 20 percent of your population is in chains. People back then saw the hypocrisy too. It made some of them uncomfortable, but not uncomfortable enough to change the law, not right away. Vermont abolished slavery on July 8, 1777, when it adopted its state constitution. After the Revolution, the other states in the North gradually required slave owners to free their slaves.

Americans had to fight another bloody war, the Civil War, before all of our people were free.

So the Americans were good guys about liberty and bad guys about slavery. Does that mean the British were bad guys about liberty and good guys about slavery?

Again, you can't look at this through good guy/bad guy glasses.

The British were not interested in freeing slaves because it was the morally right thing to do. Dunmore's Proclamation was issued to ruin the Patriot economy, particularly in Virginia, the home of many slave-owning Patriot leaders. British General Sir Henry Clinton promised "to use slaves as weapons against their masters."

Their offer of freedom was not made to everyone in bondage. If a slave owned by a Loyalist escaped to the British, he was returned to his owners and punished. Loyalists were given runaway slaves as rewards for helping the king's army. The British also sold escaped or captured Patriot slaves to their Loyalist sympathizers. Ex-slaves who came down with smallpox or typhus were abandoned by the British to die or be recaptured.

The abolition movement did grow faster in England than in America. In 1772 an English judge ruled that slavery could not exist in England itself. In 1807 Parliament banned British involvement in the Atlantic slave trade. (From 1690 to 1807 British ships carried nearly three million kidnapped Africans across the Atlantic Ocean.) Slavery was completely banned throughout the British Empire in 1833.

How was life different for slaves on big plantations, on small farms, and in the cities?

In the northern colonies, European Americans tended to own one or two slaves who worked on the family farm or were hired out. Rhode Island and Connecticut had a few large farms, where twenty or thirty slaves would live and work. Plantation-based slavery was more common in the South, where hundreds of slaves could be owned by the same person and forced to work in tobacco, indigo, or rice fields.

In most cities, slaveholdings were small, usually one or two slaves who slept in the attic or cellar of the slave owner's home. Abigail Smith Adams, a Congregational minister's daughter, grew up outside Boston in a household that owned two slaves, Tom and Pheby. As an adult, she denounced slavery, as did her husband, John Adams, the second President of the United States.

Historians recently discovered the remains of slaves found in the African Burial Ground near today's City Hall in New York City. By studying the skeletons, scientists discovered that the slaves of New York suffered from poor nutrition, disease, and years of backbreaking labor. Most of them died young.

What were the differences between servants, indentured servants, and slaves?

Servants were usually working-class white people, often recent immigrants, who were paid wages for their labor. Servants could quit their jobs if they wanted.

An indentured servant was a person, usually white, who promised their labor for seven years or so, often in exchange for passage to America. If they left their master before their term of service was up, they could be arrested. They did not have all of the freedoms of a nonindentured white person, but they had many more rights and protection than slaves.

Slaves were people of African descent who were not paid for their work and had to do everything demanded by the person who owned them. They had no rights and little protection from cruel treatment and inhumane living conditions. Slaves were not allowed to marry and children were frequently sold away from their parents.

Why don't we hear much about the Revolution in New York City? What was the city like back then?

Maybe because the British occupied the city for nearly the entire war.

Before the Revolutionary War began, New York was the second largest city in the American colonies with approximately 20,000 residents, smaller than Philadelphia (34,000 residents) and larger than Boston (15,000). It took up less than a square mile at the southernmost tip of Manhattan, then called York, or New York Island, stretching a little more than a mile north to south, and about a half mile, east to west.

The rest of Manhattan, called the Outward, consisted of forest and marshes dotted with small hamlets, such as Greenwich Village, farms, and a few grand summer estates. Fort Washington, eleven miles to the north of the small city of New York, was located between what we today call West 183rd and West 185th Streets, in the Hudson Heights neighborhood. Today's New York City Hall, where Broadway, Park Row, and Chambers Street intersect, was built on the area known as the Commons during the Revolution, which was then at the northern edge of the city.

When the British occupied New York and the region around it, Patriot supporters fled and Loyalists poured into the city, seeking the protection of the king's army. Life in the city was very hard for most people. They struggled to find firewood and affordable food, while the British officers and wealthy Loyalists enjoyed comfort and luxury.

The city was in a strategic position for the British, located between the Patriot hotbeds of Boston and Philadelphia, but they never figured out how to use it effectively to squelch the rebellion.

Are you sure there were slaves in New York back then?

Absolutely.

The earliest slaves were brought to New Amsterdam (later called New York) by the Dutch in the 1620s. When the British took over New York in 1664, about 10 percent of the population was of African descent.

The number of slaves skyrocketed as the British kidnapped thousands of African men, women, and children and brought them to the city. By 1737, 20 percent of the city's population was enslaved—more than 1,700 people. By the middle of the century, New York had the second highest percentage of slaves in the colonies after Charleston, South Carolina. Historian Shane White analyzed census data, tax records, and directories and found that every street in New York had slave owners on it, and most people lived a few doors down from slaves, if they didn't own one themselves.

Historians estimate that about 5,000 African Americans, nearly 22 percent of the population, lived in and around New York in 1771. Very few of them were free. By the end of the American

Revolution, thousands had fled to the British or run away, but thousands more continued to live in bondage.

In 1799 New York passed the Gradual Emancipation Act, which set out the very slow timetable for freeing the children of slaves, after they had given nearly thirty years of servitude to the people who owned them. The law was changed in 1817, freeing the rest of the slaves of New York on July 4, 1827.

On July 5, 1827, thousands of free African Americans marched down Broadway, following an honor guard and a grand marshal. In front of the African Zion Church, they listened as abolitionist leader William Hamilton announced, "This day we stand redeemed from a bitter thralldom."

The African Americans of New York were finally free after two hundred years of bondage.

Did that huge fire really destroy part of New York in 1776?

The fire was a terrible disaster that affected the city for years. No one has ever proved if it started by accident, or was the work of Patriots angry that the British had driven them out of the city. It started near the tip of the island and was spread by strong winds up the west side, burning through the night as panicked families rushed into the streets.

When the flames finally died, nearly five hundred buildings—a quarter of all the homes in the city—had burned to the ground. In the chaos that followed, no one counted the dead. They were buried as quickly as possible, then thoughts turned to survival.

With winter approaching, finding shelter for the homeless was critical. Families were forced to let British soldiers live with them, and homes abandoned by fleeing Patriots were taken over by the army. Poor people lived in the remnants of cellars and built so many hovels in the burned-over district that it was known as "Canvastown."

Since the Revolution, Manhattan has expanded, reaching farther into the two rivers that flow by it as developers added landfill so they could erect more buildings. Two centuries after the war, the World Trade Center Towers were built. Part of the complex stood on the land that was devastated during the Great Fire of 1776. When the World Trade Towers were destroyed during the terrorist attacks on September 11, 2001, the same region of the city suffered.

St. Paul's Chapel, a small Episcopalian church in that neighborhood, somehow survived both disasters.

Were conditions for the American prisoners of war really that bad?

The conditions suffered by the American soldiers captured by the British in and around New York were almost too horrible to describe. They were stuffed into jails, churches, warehouses, and decrepit ships in the harbor and left to rot. Their cells had no heat. They used a corner or a bucket for their toilet and were never allowed to bathe. They did not have blankets, warm clothes, or medical care. They had to drink dirty water. Their meals were raw pork, moldy biscuits infested with maggots, peas, and rice.

About half of the two thousand Americans captured at Fort Washington died from disease and starvation within weeks. If the British had not allowed the citizens of New York to bring blankets and food to the prisoners, the death toll would have been higher.

Captured officers, however, were treated differently. They were allowed to stay in boardinghouses, to work, and to walk around the city as long as they did not try to escape. The British felt that officers were gentlemen and deserved to be treated according to their higher social class.

More than 10,000 American prisoners of war died in British captivity.

What happened to King George's head?

After the Declaration of Independence was read to a crowd of Patriots on July 9, 1776, the excited Americans rushed down Broadway to the Bowling Green and pulled down the gilt-covered lead statue of King George and his horse. The statue was dragged up the length of Manhattan to Fort Washington. Some historians believe that the king's head was displayed in front of the Blue Bell Tavern, near what is today the corner of Broadway and 181st Street.

Most of the statue was melted into 42,088 bullets by the women of Litchfield, Connecticut. Other fragments of the statue were stolen and hidden. Over the next hundred years, pieces of it turned up in fields and swamps. A number of families kept bits of the statue as a reminder of the day.

Loyalist spies were outraged at the treatment of the image of their king. They stole back the head and delivered it to Captain John Montresor, a British engineer. Thomas Hutchinson, former Loyalist governor of Massachusetts, claimed he saw the head—the head of the statue, that is—in London, England, in 1777. He said the nose didn't look so good.

ACKNOWLEDGMENTS

I was blessed by the kind assistance and advice of many fine people as I worked on this book.

I am extremely grateful to Christopher Paul Moore, historian and research coordinator for the Schomburg Center for Research in Black Culture; Sherrill D. Wilson, PhD; and Kathleen Hulser, public historian of the New-York Historical Society, for reviewing the manuscript for historical accuracy. Any mistakes of fact or interpretation that remain are mine alone. Special thanks go to Judith van Buskirk, PhD, professor of history at the State University of New York at Cortland. Not only did Dr. van Buskirk read the manuscript, but she generously allowed me access to her own research notes. Thanks also to Sheila Cooke-Kayser, educational specialist at the Boston National Historical Park, for sending me a copy of the National Park Service's report, "Patriots of Color." Thank you Forrest Ainslie of Philadelphia for the information about the treatment of epilepsy during the Colonial era and Tobias Huisman in the Netherlands for help with the Dutch translation.

The African Burial Ground National Monument pays tribute to the thousands of New York slaves who lie buried in lower Manhattan. Deep thanks to Park Supervisor Tara Morrison for managing the magnificent monument and for helping me find the proper experts to review this book. Thanks also to the Gilder Lehrman Center for the Study of Slavery, Resistance & Abolition and the New-York Historical Society for providing online and real-world resources that helped me grasp the insidiousness of slavery during the American Revolution.

Amy Berkower of Writer's House is not just my wonderful agent, she is a trusted and much appreciated friend. Because of her efforts, I have a wonderful team to work with at Simon & Schuster. I extend my deepest thanks there to Rick Richter and Rubin Pfeffer for allowing me to pursue my dream of seeking out the seeds of America's stories. Lizzy Bromley is responsible for the elegant design of this book, and Christopher Silas Neal created the breathtaking cover. I am honored that their work graces my story. Thank you also to editorial assistant Julia Maguire for steering a river of paperwork safely past shoals and rapids.

Of all of the books I have worked on with my brilliant editor, Kevin Lewis, this is the one that lies closest to our hearts. Thank you, Kevin, for the long conversations about our nation's history, the scars and legacy of slavery, and our responsibilities to our readers. Kevin also gets a loud "Huzzah!" for his careful reading of all the drafts of this story and for encouraging me to take it to the next level.

Authors of historical fiction would be out of a job were it not for the angels who are disguised as librarians. Thank you to the staffs of the Penfield Library of the State University of New York at Oswego, the Bird Library of Syracuse University, and the New York North Country Library System. Special thanks to the charming and patient women of my hometown library, the Mexico Library in Mexico, New York.

My friends and fellow authors Deborah Heiligman and Martha Hewson again offered suggestions about the early drafts of the book. Thank you, Genevieve Gagne-Hawes, for your insight; Greg Anderson for saving me from comma embarrassment; and to my younger early-draft readers: Tess

Kallmeyer of California and Will Hoiseth of Wisconsin, Poland, Peru (and wherever else his family lands), for much appreciated early encouragement and suggestions.

Thank you, Mindy Ostrow and Bill Reilly (owners of the best bookstore in the country, the River's End Bookstore in Oswego, New York), for letting me write the opening pages of this story in your magic writing chair. It worked again. I also send thanks streaming through the ether to the readers of my blog for encouraging me more than they realized.

A note to our long-suffering children: Christian, Meredith, Jessica, and Stephanie. You will never again have to say "Are you *still* working on that book?!" about *Chains*. You will have to say it about my new project. Thank you for pretending to be fascinated by the historical trivia that I have been boring you with for years.

If you look carefully, you will see the faint outline of my husband, Scot Larrabee, on every page of this story. Scot did all the driving to libraries to fetch books. He brewed me gallons of tea and coffee, reheated countless meals, and never complained when I talked about the story in my sleep. Most importantly, he keeps me safe through the storms of doubt and frustration that periodically crash into my soul. Thank you, my dear, for simply everything.

READING GROUP GUIDE

Discussion Questions

1) Describe the life of slaves in the American colonies in the 1700s. Discuss the difference between a servant and a slave. How did Miss Mary Finch's view of slavery differ from that of most slave owners? Why does Mr. Robert accuse Isabel of lying when she tells him that she read Miss Mary's will? Explain why Pastor Weeks thinks that teaching a slave to read only "leads to trouble."

2) Mr. Robert collects Isabel and Ruth on the day of Miss Mary's funeral. Why aren't the girls allowed to take personal items with them? Explain the symbolism of the seeds that Isabel hides in her pocket. She plants the seeds, and one day finds that the plants have died. What do the dead plants represent? There is another plant metaphor in the novel. Explain what the mayor of New York means when he compares the rebels to vines.

3) Role models may be found in real life and in stories. How are Isabel's momma, and Queen Esther from the Bible, her role models for bravery? Discuss the connection between bravery, courage, and fear. What is Isabel's first act of bravery? Discuss her most fearful moments. How is her bravery and courage fueled by her fears? How does she become bolder and braver as the novel develops?

4) The American Revolution was about freedom and liberty. Mr. Lockton, a Loyalist, thinks that freedom and liberty has many meanings. Define freedom from his point of view. How might the Patriots define freedom and liberty? Isabel has lived her entire life in bondage, but dreams of freedom. What does freedom look like in Isabel's mind?

5) Discuss why Curzon thinks that Isabel will be a good spy. At what point does she accept his offer? Isabel later feels betrayed by Curzon. Why does she feel this way? How is Curzon betrayed by Colonel Regan? At what point does Isabel understand that Curzon's dream of freedom is the same as hers? How does this realization help her forgive him? At the beginning of the novel, Isabel needs Curzon. How does he need her at the end of the novel?

6) Isabel encounters a woman in the street singing "Yankee Doodle," and realizes that the woman is a messenger. What is the message? Colonel Regan gives Isabel the code word "*ad astra*" to use when entering the rebel camp. The word means "to the stars" in Latin. Why is this an appropriate code word for the rebels? How does this word foreshadow Isabel and Curzon's ultimate escape to freedom at the end of the novel?

7) The mayor of New York, a Loyalist, says, "The beast has grown too large. If it breaks free of its chains, we are all in danger. We need to cut off its head." Who is the beast? Who is the head? Why is Lockton so adamantly opposed to the mayor's proposal?

8) Isabel says, "Madam looked down without seeing me; she looked at me face, my kerchief, my shirt neatly tucked

into my skirt, looked at my shoes pinching my feet, looked at my hands that were stronger than hers. She did not look into my eyes, did not see the lion inside. She did not see the me of me, the Isabel." What is the lion inside of Isabel? What does Lady Seymour see in Isabel that Madam Lockton doesn't see? How does the "lamb" in Lady Seymour help the "lion" inside of Isabel escape?

9) Explain the following metaphor: "Melancholy held me hostage, and the bees built a hive of sadness in my soul." What precipitates such sadness in Isabel? How does the hive grow bigger before Isabel learns to destroy it?

10) The old man that Isabel calls Grandfather says, "Everything that stands between you and freedom is the river Jordan." He assures her that she will find it if she looks hard enough. What is the figurative river Jordan in the novel? Discuss all of the tributaries that feed into Isabel's river Jordan.

11) The bookseller gives Isabel a copy of *Common Sense* by Thomas Paine. He advises her that the words are dangerous and that she should commit them to memory. At what point does she understand Paine's words? How does the book give her courage?

12) What does Isabel mean when she says, "I was chained between two nations"? There are several references to chains throughout the novel. How is the word "chain" used as an antonym to the word "freedom"?

Turn the page for a sneak peek at
what happens next to Isabel and Curzon in
Laurie Halse Anderson's sequel to *Chains*,

FORGE

Available October 2010!

PRELUDE

Sunday, January 19, 1777

"We have it in our power to begin the world over again. . . .
The birth-day of a new world is at hand."
–Thomas Paine, Common Sense

"CAN YOU WALK?" SOMEONE ASKED ME.

My eyes opened. I blinked against the bright light and squinted.

I was sitting in a rowboat half pulled onto a snowy riverbank. The cold was a beast gnawing at my toes and fingers. It bit so hard that my bones ached and my head seemed filled with ice.

I closed my eyes and struggled to think clearly.

This is a fantastical dream. In truth, I am still a prisoner of the war, held in the Bridewell.

I sniffed. The air here was cold but clean, without the stink of jailed men and death.

No matter. 'Tis still a dream.

I drifted back toward sleep.

"Curzon!" Someone twisted my ear. "I beg you!"

I flinched and rose out of sleep.

"Open your eyes!" the voice commanded. "We must hurry away from here!"

I blinked again. Before me sat a girl, her right cheek scarred by a branding iron, her eyes swollen with fatigue.

'Twas Isabel, who was my friend.

I blinked for the third time and took a deep breath. The cobwebs slowly fell from my mind. Isabel's raw hands lay in her lap, bleeding from open sores and torn blisters. The handles of both oars were bloodstained, where she had gripped them.

Like a flint hitting steel, a memory sparked, then flared.

Isabel had freed me from the Bridewell. She'd rowed a boat, this ancient boat, all night long. Rowed us away from Manhattan, the British Army, and those who owned us.

The memory exploded.

We are free!

I stood, legs quivering, head pounding, heart leaping. "You did it! How? Don't matter. Country, you did it!"

She shook her head violently and pulled me back down to my seat, a shaky finger on her lips to quiet me. "Hush!"

"But it's wondrous," I said, voice low. "Is it not?"

"Yes," she whispered. "No." The wind swirled a veil of snow between us. "Perhaps."

"Do you know of a safe house hereabouts?" I asked. "The name of folks who would help us?"

"No," she admitted. "There was no time for planning. We have a handful of silver coins, some meat, and a map." She wrung out the water from the bottom of her skirt. "I forged myself a pass, but I fear the river has ruined it. And we must find a way to walk ten miles a day, if we're to make Charleston by April."

"Charleston?" Did she say Charleston? South Carolina would mean certain disaster. Had she injured her reason? "We have no business there, Isabel. We should make for Philadelphia."

"Yes, we do," she said. "That's where Ruth is."

I knew then that Isabel's mind had been addled by the exertions of our escape. Her little sister had been sold away to the islands. The child was likely dead, but I could not bring myself to say this to Isabel. Not right then.

The river gurgled and tugged, trying to pull the boat back into the current. I clutched at the sides of the unsteady craft and shivered. Isabel had brought us thus far. Now it was up to me.

But how?

We were escaped slaves, half-froze and exhausted. We needed to warm ourselves, sleep, and eat. But above all, we had to stay hidden. The business of returning or selling runaways was profitable for both redcoats and rebels.

I tallied our advantages: little money. Food enough for a few meals. Disadvantages: no horse. No gun. No one to trust.

A large piece of ice floated down the river as the second truth crackled in me.

This freedom could kill us.

CHAPTER 1

Tuesday, October 7, 1777

"BEGIN THE GAME."
—ORDER OF AMERICAN GENERAL HORATIO GATES
TO START THE SECOND BATTLE OF SARATOGA

THOUGHTS OF OUR ESCAPE WERE STILL tormenting me nine months later, long after we'd argued and fought and stolen from each other. Long after Isabel ran away from me.

I twisted my ear so hard it was near torn from my head.

Enough of that, I swore. *No thoughts of Isabel. Not whilst there are bears and wolves about. And not until you find that blasted apple tree.*

I studied the forest around me, uncertain about where I was, where I ought be, and how I would ever get out.

I was lost.

Again.

Lost in a dark forest inhabited not only by ravenous creatures, but also by the British army, which was feeling desperate, and the American army, which was spoiling for another fight.

I rubbed my sore ear and swatted at a persistent hornet.

Tho' lost, my situation was not yet perilous. The animals I most feared would not start hunting for hours and the armies fought their little skirmishes close to the river. I had taken great care to avoid the river.

My most immediate danger was that of starving to death, for I had not eaten since dinner the night before. There was also a fair chance that the cabbage head who was my boss had discovered I'd forgotten to arrive for work.

Again.

This time he would surely beat me, then fire me, then abandon me in the wilderness with two irritated armies, bad food, and a forest filled with bears and wolves fond of the taste of fifteen-year-old boys.

But if that be my punishment, I'd take it. Long as I could find me those apples first.

I walked an hour or more. I was born in Boston and knew every street and alleyway there, as well as those of New York City. I preferred cobblestones to fallen leaves, proper houses to tents. Walking alone in a forest made me uneasy.

I was unsure of the names of the trees that rose above me and blocked my path with their lower branches. Some had yellow leaves. Others red, for it was autumn and that was the way of trees in the north of New York state. None had apples hanging from their limbs. I saw no fruit of any kind, no sign of an orchard, tended or overgrown.

I walked along a ridge, then investigated the far side of it. All I found was a field of prickly thistles. I walked to the north end of the ridge and headed down a deep ravine. Surely an apple tree this spectacular, this monumental, would not be hard to miss.

I'd heard about this tree from several fellows at camp. A graybeard from Connecticut said it was the biggest tree he ever saw. Two brothers from Weymouth claimed the apples shined like gold and tasted like honey. The men of the northern army had camped here for near a month and everyone was tired of boiled beef and hardtack.

I aimed to find those magical apples. I'd stuff full the two sacks I stole from the supply tent, and sell my treasure after dark, moving from regiment to regiment in the firelight. My apples would transform into coin. The more coin I collected, the closer I'd be to–

Craaaack.

Gunfire? Couldn't be. I was well clear of the territory patrolled by the riflemen and scouts.

Crrr-ack.

Heavy boots crashed through the forest. Voices shouted.

Unless I'd gotten turned around the wrong way.

Crrrr-ackBOOM!

An angry hornet hissed past my ear and smacked into the tree trunk behind me with a low thump.

A British redcoat appeared from the underbrush, breathing heavy as a racing horse and heading straight for me. When he laid eyes upon my form, he spun a quarter turn and scrambled up the side of the ravine. Three more soldiers followed on his heels, all wearing the red uniform of King George, their canteens and cartridge boxes bouncing on their backsides.

There was a flash and a *crrrr-ackBOOM* from the undergrowth across the ravine. Another angry hornet flew past.

Only 'twas no hornet. 'Twas a musketball, lethal and fat enough to blow a hole clean through my middle or rip off my arm. I crouched low as I could in the brush to avoid becoming a corpse.

A dozen rebel soldiers appeared. They paused, seeking the path of the British they'd been chasing. A redcoat peered over the edge of the ravine and was spotted by the rebels.

The man with an officer's ribbon on his hat hollered, "Make ready!"

As the Americans reached for their powder horns and shot bags, there was a commotion above. The British lined up in formation, a half dozen of them now, their muskets already loaded.

"Present!" yelled the American as his men scrambled to prepare their weapons for firing.

"Present!" the redcoat officer screamed.

All the men on both sides brought the stocks of their muskets up to their shoulders and sighted down the barrels at their enemies. I lay in the middle of the field of fire.

I pressed my face into the earth, bracing for the feel of a bullet crushing flesh and bone. I could not pray, could not plan a course of escape, could not command my limbs to move. I could only think of the wretched, lying, foul, silly girl who was the reason I was lying in the mud, about to be slaughtered.

I thought of Isabel and I missed her.

"FIRE!"